MW01242914

Tone Dead

Another Laura Kenzel Mystery
with Rascal and Mischief

10-27-08

By

Mary Lu Warstler

PUBLISH AMERICA

PublishAmerica
Baltimore

© 2008 by Mary Lu Warstler.
All rights reserved. No part of this book may be reproduced, stored in a retrieval system or transmitted in any form or by any means without the prior written permission of the publishers, except by a reviewer who may quote brief passages in a review to be printed in a newspaper, magazine or journal.

First printing

All characters in this book are fictitious, and any resemblance to real persons, living or dead, is coincidental.

PublishAmerica has allowed this work to remain exactly as the author intended, verbatim, without editorial input.

ISBN: 1-60672-470-3
PUBLISHED BY PUBLISHAMERICA, LLLP
www.publishamerica.com
Baltimore

Printed in the United States of America

To
Those who struggle to make the Church
All that God intended it should be.

Acknowledgements and Word from the Author

No one writes a book in a vacuum. While I spend many hours in writing, editing, and re-writing each work that I send to a publisher, others also spend hours in editing, analyzing, and making suggestions to improve my efforts. I want to take a few words to thank those who have helped in that area of my writing. Recently a very good friend, Don Shilling, offered his experience in editing and has been a tremendous help in pointing out areas that need work. Thank you to Don, a former District Superintendent—obviously much different from *Bill Collins!*

My family has been more help than I can ever express. I could not have progressed as far as I have without their help. My son, Timothy Warstler has been my editor from the time I started writing and we have both learned a lot in the process. My daughter, Martha Coleman, Assistant Director, Technical Services for First Regional Library in Hernando, Mississippi, has given me many technical, as well as, practical suggestions. Since I began writing, my other daughter, Liz Flaker has become a Registered Nurse. She has been an invaluable source for medical questions. My son, James Warstler has given me so much technical support for my computer that I could not have even sent a single manuscript to a publisher without his help. And of course, my husband, Rodney, has graciously given me time to write by taking over many of the time-consuming, but necessary, household chores. I give to all my family my heart-felt thanks for their encouragement and help along the way.

Writing fiction is as much fun as reading it—at least for me it is. In this day of *reality shows*, many folks want something that is *real*. There is often a fine line between fiction, fantasy, and science fiction. But I have found that is also true in real life. Often, truth is certainly stranger than fiction.

While I have never heard an animal speak human words, my male Siamese comes pretty close to it sometimes. He makes himself understood in more ways than speaking. I grew up in a family that commonly acknowledged

5

dreams, visions, and ESP. With a sense of imagination, it is not difficult for me to believe that children and animals have a special rapport and they understand each other; we often know some things without knowing why we know them. Therefore, if you find the antics of Rascal and Mischief more unreal than your animals, that's all right. They are different. They are fictional. They are special.

Again, I would have to say, that while I wish I could have the faith and courage of Laura Kenzel, she too is fictional. She is not an autobiography of me—not even close. All churches have folks that are saints and some that are sinners. That is what makes the church so special—we can still work and love together.

While I have had some District Superintendents with whom I have disagreed, and some whom I felt dealt unfairly with the churches, I have always supported them because they do the best they can in a very difficult job. I certainly do not envy them! But in over fifty years of ministry (mine as well as my husband's), I have NEVER—let me repeat that—NEVER met a District Superintendent (or even a minister) who even came close to being as mean and nasty as Bill Collins. I have known several Bishop's who have been as kind and gracious as the Giles and I thank God for them. The church is very dear to me, and leadership is difficult.

As you read these pages of the third Laura Kenzel mystery, may you find a sense of hope in a troubled world. May you see the importance of forgiveness, no matter how difficult it may be. May you seek to live a life of faith and courage wherever you may be.

Mary Lu

Primary and Secondary Characters

One suggestion I received asked that I list the main characters since they appear in all three Laura Kenzel novels.

Reverend Laura Kenzel—middle-aged widow, pastoring her first church in Cottonville, Ohio.

Rascal and Mischief—two Maine Coon Cats that Laura and Jerome rescued from the church belfry. They are intelligent, trained show cats that have adopted her and become her protectors.

Shebop—Laura's Chevy Chevette that has been her "friend" since she went to Seminary.

Detective Steve Morgan—Laura's fiancé, Homicide Detective for Glenville and the county. Does some FBI undercover work for his friend, Commander George Burton.

Cottonville Police Chief Todd Williams—friend of Laura's, engaged to marry Carolyn McMichaels.

Carolyn McMichaels—Jerome's mother, Todd's fiancée.

Jerome Nicholas McMichaels—Carolyn's ten-year old son, who helped Laura find the cats. He becomes best friends of Laura's grandson **Joshua Stewart**.

Joshua Stewart—Laura's ten-year old grandson who is staying with her for a year.

Sophia Dugal—Carolyn's mother; Jerome's grandmother.

Norman and Susan Stewart—Laura's daughter and son-in-law. They left Josh with her for a year while Norman is teaching in Germany.

Cora Duncan—Laura's prayer warrior who always seems to know when Laura needs special prayers.

SaraBelle Cotton—Ninety-one year old founder of Cottonville who has become a very close friend of Laura's.

Dorothy Barker—Church secretary who has become Laura's friend.

Mark Goodwin—Todd's right hand man.

Colin Jacobson (AKA Reverend William [Bill] Collins)—an obsessed killer who is determined that Laura will not marry Steve.

Hugh Jacobson—brother of Colin

Fred Martin—trustee of the church, jokester, friend

Martha and Frank Jennings—neighbors of Laura, also part of the church leadership.

Bishop Matthew and Helen Giles—Laura's bishop who comes to marry her and Steve.

Joe and Clarissa Baldwin—Steve's partner in Glennville Police Department and close friend.

All characters are purely fictional and bear no resemblance to anyone living or dead, except Cora Duncan who is based on the life of a very good friend who was my prayer warrior in ministry. Others are composites of church people in general—some I've known, some I've heard and read about. The character of Bill Collins/Colin Jacobson is purely imagination. Rascal and Mischief are also figments of my imagination based on research for Maine Coon Cats. I have never owned one, but know people who have. They are truly beautiful animals.

Prologue

Although only a few days into September, the log cabin deep in the woods gave the impression of a cold, dark day, not unlike early November. Except for the occasional visit of the Jacobsons, the cabin had sat uninhabited for nearly a century. Colin Jacobson and his brothers knew of the place from the time they were able to steal a car and drive around southern Ohio looking for whatever trouble they could find. The abandoned cabin became their private hideaway.

Chipped mortar between logs; cracked, sooty windows; and a loose shingle or two on the roof made no difference to the brothers. They needed only a hidden shelter from erratic Ohio weather. Only the brothers ever went there.

This time, however, was different. Colin was in the Chillicothe prison. Hugh alone, waited for a stranger. Pacing the dirt walk in front of the cabin, he stopped occasionally to listen for an approaching car. He was nervous about this meeting.

I shouldn't be meeting a stranger here, he thought, not at our secret place and certainly not in broad daylight. Colin never worked with anyone outside the family before. If he hadn't lost his senses and killed Randy…Oh, well, that's water over the dam.

Hugh continued to pace—to listen—to think. Colin never trusted *any*one before. Now here I am waiting for some relative of a gangster he met in prison. Can we trust him? Probably not, but what's the choice. I'll just have to keep an eye on this man called *Killer*. But, what if this is a setup? What if the man's a cop? What if…?

Hugh shook his head and paced some more. He wanted a cigarette, but Colin had forbidden smoking near the cabin. "Too much danger of forest fires," he'd said. So he paced and waited until finally, the hum of a well cared for engine signaled the approaching vehicle. The spot of dust on the horizon grew bigger. Hugh shaded his eyes against the afternoon sun and watched the black sedan approach. Then he stepped toward the drive to greet this stranger from New York.

* * *

Inside the cabin, the man called Killer and Hugh Jacobson sat on the rickety chairs. Hugh poured coffee from a thermos into cracked cups from a cupboard. Killer looked at the cups with disgust.

"No one told me I'd have to live like a mountain pauper." He sat on the edge of his chair, careful not to get any more dust than necessary on his black pinstriped, silk suit.

"We don't *live* here," snarled Hugh. "This is just a meeting place."

"So where is this job you want done? My uncle said you need someone taken care of."

"I've got most of the details, but my brother Colin will give us the final word."

"So where is he?"

"He's still in prison."

"He's running this show from there?" Killer gave Hugh an incredulous look that clearly said he didn't like this setup one bit.

"He'll be out in a few days. Our job is to kill the dame then slow down the investigation until he can break free."

"So who do I kill and when do I get paid?"

"We start immediately and you'll get paid when Colin gets here. There's this woman who was involved with the local funeral director. She knows too much and just might start talking to the wrong people. But there's more to the plan than killing her. It's a little complicated so listen closely."

Hugh then described Colin's plan to kill Judy Franklin and cause Laura Kenzel trouble at the same time. Then they were to masquerade as Assistant District Attorneys, make more trouble for the Chief of Police and his fiancée and do whatever was necessary to keep Homicide Detective Steve Morgan out of the way.

"Why not just kill Morgan?"

"Because my brother is obsessed with getting Morgan's girl and watching Morgan suffer in the process."

Killer guffawed then broke into a mixture of laughing and coughing. "I think I'm going to like your brother, but will anyone believe such a stupid…?" Killer jumped to his feet, kicking over his chair, as Hugh drew his knife and lunged toward him.

As natural as breathing, Killer grabbed Hugh's wrist. They glared at each other over the corner of the table—neither willing to back down.

"Don't you *ever* say anything like that to my brother," Hugh spoke through clenched teeth, "or you won't ever say another word at all. Don't matter if *we* think it's stupid. Colin says do it; we do it."

"All right. All right," said Killer twisting Hugh's arm aside until he dropped the knife. As long as I get paid, I'll do as the man says."

"Fine just so we understand each other." Hugh continued to glare as he stooped to pick up his knife, keeping his eyes on Killer.

As if the scene had never taken place, Killer asked, "How's he going to get out of there and get to this little Cottonville berg…?"

"He's got a plan. He'll make it."

One

Josh stuffed the last bite of toast in his mouth as the phone rang in the living room. "I'll get it," he yelled and jumped up from the table, tipping his chair, righting it, and getting to the phone before the third ring.

"Slow down, Josh," Laura said following him to the phone in case it was one of her parishioners instead of Jerome.

Josh pushed the speakerphone button. "Ready to go?" The excited voice at the other end filled the room.

"Yeah, meet you at the square in five minutes," said Josh.

"Okay. Don't forget your lunch money and books and things."

"I got my back pack. Are you sure we'll be in the same class?"

"Yeah, I had my mom check. Let's go. Don't want to be late the first day."

"Five minutes at the square. See you there."

Josh tapped the off button, grabbed his backpack from the couch and started for the door. Rascal and Mischief, the two Maine Coon Cats that had chosen to live with Laura, jumped in front of him, preventing him from opening the door.

"Did you forget something, Josh?" Laura smiled at his perplexed expression.

"I don't think so," he said. Rascal smacked him sharply on the ankle. "Oh, yeah," he said grinning. He ran back to give Laura a hug. "Sorry," he said giggling. "Guess I'm too excited."

Laura hugged him back. "Are you sure you're not too excited to find your way to the square?

"Rascal and Mischief won't let us get lost."

"Are they going with you?" Laura was surprised, although she shouldn't have been.

Josh giggled. "I don't know, but they're already on the porch waiting."

"Maybe they…" Laura thought better of saying they should stay home. Rascal and Mischief set their own rules. She just hoped they came back home. "If they stay, have the secretary call me, so I won't…"

"Yeah, I know. So you won't worry." Josh grinned and ran out the door. Laura stood on the porch and watched until he turned the corner, Rascal and Mischief on either side of him. Had it only been three months since Susan and Norman left Josh with her. She smiled at the excitement of both boys. Josh, her grandson had never attended public school with other children. Susan brought tutors to their apartment, not wanting Josh to mingle with *riff-raff.*

Jerome McMichaels never liked school and preferred to go fishing whenever he could until the bomb scare last spring. Often folks meeting the boys for the first time thought they were brothers. Even Laura couldn't believe the resemblance—both were ten, about the same height and build, both had red hair, although Jerome's was a bright red and Josh's was more like her dark auburn color, Jerome had green eyes and Josh brown like her own. They were in the same grade and would be in the same class at Grayson Elementary School.

Laura returned to the kitchen and began to clean up after breakfast. Memories pushed aside her immediate plans. Susan and Norm had left soon after Memorial Day for Germany where Norman would be teaching in a university and Susan would pursue art classes. Laura believed they should have taken Josh with them, but, as Norm told her, he and Susan were experiencing difficulties in their marriage and needed time alone. Laura was glad for Josh's company for a whole year. He had certainly grown—emotionally and physically—over the summer filled with danger and intrigue. But through it all, Josh was learning to live like a "normal" little boy.

Drawn from her reverie by the ringing of the phone, Laura returned from grandmother mode to pastor mode as she answered. "Good morning, Reverend Kenzel speaking."

"Good morning, Love. I hope this doesn't mean more trouble for you, but the Lord said I should call and remind you I'm praying for you. Whatever happens, please know that I do pray every day and often. Dear God…," Cora Duncan never explained herself. She just prayed. "Whatever my dear friend needs, give her the assurance of Your love which surrounds her. Amen."

Laura replaced the phone knowing there would be only the dial tone. Cora called her often just to pray—usually when trouble was imminent. Feeling certain those prayers had helped her through many ordeals of the past, Laura dropped to her knees. "Lord, thank you for Cora. You have given her insight and wisdom that somehow I seem to miss. Maybe I'm too busy, or too wrapped up in what is happening to see the full picture. Whatever the cause, I thank You for her gift. Whatever is coming, give me the strength to see it through. Amen."

Laura heard the screen door open and close. Since there were no footsteps, she knew Rascal and Mischief had returned. She breathed a small sigh of relief and rose. She combed her long slender fingers through her short auburn hair, picked up her briefcase and started for the door. She glanced at Rascal and Mischief. "Well, kitties, what are we in for now? Cora's prayers are powerful, but then they need to be. She always seems to know when trouble is coming our way. Whatever, we are covered by her prayers. Are you staying here and sleeping, or going with me today?"

Rascal and Mischief blinked their emerald green eyes and ran around her as she opened the door. By the time she crossed the porch to the driveway, the Maine Coon pair sat at the church door waiting for her.

"Good morning, Dorothy," Laura called as she entered her office through the Alpha Room—the gathering area behind the sanctuary that served as an overflow.

Dorothy Barker, part time secretary, had worked from her home to keep the church together during the two-year period when strange things were happening at the church and weird, scary noises floated daily from the belfry. Police Chief Todd Williams had even found one pastor hanging in that tower. Until Laura Kenzel came to Cottonville and refused to be frightened off, no pastor would stay more than a few hours. Laura discovered the cats in the belfry and helped Todd and Detective Morgan get rid of the drug gang who scared pastors away. Once she felt safe, Dorothy returned to her office at the church. She and Laura had become good friends.

Although opposites in many ways—Laura, a trim five six; short auburn hair, brown eyes; Dorothy a plump five one, long brown hair, gray eyes; both tended to be perfectionists when it came to messages from the office. Dorothy was quiet and efficient with the computer; Laura was adequate for her needs. They each respected the other's work time, but took time each day to visit and learn to know one another. Dorothy didn't mind the cats in the office. They usually stayed with Laura, but occasionally they would wander around the church, including Dorothy's office.

"Good morning, Pastor," Dorothy called back from her computer, spinning her chair around with her back to the computer as Laura walked through the connecting doorway.

"It was such a beautiful day," said Laura, "I was tempted to pull a Jerome and play hooky after I got Josh off to school.

"That's not a good idea after convincing him not to do it any more," said Dorothy.

Laura grinned. "I know, that's why I'm here."

"How did it go—getting Josh off to school? It has to be difficult for him never having gone to public school—except those two days last spring when he went with Jerome. But that wasn't really going to school."

Laura grimaced at the memory. "You're right. Those two days were not even close to normal school days—especially with a bomb scare. But Josh was excited this morning."

"A little different from his summer schedule, I expect," said Dorothy.

"Yes, I'd forgotten how much tension comes with getting a child off to school—making sure he has breakfast and all his stuff together and isn't too early or too late. Susan was constantly missing her bus. At least I don't have *that* worry with Josh."

"Too bad he couldn't have gone to Europe with his parents, but it sounds like he'll have a lot more fun here—especially with that Jacobson nut behind bars now."

Laura nodded and shivered. Colin Jacobson, alias Bill Collins, her ex-district superintendent, had tried several times to kill her. Even though he was now serving a life sentence, Laura had a prickly feeling in her soul. He was as slippery as mercury and twice as deadly.

Dorothy sought to change the subject. "Wasn't that a marvelous Labor Day celebration yesterday? I love parades and picnics and fireworks."

"It was spectacular all right. I've never lived in a community that celebrated holidays the way Cottonville does. Have they always been so...extravagant?"

"They've celebrated like that forever," said Dorothy. "I remember going to the park as a child and all the tables loaded with casseroles, cakes, pies, and anything else that was edible. Then they expected us to run races and relays after stuffing ourselves." She laughed and Laura joined her.

"Maybe they knew that people, even children, needed to exercise all that food away."

"Maybe so, but it sure is hard to get back to work after a day like that." Dorothy looked past Laura into her office. "Did someone follow you in this morning? I thought I saw movement at the door. We don't need anymore mysteries around here with a big wedding coming up and everything."

Laura glanced at Rascal and Mischief as they jumped to Dorothy's desk and blinked their green eyes at her. "They got in the habit of coming with me when they needed to protect me. Besides, they like to be where the action is. They went to school with the boys this morning and returned to *help* me here."

16

The sound of organ chords and arpeggios drifted from the sanctuary. Both cats turned their heads; their ears perked and alert. As if they were one animal, not two, they flew from the desk and bounded out of the office toward the music.

Dorothy lifted her eyebrows. "They like music?"

"Maybe, but with them you never know. They might just want to watch Karen's fingers running over the keyboards."

"At least we don't have to worry about that psycho stalking us," said Dorothy.

"All I have to worry about now is the town's biggest wedding since SaraBelle Cotton's wedding some seventy years ago," said Laura.

Dorothy nodded knowingly and Laura started back to her office. She froze in her tracks. A horrible screeching noise came from the sanctuary.

"What is that?" Dorothy shivered. "It sounds like the noise we used to hear from the belfry before you found the cats."

Laura realized she was holding her breath and exhaled. "It *is* the cats," she said. "Apparently they want to sing with the music."

The music stopped. Karen Markley, the pretty, very talented, young organist, appeared at the office door. She had pulled her long blonde hair into a modified ponytail; her blue eyes sparkled. At twenty-five, she could have passed for a teenager.

"Pastor," she said with as straight a face as she could muster, "I know your cats are smart and can do a lot of things, so please don't misunderstand me. They try, but they are hopelessly tone deaf. Do you think you can get them out of there so I can practice?" Then she broke into laughter. "I know they want to sing, but I really have to work on some of this music for the big wedding."

Dorothy was laughing so hard she reached for a tissue to dry her eyes. "Maybe you need to take them on the road, or give them singing lessons," she said. "Maybe they miss their old way of life."

"I doubt that," said Laura. "They haven't had it so good and they know it."

Memories flashed through her mind like a slide show projected on the wall: Jeb Little, who had owned the trained show cats, lying in a pool of blood; Rascal and Mischief chained to the wall of the belfry; Jerome climbing up to rescue them. She blinked the images away.

"I'll see if I can get them to come and help Dorothy," she said over her shoulder, and started for the sanctuary.

17

"Oh, no you won't. I'll lock my doors," Dorothy called after her.

Laura walked down the aisle with Karen. The cats sat on top of the organ, staring at the pipes high above them.

"Rascal! Mischief! Come on kitties. Karen doesn't need your help this morning." They continued to stare at the pipes.

"Don't even think about trying to jump up there," Laura said sternly. "I don't want to have to call the fire department to get you down. Come on; let's find something else to do."

They continued to sit and stare. Laura frowned. The familiar chill of foreboding flooded over her.

"Do you suppose there's a mouse up there?" Karen shielded her eyes with her hand as if looking into the bright sun. The pipes were behind a crisscross of intricate woodwork. Even if something were up there, she couldn't have seen it.

"Play a few scales. Maybe that will scare them away—the mice that is, not the cats. I don't think they scare easily."

"Worth a try," said Karen. She ran her fingers over the keyboards until she hit a key that jarred the sensitive ears of both musician and pastor.

"That sounded like an off key. I didn't think these pipes could go flat," said Laura.

"Not usually, but one or two notes didn't play at all. Let me try again, slower." Karen went over the keys again, slowly, note by note. Two notes didn't play at all and two more sounded muted.

"Oh, no," wailed Karen. "With the wedding in just two weeks, what are we going to do? It usually takes the technician a week to get out here when we call—sometimes longer than that."

"Do we have the number on file?" asked Laura

"It should be—Melody Brothers, Organ Tuning and Repair Service. Do you suppose that's what those cats were trying to tell us?"

Laura felt the shiver down her spine again. "I hope that's all."

"Maybe a mouse is building a nest in one of the pipes," Karen suggested.

"Maybe," said Laura. "I'll have Dorothy call. See if you can work around those notes. I'll be right back."

She turned to the cats and added, "Good kitties, no more singing for now."

She started back to the office and Karen looked for ways to work around the stuck keys. The cats eased down on their tummies, tucked their front paws under them, and dozed.

Two

"Dorothy," Laura said as she entered the office again. "See if you can get Melody Brothers on the line for me. We have problems with the organ."

"Sure thing, but it usually takes them at least a week to get out here." She was dialing as she talked. "Hello, Melody Brothers? This is Cottonville United Methodist Church. We are having a problem with our organ and...just a minute, please."

Dorothy put her hand over the phone and turned to Laura. "She said they are so far behind that it will be at least a week before they can even think about it—said I should call back next week."

Laura took a deep breath and reached for the phone. She spoke as pleasantly as possible. "Good morning. This is Reverend Kenzel speaking. I need to talk to the person in charge."

"Sorry, Pastor," said the voice at the other end. "It won't make any difference who you talk to. We can't do anything for at least a week, maybe a week and a half."

"Are you the manager? Owner? Secretary?"

"I am the Scheduling Secretary. Nothing goes in or out without my knowledge." The voice had an angry, defensive edge to it.

"Do you have a name, or shall I just call you Scheduling Secretary?" Laura hated it when she became sarcastic, but this woman was going to be impossible.

"I am *Ms.* Brummelside, and pastor or not, you are wasting my time."

"*Ms.* Brummelside, I'm sorry I'm wasting your time, so let me talk to one of the Melody brothers and you can get back to your scheduling."

"That is impossible. They have more important things to do."

"More important than speaking to a client? Very well, I'll call information for their home numbers and reach them at their dinner hour."

There was a long pause at the other end. Laura heard no dial tone. They were still connected. Dorothy watched with her mouth open and her eyes wide. This side of her pastor she had never seen.

"Ms. Brummelside? Are you still there?"

"Yeah, I'm here." The tone was sulky.

"And?"

"Hold on I'll see if Bryan is available, but he will tell you the same thing."

Another long pause then a man's voice answered. "Good morning. Pastor Kenzel, is it? Bryan Melody here. Ms. Brummelside tells me you want a technician immediately. I'm afraid that is impossible. You see…"

"No, Mr. Melody. I do not see. I have a wedding for one of the most prominent men in our community in less than two weeks and that organ *will* be working. Not only will it be working for the wedding, but it will be working by tomorrow morning so my organist can properly prepare."

"Reverend Kenzel you don't understand…"

"Mr. Melody, I understand perfectly. I realize you are behind in your calls. Maybe you need to computerize your scheduling. I also understand you sold us this organ with the promise that we would be able to get repairs, if, and when, we needed them. And, I understand that this is a very expensive organ and to replace it would be very costly. But, Mr. Melody, please hear me very clearly, if a technician is not out here this afternoon, we will replace the organ with a new one and you will *not* be the installer. Do you understand *me*, Mr. Melody?"

"You're bluffing." He didn't sound too sure of that.

"Try me," Laura said through clenched teeth.

There was a long pause, then the man's voice again sounding controlled and angry. "I understand you very clearly, Reverend Kenzel, but… Oh, wait a minute, George just walked in. He isn't supposed to be back from vacation until next week. He'll be there around one o'clock this afternoon. Will that be soon enough?"

"Thank you Mr. Melody, I can work around that. Nice talking to you. Goodbye." Laura handed the phone back to Dorothy. "Close your mouth, Dorothy. There are still flies around."

Dorothy's mouth snapped shut. Her surprise and awe at her pastor's way of handling the difficult Bryan Melody gave way to laughter. "I sure would like to see the look on Ms. Brummelside's face," she said, wiping the tears from her face.

"Someone will be here at one," said Laura feeling drained. She hated confrontations. "I'll be here to see that he gets in to do the work."

"One question," asked Dorothy still chuckling as Laura started to her office. "What would you have done if he had called your bluff?"

"We'll never know will we?" Laura grinned and went to tell Karen and gather her cats.

Three

Lunch finished; table cleared; dishes washed and put away; Laura glanced at the clock and started for the door. "All right, kitties. I need to meet George—whoever he is. Are you coming with me, or taking a nap?"

Two balls of blended gold, orange, and black fur lay entwined like one large fluffy pillow on the couch. As Laura closed the door, however, Rascal and Mischief, raccoon-like tails in the air, streaked across the porch toward the church. When she reached the church door, Rascal already had his paws on the door.

Laura sat at her desk and turned on her computer while she waited for George. Uneasiness nagged her. She had been far more authoritarian than was her normal custom with Ms. Brummelside. What would she do if George didn't show up? She would have to work out something.

The townsfolk liked Todd and Carolyn. Laura smiled as she remembered when she first met Todd Williams, Cottonville's Chief of Police. His appearance had challenged her preconceived notion of a small town police chief. He was a tall slim, muscular man in his mid to late thirties, not short and chubby, as she would have thought. Instead of a shiny pate, he had a full head of brown wavy hair that looked windblown much of the time.

He and Carolyn had been high school sweethearts but Todd went to the Wheeling Police Academy and Carolyn ran off with Doran McMichaels. She returned to Cottonville two years later with a son. They had ignored each other until Jerome was beaten and threatened for helping Laura find the cats last spring. The trauma brought them together again and they deserved a beautiful wedding, complete with organ music.

Laura blinked; fish swam before her eyes on the monitor while the computer hummed waiting for her to engage it in something more productive. Mischief jumped up and down near the door; Rascal had his paws on the doorknob.

"What in the world is wrong with you guys?" Then she heard what they'd heard before her, someone walking in The Alpha Room. She opened the door just as a man with a toolbox in one hand was about to knock at the door with the other.

"Oh, I'm sorry," he said. "I hope I didn't startle you. I'm George Melody. I understand your organ is on the fritz."

George Melody was nothing like Laura had pictured him to be. His tousled brown hair above his narrow forehead, brown twinkling eyes, and his Leprechaun grin made him seem like a kid just out of high school, not old enough to be an organ technician.

"You didn't startle me," she answered. "I was expecting you. Although I must say, I was expecting someone much older."

"I'm old for my age." He grinned. "I was an afterthought, I guess, but I am one of the brothers and they have to let me work." He laughed at her expression. "It's all right—really. I do know my job. I've been playing in and around organs since I was, oh, about three, I would guess. Now, what seems to be the problem?"

"I really should apologize for my behavior this morning," said Laura, "but it's rather critical and…"

"No need to apologize." He laughed—an infectious, mirthful sound. "Actually, you made my day. It was the first time I've ever seen Ms. Brummelside at a loss for words. I came back from vacation early because I was bored, so I'm glad you called. Now, let's see what's wrong with this baby."

They walked toward the organ as they talked. Rascal and Mischief ran ahead and were sitting on the organ looking up at the pipes. Laura smiled at his expression. "They were doing that this morning. I think the problem is about there." She pointed to the spot where the cats were staring.

"Do you always keep cats around to flush out your problems? Those beauties look like they wouldn't take any nonsense from anyone, or anything."

"Meet Rascal and Mischief," she said, "And I don't think you would want to cross them, or try to harm me," Laura said. "They're my protectors. They've saved my life more than once."

"I don't doubt that at all. They are fine, intelligent looking animals."

"Kitties, this is George. He is going to fix the organ."

"Meow?" answered the Maine Coon duet. Then they winked at George and returned to their vigil of the pipes.

George shook his head, picked up his toolbox, and headed for the door behind the organ. Laura heard him going up the steps to the platform where he could work. Then he stopped and whistled a low long sound of surprise.

"Eh…Reverend Kenzel, I think you better call the police," he called down to her.

"What is it, George?" Laura had a sinking feeling that she really didn't want to know. The cats had settled down on the organ, their job done.

"There seems to be a dead woman lying across the pipes. That would certainly make for a tone dead pipe."

"Come on down, George. I'll go call." Now she understood Cora's call.

George returned to the front pew looking pale and more than a little shaken.

"Will you be all right while I call Chief Williams? Maybe you should come with me and lie down on my couch."

"I'll be all right," he said. "I just never saw a dead person before—especially like that."

Rascal and Mischief leaped from the organ to the floor then to the pew on either side of George.

"Looks like they'll take care of me," he said and tried to smile.

"I'll bring you some water," said Laura then hurried back to her office and called Todd's office. He answered on the first ring. Laura wasn't prepared—would she ever be?

"Todd, this is Laura. We have trouble at the church."

"Karen talked to Carolyn this morning. She said you were having problems with the organ. Didn't the repair man show up?"

"Oh, yes, he's here and he found the problem."

"So, what can I do for you?"

"Todd, the problem is a dead woman across the pipes."

"Laura! Don't kid me about…never mind. You would never joke about that. Be there in three minutes flat, or sooner."

A small town like Cottonville had its advantages. The police station was only a couple of blocks away from anywhere, so Todd and his men were there in minutes. George still sat on the front pew and sipped the water Laura brought him. He was still pale, but looked less likely to pass out.

"I just went up there to see what was causing the dead tone and there she was," said George as Todd recorded his statement. He seemed almost calm.

"You don't seem very upset," commented Todd.

"Looks can be deceiving," he answered somberly. "Having two, much older brothers, who were always giving me a hassle, I learned to hide my feelings. But, believe me, I wouldn't want to experience that again. I don't understand how *she* can be so calm." He nodded toward Laura, who had sat in a pew a few rows back to wait and watch.

Todd shook his head. "You would if you'd been around here the last four months. She's contended with more than her share of dead bodies, as well as coming close to being one herself a couple of times. Someone is going to a lot of trouble to get rid of her one way or another. Like you said, looks can be deceiving. She isn't as calm as she looks."

"Did those cats actually save her life, or was she just putting me on?"

"Oh, they certainly did. And if they said there was a dead body up there, they knew what they were talking about—or meowing about."

"Well they definitely knew something was up there," said George, "and they were perfectly willing to let me be the one to find out what it was. Do you suppose I can get up there any time soon and finish my job?"

"Should be about an hour," he said. "The coroner will check her out. Then they need to get some pictures and any fingerprints."

Laura joined them. "I'm sorry I made such a fuss and now you can't even do your job."

"Oh, I would say I've done a good day's work. And I'm certainly no longer bored, but I think I could use some coffee. Is there someplace I can get a bite of something while I wait?"

"Sure, Charlie's is just a couple of blocks from here."

"Oh, yeah, out by the park. I remember passing it on the way in. I'll go get my stomach settled. Maybe the pipe loft will be clear when I get back. All right if I leave my toolbox here?"

"Sure, and thanks for being so understanding George. Tell them at Charlie's to put it on the church's bill. We owe you big time."

One of the outer doors closed and Laura turned as someone else entered the sanctuary.

24

Four

"Pastor," called Karen coming down the aisle, "did we get it fixed, yet? Can I practice?"

"Sorry Karen. We did and we didn't. George found the problem, but it happened to be a dead woman on the pipes. Now we have to wait for Todd to finish before George can get back up there to see if there's any damage."

"How awful! But who is George?" Karen looked past Laura at the young man who stood behind her.

"This is George Melody from Melody Brothers. He's the one who found the body. George, this is Karen Markley, our organist."

George stared with his mouth open.

"George? Are you sure you're all right?" asked Laura. At least he wasn't pale now—a little flushed, maybe, but he seemed all right.

"What? Oh, yes, I'm fine. I just have never seen…a *young* organist. Most are…older…eh…ladies."

Karen laughed a soft giggly sound like a teenager. "I guess we're equal then. I've never seen a *young* organ technician either—especially a *handsome* one."

"Getting a little deep in here isn't it?" commented Laura. "Karen, why don't you take George over to Charlie's while Todd finishes up here? He needs some coffee and maybe a bite of lunch."

"I just had lunch, but I would be happy to keep George company…maybe even indulge in a cup of Charlie's coffee and apple pie." She grinned at Laura.

The women in the church were always trying to fix Karen up with somebody's cousin, brother or nephew. They couldn't understand why a beautiful young girl, like Karen Markley, wouldn't want to find a nice catch and move away from such a small town. She had too much talent to waste on Cottonville. Laura had never agreed with them, reminding them she would find someone in her own good time if that's what she wanted. As far as her talent,

Laura sort of agreed. Karen was certainly talented, but then Cottonville needed a good organist as well as the larger city churches.

Love? Only time would tell, but Karen and George certainly seemed to like each other—more than just professionally.

"It sure beats death and violence, huh kitties?"

They blinked, as if they had read her thoughts, and trotted back to her office where they curled up on the couch for their afternoon nap while Laura worked at her computer. She was so involved in her work, that she was startled when Todd stepped into her office.

"We're leaving now, Pastor. I think that repairman can get up there now. Where is he, anyway?"

Laura looked at the clock. "Karen took him over to Charlie's. They should be back soon. Thanks, Todd."

"I'm sorry you have to go through this again, Laura. Steve might want to know about this."

"You think there's a connection, too?" Laura didn't really need to ask. His face expressed his thoughts. However, Todd was a little hesitant to jump to conclusions.

"There might be," he said.

"Who was she?"

"Judy Franklin."

"Phil Jameson's secretary—the one who was involved with Ed Winters?"

"That's the one," answered Todd. "Is Steve coming over tonight?"

"I'm not sure. Yesterday, he said he would be having some briefings today. He didn't go into detail. It all depends on how long the meetings run."

"He'll be over," grinned Todd, "but I think I'll give him a call anyway— unless you want to call him."

"No, you do it. I don't want to get yelled at for finding another body."

"Talk to you later." Todd started out the door, turned back to her, and nodding at the sleeping cats added, "You know, it's not a bad idea keeping them close."

"It's their idea, not mine," she answered. "I like having them here, especially when I'm here by myself."

Todd left and Laura sat at her desk trying to focus. The past intruded, stirring up more memories—some pleasant, some unwanted. She remembered the night she arrived in Cottonville and Todd had come to her home because Frank Jennings called him. He brought Detective Steve Morgan with him. Steve was on vacation and staying with Todd a few days to help him with some continuing education in violent crimes. As with Todd, Steve had challenged her idea of a homicide detective. He wore no police uniform, but was dressed in gray slacks, pale blue, shirt that he buttoned almost to the neck. He wore no tie. He was tall, taller than Todd, had dark hair that was graying around the temples. Sky-blue intense eyes twinkled when he smiled, or teased, which he seemed to do often. It was the first time since Harold's death that she had felt an attraction toward another man. She'd tried to ignore it, but…

She smiled to herself, remembering the night he captured Colin Jacobson, alias Bill Collins. He asked her to marry him. She said yes, but they would have to wait until June—when Norman and Susan were back from Germany. He had been disappointed but was willing to wait.

More memories intruded—the unwanted ones. Ed Winters, owner of Cottonville's only funeral home, had been having an affair with Judy Franklin, secretary to Phil Jameson, manager of Cottonville Savings and Loan. Phil was also in partnership with Colin Jacobson. Somehow, Phil had learned of the affair and blackmailed Ed. Randy Jacobson, Colin Jacobson's nephew, killed Ed then Colin Jacobson killed Randy. Now Judy was dead. Although she didn't want to believe there was a connection, she knew there had to be.

Laura glanced at the clock. George and Karen should have been back by now. More trouble? She got up and started toward the sanctuary. Rascal and Mischief, still curled together on the couch, lifted their heads. Their ears perked up and they jumped down, stretched then trotted after Laura. George and Karen met them in the Alpha room laughing, flushed with joy.

"Oh, Pastor," said Karen when she saw Laura. "I hope we didn't keep you here waiting for us. We were talking and the time just sort of slipped away."

"Sorry, Reverend Kenzel, it was my fault." George had definitely lost his pallor and looked like the young man she met earlier. "I don't often have a chance to talk to someone my age that understands what I'm talking about—and really cares about it. I'll get right on that organ then Karen is going to play it for me—that is if you don't mind."

Laura smiled at them. "Why should I mind? And no, you didn't keep me waiting. I was working and just decided I needed to stretch a little. I'm almost done and Josh will be home from school soon, so I'll be leaving. Do I need to leave Rascal and Mischief here to chaperone?"

Karen and George looked at one another then laughed.

"I think I can handle him, Pastor."

"You got that right," answered George. "We'll be good."

"Then you get to your work and I'll take my protector cats and go home. Leave the bill on the secretary's desk."

"What bill? How can I charge for the most interesting day in my life?" George laughed and started for the steps to the pipes whistling a tune from *The Sound of Music.* Had he forgotten his previous encounter up there? Or was he *whistling in the dark* so to speak.

Laura started home, but Rascal and Mischief left her and took off toward town. Probably going to meet the boys, she thought with relief.

Five

Laura glanced at the clock as she spread the peanut butter and jelly and set two glasses of milk on the table. The boys will be here…the front door burst open before she finished her thought. Josh and Jerome ran in giggling. Rascal and Mischief raced up and down the stairs, up and over furniture, and landed on a shoulder of each of the boys. They all fell to the floor rolling and tumbling; laughing and chattering. Laura laughed with them. Finally, they got up, brushed themselves off and headed for the kitchen.

"How was your first day of school, Josh?" she asked.

"It was great! I never knew there were so many kids who didn't know any more than I did. Jerome and I are in the same class, but our teacher, Miss Campbell, said if we didn't stop talking to each other, she would put one of us in another room. We don't want that, so we tried real hard. We asked her to move us to different parts of the room so we wouldn't be tempted."

"Did she do that?" Laura wasn't sure how a teacher would react to a child telling her how to run the class.

"Yeah," answered Jerome. "She thought that was pretty clever of us to think of it."

I must remember to send a thank you note to that teacher, thought Laura.

"Did anything exciting happen here?" asked Josh.

"Well, the cats went to the church and tried to sing with Karen. She said they were tone deaf. But, they were more interested in the pipes."

They boys giggled and went to the sink to wash their hands.

"You mean those pipes way up by the ceiling where the sound comes from?" asked Jerome.

"That's the ones."

"What was there?" Josh knew the cats well enough by now to know that when they did something unusual, it was for a reason. He wiped his hands and handed the towel to Jerome.

Laura hesitated, took a deep breath, exhaled slowly then answered. "There was a woman's body lying over the pipes." For most ten-year olds this would be off limits for conversation, but these two had been so close to life and death in the last four months, she treated them as she would adults.

"Anyone we know?" Jerome asked sitting at the table.

"Judy Franklin. She worked at the bank."

"You mean the one whose place my mom took?" Jerome looked surprised, but also a little sad. He at least knew who the woman was.

"Afraid so."

"How awful. Does Mom know?" Jerome was very sensitive, especially where his mom was concerned.

"Probably. Todd was there."

They sat there for a minute, shaking their heads and taking in what Laura had told them. Then like the ten-year olds they were, the subject went to matters that were more important.

"Did we get any mail?" Josh asked around a bite of sandwich.

"We? Since when does Jerome get his mail here?" Laura smiled at them.

"Since we ordered our super-duper code rings together. We had them sent here in case his mother or grandmother wasn't home and the package was too big to fit in the mail slot."

"Ah, so that's what these packages are," Laura said as she got up to get two small boxes from the counter top. "What are these rings? How do they work? Show me."

"Gee, Grandma, you're as bad as Jerome. You have to wait until we get the package open first." Josh giggled as he tore at the wrappings.

"Oh," they both sighed with pleasure as they pulled the gold colored rings from the package. The large stone on top lifted and a tiny roll of paper was inside. They each unfolded their own and discovered they were just alike, except for the color of the stone on top. The paper gave instructions for developing a code.

"Come on Jerome, let's go show Grandma Sophia. I'll be back in time for supper," Josh called as they ran out the door, Rascal and Mischief right behind them.

A little later, as Laura was preparing salad for dinner, the phone pealed for her attention. She set aside the salad and hurried to beat the answering machine. I've got to get a phone in the kitchen. It wasn't the first time she thought about that—probably wouldn't be the last time, either.

"Good afternoon, Reverend Kenzel speaking."

"Laura?"

"Steve! I thought you would be busy all day."

"I just talked to Todd. I need to meet with him tonight."

"Your meetings are over?"

"For today, anyway. Got room for one more for supper? Sounds like we need to talk, too."

"There's always room for one more."

"How was Josh's first day at school?"

"It was wonderful. They were both so excited. Oh, and they got the super-duper code rings they ordered a couple of weeks ago. They'll want to show you how they work."

"Sounds like I'm going to have to do some finagling to get you alone for a few minutes tonight."

"Maybe."

Laura smiled to herself and went back to preparing dinner. A dead woman in her organ loft was not going to put a damper on her life. Colin Jacobson was in jail, one brother and a nephew were dead, only Hugh was still out there somewhere. But he couldn't do anything without Colin telling him when and how. There just couldn't be any connection between this murder and the others. It had to be purely coincidence. But, somehow, a feeling of *deja vu* and ghosts of murders past began to haunt her.

Six

"Good morning, Dorothy." Laura set her briefcase beside her desk and was surprised that Dorothy didn't answer. Must be on the phone, she thought. She followed Rascal and Mischief into Dorothy's office just as Dorothy replaced the phone in its cradle on her desk and reached for a tissue.

"Dorothy, are you all right?" Laura asked moving closer to the desk.

"Oh, Pastor," she cried. "Is there ever going to be an end to the nightmare we've lived with for so long?"

Laura had a sinking feeling in the pit of her stomach. Maybe she didn't want to know, but she had to ask. "What is it Dorothy? Who was on the phone?"

"That was Carolyn. She wanted to talk to you. I didn't hear you come in. I'll call her right back for you."

"First, tell me what's happening. Just talking to Carolyn shouldn't send you into tears—not those kinds of tears anyway." Dorothy was an emotional person who often shed a few tears of happiness for other's joys. These were not tears of happiness.

"That woman who was found here yesterday, she worked at the bank."

"I know."

"When she disappeared last week, Mr. Gordon, the new bank manager, asked Carolyn to take her job."

"I don't understand. Why should that…? Oh, no, surely they don't…" Laura's face reflected the horror of what she was thinking. Somehow, someone was pulling Carolyn into the Jacobson mess.

Dorothy nodded her head and blew her nose. "The woman's husband is accusing Carolyn of all kinds of things, including murder. Todd is threatening to turn in his badge before he will arrest her. Mark says he won't stay on without Todd and he certainly won't arrest Carolyn. It's such an awful situation. Mr. Gordon suspended Carolyn because the DA's office said they are indicting her for murder. She's at home. I'll call her back for you."

"No, don't call her… Second thought, call her. Tell her I'm on my way over there. If anyone else calls, I'll return the call later. If Steve should call, tell him what you told me and where I've gone."

"I've known Carolyn since we were kids. She couldn't even kill a bug without going to pieces."

"I know, Dorothy. Surely, there are other suspects. Todd will work it out. If he can't be objective, Steve will…" She realized that Steve also might be too close to be objective. After all, he would be the best man at the wedding. "We'll work it out one way or another. Call SaraBelle, Martha, and Cora. The rest will get it on the grapevine. Those three will know what to do to get the prayer wheels turning. I'll be back as soon as I can."

Strains of Bach drifted from the sanctuary into the office and Dorothy turned her head in that direction, listening. "Didn't that man from Melody's fix the organ yesterday?"

"I thought so. It sounds good to me. Why do you ask?" Laura asked as she too listened to the beauty of the music that contrasted so sharply with the news she just received.

"Well, he's back this morning. I just heard him come in with Karen. I hope there's nothing seriously wrong with the organ."

Laura chuckled in spite of the horrible news Dorothy had just given her. "It might develop into something serious, but I don't think it's the organ—more likely the organist and technician. Karen and George hit it off as if they'd been friends forever. He seems like a really nice young man."

Dorothy smiled. "Really? Karen and…?"

"Sure looked like it to me. There are always causes for celebration, Dorothy, so keep your faith up. Talk to you later."

Laura could have walked to Carolyn's house from the church, but she might need her car later. She opened the driver's door and two furry blurs shot past her into the back seat. She sighed. "Trouble ahead? If you guys sense I need you, it must be bad." Rascal and Mischief stared ahead, waiting for her to start the car.

"Shebop," she spoke to her car as she slid behind the wheel, "here we go again. If only people were as faithful as cars and cats," she glanced in the mirror at Rascal and Mischief sitting like a king and queen surveying their kingdom, "we wouldn't have so many problems."

Even though Laura knew God was already ahead of her—After all, He had alerted Cora, who had given her another brief call before she left the house this morning—she needed reassurance.

"God, give me the wisdom to know what to say. Don't let me lose my temper. I want to be a help, not a hindrance. And Lord, give Carolyn the strength she needs to get through this—and Todd and Jerome." Laura sighed. "Jerome is just a kid and he's already seen far too much violence and heartache."

* * *

When Laura arrived, Carolyn flew sobbing into her arms before she hardly had the door open. Laura held her until Carolyn was able to breathe without gulping air. Wiping her eyes and blowing her nose, she tried to laugh as Rascal and Mischief squeezed past them into the house, swiping her legs with furry tails.

"I'm sorry, Pastor. I'm such a mess. After all the stuff you've been through and I go to pieces with one little bit of bad news."

"Carolyn, being accused of murder is not a small matter. This is serious. You have a right to fall apart. I'm not sure that I would handle it any differently."

Carolyn glanced down at the cats who sat staring at her. "Do you always take your body guards with you when you call on those accused of murder?"

Laura smiled. "You should know by now that the cats make their own choices. They didn't ask. They just flew into the car and came."

"Come on in and sit down," Sophia called from the kitchen. "I've got the kettle on to make a pot of tea. I can always think better with a cup of hot tea in my hand."

Carolyn rolled her eyes and shook her head. "Mother is trying so hard to be brave, but I know she's scared to death."

"I'm sure she is," Laura said as they walked to the kitchen trailed by Rascal and Mischief.

"A cup of tea sounds great to me," she told Sophia.

The kitchen was a roomy place with lots of windows and lace curtains that let in the sunlight. Carolyn had worked hard to make this little house a home for herself and Jerome. They liked the location, so she and Todd planned to live there after they were married.

Carolyn got cups from the cabinet while Sophia poured steaming water in the teapot. Laura noticed, not for the first time, how much Carolyn looked like her mother. Both were medium height with hazel eyes. Sophia's hair was now nearly white and Carolyn's a light brown with a slight tint of red.

Sophia poured a cup of tea for each of them and set a saucer of milk down for Rascal and Mischief. The women sat around the table to talk while Rascal and Mischief sat on the floor near Laura. They watched and listened with ears twitching.

"Now," said Sophia, "we need to keep our heads. We all know you didn't kill that woman, Carolyn, so we have to concentrate on checking our facts. I'm sure the evidence will show that you had nothing to do with the murder. Just because the woman's husband is hurting and needs to find someone to blame, doesn't make a case against you. He's probably feeling guilty because she found it necessary to have an affair with Ed Winters."

"You know, Carolyn, I think your mother has a point. The first thing they will look for is an alibi. Before we can know that, we need to know when she died. Did Todd say?"

Tears ran down her face again as Carolyn tried to answer. "He couldn't talk to me about it. He wanted to, but he is under some kind of court order not to even speak to me."

"Court order? What kind of court order? From who? Or Whom? Or whatever? I never heard of such a thing!" Anger spilled out with each word.

"The Prosecuting Attorney got Judge Walker to issue some kind of restraining order to keep Todd from talking to anyone until things are sorted out."

"That doesn't make any sense at all. Can I use your phone?" Laura moved toward the phone, a confused expression spreading across her face.

"Sure, but it won't do any good to call him. He can't talk to you either." Carolyn looked up at her, tears stopped for the moment. She dabbed at her eyes with a tissue and blew her nose.

"How did you find this out? Did Todd tell you?"

"No, he couldn't even call me. He had Mark do it. Mark said if Todd talked to me, we would both be in trouble. He said Todd would call me later, even if he has to turn in his badge to do it."

"Trouble? How? With whom?" Laura picked up the phone and dialed.

"Morgan here."

"Steve, I need some help."

"No more dead bodies, I hope," he answered cautiously.

"No," she said, "I wish it were that simple. Have you talked to Todd today?"

"No, I was just going to call him. What's up?"

"Carolyn is under suspicion for the murder of that woman, Judy Franklin."

"What?" She could hear the disbelief in his voice.

"It seems the Prosecuting Attorney has gotten some kind of order from Judge Walker to keep Todd from talking to anyone connected with the case—including me and probably you. He can't talk to Carolyn about anything at all. None of this makes any sense—the Prosecuting Attorney, the judge, the order. We know she didn't do it, but we don't even know when the woman was murdered. Am I making sense? I feel like I'm in the midst of a badly written mystery farce. It's all so preposterous."

"You're right. It doesn't make any sense," he replied. "I never heard of that kind of an order. You want to know the time of the murder. I haven't got that information, Laura."

"They haven't given you orders not to talk to me, have they? You would at least tell me if they did, wouldn't you?"

"What kind of heel do you think I am?" He was almost angry.

"I'm sorry I'm just so confused I don't know what to think. Todd has orders not to talk to Carolyn. Mark called her for him. I know you wouldn't do that to me if you could help it, but… It's all so bizarre. Please, Steve, help me to understand this."

"Laura, I'm sorry I snapped at you. You're right. This is preposterous. If I call Todd…I don't believe either the Prosecuting Attorney or Judge Walker have anything to do with this. Let me think about it. I'll see what I can find out and call you back. Are you at the office?"

"No, I'm at Carolyn's. Thanks Steve."

"I'll talk to you in a few minutes."

"I gather he hasn't talked to Todd today. He doesn't know what's going on—or he can't say." Sophia said as she refilled their cups.

"He doesn't know anything. He was just going to call Todd. He doesn't believe the Prosecuting Attorney or Judge Walker have anything to do with what's happening here. He'll call me back."

"I just don't understand," cried Carolyn. "I hardly knew the woman. Oh, we were friendly at the bank, but not socially. I don't know her husband at all—not even his name."

"Carolyn, I hate to even think this," Laura was hesitant, "but I have a feeling it's all somehow connected with what's happened before. It's not you they are after, it's me. By hurting you, they're hurting me."

"Laura, you can't mean that." Sophia stared at her.

"I don't know what to think, or what I mean. It's just a gut feeling. I…" Rascal and Mischief growled as if agreeing with her.

The phone rang.

"Hello," said Sophia. "Sure, Steve, she's right here." She handed the phone to Laura.

"I've got to talk fast, so don't interrupt me. The woman was Judy Franklin, who worked at the bank. She disappeared last Thursday. The coroner said she died approximately midnight Monday. She was strangled somewhere else and carried up to the loft. Her husband, Robert, is accusing Carolyn, because Carolyn took the job Judy had. He also said Judy told him Carolyn accused her of having an affair with Ed Winters and others, including Todd."

"But that's…"

"Don't interrupt. Robert said Judy also told him she and Carolyn had words on Wednesday about Todd. The woman's brother is here from New York and declares he witnessed her telling Robert this. They told Judy she should file a complaint against Carolyn, which she said she would the next day. She thought she might try to talk to Carolyn Wednesday night. She disappeared—didn't come home. They never saw her again until yesterday at the morgue. That's about all I could learn. The husband also has a motive if she was sleeping around the way they say she was. Laura, here comes the man who claims he's from for the Prosecuting Attorney's office with my orders. Hang loose until we can get this charade untangled. Don't talk to him if you can avoid it." Steve changed to a more professional tone. "That's the best I can do for you, Sir. Hope you find your dog soon. Goodbye."

Laura stood holding the buzzing phone then turned to the waiting women and repeated what Steve had said. "The man claiming to be from the Prosecuting Attorney's office came in while Steve was talking to me."

Seven

With ears twitching and tails slapping the floor in agitation, Rascal and Mischief watched as if they knew something the women didn't know. Their behavior concerned Laura, but she didn't want to worry Carolyn and Sophia any more than they already were. She would simply keep an eye on Rascal and Mischief and follow their cues.

"All right, we still don't know much," she said, "but we do know more than we did." Laura pulled a note pad and pen from her purse. "Someone strangled the woman around midnight Monday, after all the celebrations and fireworks, maybe even during the fireworks. She was a small person, but it would still take some strength to carry her dead weight up those steps to the pipe loft."

"How did they get into the church?" Sophia refilled their cups.

"Not too difficult," said Laura, "with so many doors and windows on or near the ground level. Todd's men went over the entire building and found a window in the furnace room that looked locked, but wasn't. Probably been that way since Jeb Little camped in the belfry with the cats." Laura paused, took a sip of her tea. She frowned, not at the tea, but at her churning thoughts.

"Todd and I were at your house until around one a.m. Monday," said Carolyn with a sense of dawning hope.

"That's right," said Laura. "Sophia, you took Jerome home after the fireworks and put him to bed since Tuesday was the first day of school. Josh went to bed soon after Jerome left."

"You, Steve, Todd and I talked, listened to music, and played some board games after that," said Carolyn.

"Todd knows that, but he's probably too stressed to think clearly." Laura took another sip of her tea.

"Is this normal procedure? Preventing people from talking to each other, I mean." Sophia frowned.

"No," answered Laura, "that's what doesn't make any sense to me. It's almost as if someone—the prosecutor, judge, or someone who wants us to think it's them—is trying to slow down the investigation. The question is, why? Anyone who takes over from Todd will learn the truth immediately."

"What about her husband? Is he a suspect at all?"

"He was. Her brother from New York swears that Robert Franklin is innocent." Laura let her thoughts roam then said, "I would like for the cats to meet her brother."

Carolyn gave her a confused look. "Why on earth would you want that?"

"They've never been wrong about character assessment yet. Did I tell you what they did yesterday?"

Rascal's and Mischief's ears perked up at the mention of their names.

"No," Sophia and Carolyn both answered.

"Well, they went with me to church like they usually do…" Laura told them how they had discovered the body; how they had instantly taken a liking to George; and how George and Karen had hit if off immediately. "As a matter of fact," Laura added, "George was back this morning. The organ is fixed, but I am sure he found something that needed cleaning. Of course Karen was there too."

"Oh, that's wonderful," exclaimed Sophia. She was one of the women who had tried to play Cupid for Karen.

"Mother, don't even think about interfering. It sounds like Karen is doing very well on her own."

"Would I do that?" Sophia asked innocently.

"You would if you had half a chance," Carolyn accused with a note of sarcasm.

"I don't think this budding romance is going to need any outside help," Laura said.

"Well," said Carolyn sobering and sighing deeply, "it's good to know life is still good somewhere, but where do *we* go from here? What's next? I can't just sit here worrying and waiting for someone to arrest me."

"Do you have a lawyer? I don't think you'll need one, but it's better to be prepared."

"I've never needed a lawyer before," Carolyn answered. "Cottonville's only lawyer got himself killed earlier this summer. Remember? Of course, I wouldn't have gone to him anyway."

"How could we forget?" Laura shuddered at the remembrance of Rascal and Mischief unearthing his body in her garden.

"Actually, Mike Atkins wasn't a bad person until he got mixed up with the Jacobsons," said Sophia. "Still he didn't deserve to be murdered and left in Laura's newly plowed garden last spring." Sophia was thoughtful for a minute then added half jokingly, "You know, a person could get a little paranoid about holidays around here—Mother's Day, Memorial Day, and now Labor Day."

Laura felt a chill slide down her spine but forced a smile at Sophia's feeble attempt at humor. The ringing phone saved her from having to comment. Sophia reached for it.

"Hello," she answered then laughed. "You got the right number, SaraBelle. This is Sophia. Carolyn is right here." She handed the phone to Carolyn.

"SaraBelle! How good of you to call... Well, yes, I guess you could say I'm in a little hot water and it feels like it's getting hotter... You do? ...Oh, I couldn't... Well, all right. Thank you, SaraBelle. God bless you. Bye." The tears were streaming down her face again when she turned back to her mother and Laura.

"What is it darling," asked her mother. "What did SaraBelle say?"

"She thought I might need a lawyer, so she called her attorney from Glenville—James Coffman. He's on his way over right now. She's paying the bill. Wouldn't take no for an answer. Oh, Mom, why do people treat me so good, when I've been so bad?" More tears streamed down her face.

"Carolyn, you haven't been bad," Sophia protested. "You made a mistake when you ran away with the McMichaels' boy, but that was over ten years ago. People in Cottonville love you. Accept their love and be grateful."

"She's right, Carolyn," said Laura. "Don't deny SaraBelle and others the joy of doing something for you. It's their gift. Accept it."

"I just wish I didn't have a need for that kind of gift."

"Try not to worry about it. Be honest with your lawyer," Laura advised. "I'm sure he'll be able to work this out for you. SaraBelle doesn't employ second-rate people in anything she does. Did she say when she called him?" Laura was checking her watch to see if she had time to stay and wait, or if she should go.

"She didn't say. She did say he should be here any time, so I gathered she called him earlier."

"Probably about the time I left the office. I told Dorothy to call her. I think I..." Laura paused at the knock on the front door. She looked at the other two women.

"I'll get it," said Sophia started to the living room. Laura and Carolyn followed. Rascal and Mischief zipped past Sophia and placed themselves between her and the door. Rascal began pawing at the screen door handle.

A man in a dark blue, pinstriped suit stood on the porch with his fist raised to knock again. He doesn't look like the kind of lawyer SaraBelle would hire, Laura thought. He reminds me more of a gangster in an old movie. Something is dreadfully wrong here. She glanced down at Rascal and Mischief. Their fur stood on end, ears laid back. Mischief sat with her tail thumping the floor while Rascal continued to try to open the door.

Thinking he was the lawyer SaraBelle had sent, Carolyn smiled and reached around her mother to open the door. "Mr. Coffman? I'm Carolyn McMichaels."

"Well, Ms. Carolyn McMichaels, I don't know who this Coffman is, but I hope you're happy now that my sister is dead. You're going to pay for it; believe me, you *will* pay. You'll be lucky if you get out of jail in time to see your grandchildren married."

Laura eased in front of Carolyn, who had turned ashen and laid her hand over the door handle. "Who are you?"

"None of *your* business, *Reverend* Kenzel. She's going to pay for my sister's death. And if you don't want your reputation to be ruined, I suggest you stay away from her. Everyone she loves will feel what she's done."

"I think you better leave before I open the door for my cats. I don't think you want to meet them." Laura spoke with controlled anger. Rascal and Mischief growled and snarled pawing at the door that Laura held tightly shut. Rascal would open it if she let go.

"You better listen to her, Mister. Whoever you are, you have no right harassing my client." Laura had been watching the man so closely she hadn't seen another stranger approach. The deep male voice startled her. She glanced from the sneering brother to the man behind him. This one was of medium height, about forty years old, trim, fit figure, in gray slacks and light green golf shirt. He stood with feet apart and hands on hips.

"Who's afraid of cats?" The sneer seemed pasted to his face. He turned to the new stranger. "And who do you think you are—some big shot lawyer? Well we'll make mincemeat of you when this case comes to trial." The man glared and Laura had a sudden feeling of premonition or insight. She didn't know *who* the man who claimed to be the "brother" was, but she knew who had sent him.

"In case I didn't make myself clear," said the lawyer, "you have three seconds to be off this property or you will face charges of harassment and trespassing. And in the event you can't count that high, I will assist you—one; two."

The man, who the women assumed was Judy Franklin's brother, sneered obviously with no intention of leaving right away. "No big shot, small town lawyer, or preacher,"—He glared at Laura—"is going to tell me what to do."

"Three," said the lawyer, but before he could say, or do anything more, Rascal smacked Laura's hand away from the door. It flew open and two felines with backs arched and fur on end stood hissing before the intruder. His eyes widened and he began backing down the steps, not taking his eyes off the cats. They inched down the path after him, hissing and snarling.

"Whoa," he said. "You didn't say they were wild cats. You wait; I'll get you for this. It's against the law to have unleashed wild animals."

"Just keep moving and they won't touch you," said Laura. "Take one more step this way and I won't be responsible for what they do."

The man retreated, got in his car and left rubber marks on the street as he took off. Rascal and Mischief shook themselves and returned to Laura.

"Would they really attack? Are they safe?" The second man looked warily at Rascal and Mischief.

"Yes, they would attack, and yes they are safe." Laura smiled. "You must be James Coffman. Talk about timing, you couldn't have timed that better if you had planned it. I'm Laura Kenzel." She opened the door for him. "This is Carolyn McMichaels and her mother, Sophia Dugal. Please come in. I'll be on my way, Carolyn. Call me if you need me."

"Thank you Reverend Kenzel—SaraBelle told me about you and your cats. I thought she was exaggerating. Maybe not. You're welcome to stay, if you want. I expect I'll want to talk to you anyway." James Coffman's smile was genuine, showing a set of beautiful, white teeth.

"Thank you, Mr. Coffman, but I think it's better if you talk with your client first. You're welcome to drop by my office later if you want to, or I can come back."

"You're right. I do need to get to know my client and hear her story. I will stop by your office later. Right now, I need to get the facts and find out where we go from here. Oh, by the way, I talked to Steve Morgan, before I came over. Someone from Judge Walker's office had just served him *orders* preventing him from talking to anyone about the case. He said you might be able to fill me in?" He gave Laura a quizzical glance.

She looked surprised then smiled. "Sure, stop by…second thought, why don't I tell you what he said now…just in case they decide to put an order out for me…on the off chance that I know something."

Eight

Laura gave James Coffman what information she had, then left intending to make hospital calls before returning home for lunch. Rascal and Mischief, however, made it very clear they didn't want her to go to the hospital. They set up a Maine Coon duet howling session until she turned back to the church.

"I'll leave you two at home when I make my calls," she said. "Do you mind if I check my messages first?" Her sarcasm was lost in the Maine Coon fur, but it lessened her irritation. "I can't believe you're so hungry you couldn't wait until I made a few calls. If I can wait, so can you."

Two sets of emerald green eyes glared at her. They turned their backs and curled into a catnap position to wait.

"No use getting too comfortable, unless you plan on sleeping there all afternoon. I'm going home for lunch in about five minutes."

Rascal and Mischief twitched their ears but otherwise ignored her.

"All right," she said. "Suit yourselves. I'll leave the window open. It doesn't look like rain." She left them in the car and went to check her messages. Her head still spinning over the bizarre turn of events, Laura approached her desk. Was the world going crazy, or was she? Steve was right. Surely, neither the Prosecuting Attorney nor Judge Walker would be involved in something so blatantly childish.

A full sheet of paper lay in the middle of her otherwise cleared desk. She couldn't miss it. Must be important. That recurring chill of foreboding sent a shiver down her spine as she reached for the note. *Tried Carolyn's but you already left. Also left message on home phone. Call the school. Urgent!*

"Now what?" Laura reached for the phone, a sense of panic twisting her stomach in knots. Was Josh hurt? It was only the second day of school. He couldn't be in trouble already. Could he?

"Good afternoon. Grayson Elementary School. Miss Richards speaking."

"Good afternoon, Miss Richards," said Laura more pleasantly than she felt. It was an hour past her lunchtime and her intuition told her she was not going to get that meal any time soon—if at all. "This is Reverend Kenzel returning your call."

"Yes, Reverend Kenzel. Mrs. Ellison our principal wants to talk to you. Please hold on while I transfer your call."

The queasiness in her stomach increased and it had nothing to do with missing lunch. After what seemed hours, Mrs. Ellison came on the line.

"Reverend Kenzel, thank you for returning my call. I'm not sure how to approach the subject, so I guess I'll just have to blurt it out as the kids say. Josh and Jerome were fighting at lunchtime. Normally we suspend students immediately for that offense. Since it's only the second day of school and understanding the circumstances of Jerome's home right now, I thought it would be better if I contacted you first. I haven't talked to Jerome's mother. I guess I hoped you would have time to…"

"I will be there in five minutes. Are the boys in your office?"

"Yes. I'm using Miss Richards' phone. I'm really sorry to bother you."

"Thank you Mrs. Ellison. You did the right thing. I don't understand what happened, but believe me I will know before this day is over. I'll see you in a few minutes."

"Thank you."

Josh and Jerome fighting? The world *is* going crazy.

Laura got in her car and glanced at the cats. Their eyes were half-open, so she knew they weren't asleep. "You knew the boys were in trouble, didn't you?"

Rascal and Mischief blinked, sat alert, ready for battle. "All right, but don't make things worse. Be good kitties." She started the car. Lunch would have to wait and so would her other calls. Forcing herself to stay within the speed limit, she was at the school within a couple of minutes.

Not bothering to find a space in the visitors' lot, she parked in front of the building. Rascal and Mischief ran ahead of her, waiting only for her to open the door. Inside she hurried down the long hall to the principal's office. Taking a deep breath, she followed the cats into Miss Richards' office.

"Reverend Kenzel, this way please." She got up from her desk and walked to the closed door with the word PRINCIPAL in bold black letters.

Miss Richards smiled at the cats who had often accompanied Jerome to school the previous spring. She tapped on the principal's door, opened it a crack and said, "Reverend Kenzel is here to see you, Mrs. Ellison."

"Show her in, Margaret."

Miss Richards stepped aside and held the door open for Laura. Rascal and Mischief trotted into the room, tails waving like battle flags. Laura followed, feeling like she was entering the lion's den or the fiery furnace. Miss Richards closed the door behind her. Mrs. Ellison's office was roomy with a large desk, a couch, a couple of overstuffed chairs, a small table with a straight-backed chair beside it. Josh and Jerome sat in the two chairs at opposite ends of the room, glaring at each other. Each sported a black eye and torn shirt. Mrs. Ellison had been sitting behind her desk, but rose when Laura entered. She walked around and extended her hand.

"Reverend Kenzel, it is so good of you to stop by." It sounded as if she assumed Laura was just in the neighborhood and decided to see how the boys were doing. Laura understood. Mrs. Ellison didn't want the boys to know she had called her.

"It looks like I chose a good time. Josh? Jerome? Is there something you need to tell me?"

Neither boy spoke. They continued to glare. Rascal and Mischief sat like stone statues—one in front of each boy—watching them. The boys were so intent on glaring at each other they hadn't even noticed.

"I wanted to see your teacher and thank her for helping you stay out of trouble," said Laura feeling like she was stretching the truth to its limits. "Maybe that is a little premature."

Both boys started yelling at each other trying to make her think it was the other one's fault.

"He started it. He said you were causing his mother trouble," shouted Josh.

"He started it. He punched me," Jerome shouted at the same time.

They continued to yell at each other, calling the other one names, accusing them of whatever they could think of.

Laura glanced at Mrs. Ellison, motioning with her hand to let her handle it then let them shout at each other for about a half a minute—long enough for her to get her own temper under control. Finally, she raised her voice slightly, emphasizing each word, "*Stop that this instant.*"

Josh and Jerome stopped, mouths open for the next verbal attack. Laura had never raised her voice at either of them before. Never! She was angry and they knew it. She had never been angry with them before either. She stood towering over them, looking from one to the other. Their lips began to quiver.

46

Nine

When she had their attention and her anger under control, Laura said more quietly, "Both of you move over to that couch." They started to sit at opposite ends. "In the middle...together."

Laura knelt on the floor in front of them, leaning back on her heels. Rascal and Mischief sat on either side of her.

"Now, we're all on the same level. I want to know what happened and why."

They both started to talk again, but she raised her hand to silence them.

"One at a time. Josh, you first."

Josh started mumbling something.

"Josh, we don't mumble when we have something important to say."

"I'm sorry." Tears started to roll down his face.

"That's a good start, Josh, but I need to know what would bring you and Jerome to blows."

"He said he couldn't talk to me any more because you were causing trouble for his mother. I said you didn't have anything to do with it and he said it was all your fault."

Laura turned to Jerome. "Jerome, did you say that to Josh?"

Jerome brushed at his own tears. "That's what the man told me. He said if I didn't stay away from Josh and you, my mother would go to jail for a long, long time. So I had to make Josh mad enough to stay away from me."

"Jerome!" Laura took a deep breath. She heard Mrs. Ellison's quick intake of breath as well. "What man told you that, and when?"

"I don't know who he was. He called me over to the fence when we went out for lunch recess. He said he was from the Prosecuting Attorney's office. Josh wasn't out yet. He was helping Miss Campbell do something."

"What did the man look like?"

"He was sort of tall. He had a dark gray or black hat and a dark colored sort of striped suit."

Laura took another deep breath, reached out to the boys, and placed a hand on each of them.

"I want you boys to listen very carefully to me. I don't know what is going on or why. Someone is playing a very cruel, practical joke. Your mother had nothing to do with that woman's death, Jerome. Someone is doing their best to make enemies of all of us—you boys, your mother, Todd, Steve, and me. I don't know who that man was, but everything he told you was a lie. Whatever is going on, I will get to the bottom of it—today. Now, I want you two to kiss and make up so I can go find out where the real problem is."

Rascal and Mischief chose that moment to make their presence known. They each jumped on a boys lap and smacked a nose with a paw, claws held back.

"Ouch," they both exclaimed together.

Laura smiled and said, "Now, kiss and make up."

"Yuck!" They both spoke as one and then started giggling. "Boys don't kiss and make up," said Josh.

"Yeah, only men and women do that. Like Todd and Mom." Jerome added.

"And you and Grandpa Steve," said Josh.

Laura laughed and heard Mrs. Ellison chuckle behind her. "All right what do boys do?"

"We give our secret handshake like this," Jerome said. And he and Josh demonstrated their secret handshake. Laura enfolded both boys in her arms and did the inexcusable. She kissed each of them on the cheek.

"Grandma!" exclaimed Josh

"Pastor!"

"You have a problem with being kissed in public? Then don't ever let me catch you in this kind of predicament again."

The cats wrapped themselves around the boys' shoulders, purred in their ears, and licked their cheeks.

"Pastor," said Jerome. "I really am sorry. I shouldn't have listened to a stranger. I should know better."

"Jerome, you are only a child. Your mom, Chief Todd, and Detective Steve have all been taken in by this very sharp, shrewd man."

"They have?"

"Yes, it's a little different story, but I'm sure it has all come from the same source and I'm going to put an end to it right now."

"Grandma?"

"Yes, Josh?"

"Is *he* behind it?"

"I don't know, sweetheart. I hope not." She knew he meant Colin Jacobson alias Bill Collins.

"Me too," he whispered.

"I think you can go back to class now, boys," said Mrs. Ellison. "But, if this ever happens again, I will have to suspend you."

"You called her didn't you," asked Josh. He wasn't angry and it wasn't even a question as much as it was a statement.

"I had to call someone," Mrs. Ellison answered.

"Thank you," said Josh. "I'm glad you did. I don't like being mad at Jerome. It hurts too much."

"Yeah, almost as much as when Uncle Jerome died," answered his friend. "Thank you, Mrs. Ellison—and thank you for not calling my mom. She's hurting too much for this."

"I know, Jerome. It will work out. She's a good woman. Now, you boys get back to class…"They started to run for the door. "…but don't run."

Mischief followed the boys. Laura breathed deeply and exhaled slowly then glanced down at Rascal who sat like a statue beside her. "Apparently, they have decided the boys and I both need watching," she said. "Do you mind if she goes to class with them. She will make herself practically invisible."

"As long as she doesn't interrupt the class, I'm sure Miss Campbell won't mind. Thank you for coming in Reverend Kenzel. I just knew there had to be something unusual that would cause those boys to fight. They're good kids. And I heard Carolyn is having a rough time right now. She didn't need to handle this too."

"I'm glad you called me. Please call any time you need my help. I love those boys as if they were my own. I can't stand the thought of them not getting along. Now I have to go confront someone else about what is going on. I hate confrontations."

"I know what you mean. Not many of us really enjoy them. I really admired the way you handled those boys. Are you sure you wouldn't like a job here as a teacher—or counselor?"

"Positive," answered Laura. "God is having a hard enough time shaping me into a pastor. I don't need to complicate things by taking on another job."

Deep in her soul, the soft chuckle confirmed her evaluation.

Ten

Laura wasn't at all sure she would make it to her car. Her knees wanted to buckle and her nerves felt like rubber bands stretched beyond their limit. She would rather go home and sit for a while in communion with God, but she had one more confrontation to make before she could do that.

Sliding across the seat, Laura gripped the steering wheel. Rascal climbed over her lap to the passenger seat since Mischief wasn't with him. Laura paused to get her bearings before starting the car. "Lord, You know how I hate this kind of stuff. What kind of man would deliberately set two young boys against each other? And why is he doing this to Carolyn? He has to be taking orders from Bill Collins. Please tell me I'm on the wrong track. Tell me it's all a big joke."

Laura waited for that soft chuckle in her soul she had learned to depend upon. It wasn't there. All she felt was an overwhelming sense of urgency.

"All right, I get the message. It's serious and I need to do something about it now. Give me strength and courage. I'm scared to death. I could land in jail."

Then she sensed the soft chuckle in her soul.

"You think that's funny, do you? Well, if I'm in jail, who will find all those dead bodies that keep popping up like mushrooms?"

The chuckle felt more like a belly laugh. Laura's heart felt a little lighter as she started her car and headed downtown for her next stop.

"Rascal, one more emotion-filled encounter, and then I hope we can go home."

He blinked, settled down on the seat, tucked his front paws under him, and closed his eyes for a quick catnap.

A parking spot in front of the courthouse was open and Laura slid her Chevette into it. Taking a deep breath to calm her nerves, she entered the city building. Rascal trotted beside her as she walked across the polished marble floor. She checked the list of offices on the brass plates beside the elevators. Judge Conrad Walker—Room 308.

"Here we go, Rascal." They stepped into the elevator and it rose smoothly to the third floor, and stopped. When the door slid open, Laura stepped out. Rascal brushed against her leg as he ran ahead.

Taking another deep breath, Laura walked down the long carpeted hall to the door marked: Judge Conrad Walker. Rascal was already there, waiting. How did he know the right door? At least he waited for me to open it.

In the waiting area, a tall, thin woman with her gray-streaked black hair pulled into a bun at the nape of her neck, sat at the reception desk. Her eyes were on the computer screen before her; she didn't look up. The nameplate said, Pauline Berry, Secretary, but Laura sensed she was more than an ordinary secretary. She was probably more of an administrative assistant.

Ms. Berry continued what she was doing as if she hadn't seen or heard Laura. Rascal sat beside the desk, the tip of his tail slapping the floor—his equivalent to Laura's impatient toe-tapping. They both knew the woman deliberately ignored them.

"Excuse me," Laura said. She'd waited long enough.

"Yes?" The woman hardly glanced up away from the screen.

"I'm Reverend Laura Kenzel and I need to see Judge Walker." The woman behind the desk would not intimidate her.

"Do you have an appointment?" Ms. Berry glanced at her appointment book which lay open beside her computer.

"No, I don't, but this is an emergency. It's urgent that I see him—today."

"Judge Walker is booked all afternoon. If you want to make an appointment, I can get you in…" She flipped through the pages of her appointment book. "…next Thursday."

"I need to see him now—today." Laura said. A sense of panic grew alarmingly in her already knotted stomach.

"That's impossible, Ms.…"

"Kenzel, *Reverend* Kenzel."

"Reverend Kenzel, it isn't possible to see Judge Walker today. He's with the Prosecuting Attorney right now and is booked for the rest of the day."

Laura looked around to determine which of the several doors might be the Judge's office. Rascal had already approached one and began working at the doorknob. Laura knew he could open doors, but had never actually seen him do it. She watched him from the corner of her eye, while trying to divert Ms. Berry. "Would you give him my name and ask him to see me for a few minutes?"

"No, I'm sorry, but he's very busy and asked not to be disturbed." Ms. Berry glanced toward the door to her right as she spoke. At that moment, the door clicked, and Rascal pushed with his front paws. Slowly it swung open.

"I'm sorry, too" said Laura, "but I simply must see him today." She moved quickly toward the door that Rascal had so conveniently opened for her.

The woman rose from her desk and moved with more speed than Laura thought was possible, but Laura was quicker. She followed Rascal into the room. Judge Walker was talking with a pretty, young woman whose pen paused over the yellow legal pad before her. The judge looked up at Laura, more surprised than alarmed.

"I'm sorry, Judge Walker," said Ms. Berry. "I tried to stop her. I pushed the button for security. I hear him coming now."

"Judge Walker," Laura said, anger and fear giving her courage, "Please, sir. I *must* talk to you. I'm willing to wait, but I have to talk to you today—as soon as possible."

At that moment the security guard rushed in, gun in hand. Rascal jumped between Laura and the guard, back arched, fur on end, hissing through bared teeth. The man pointed the gun at him ready to pull the trigger. Laura grabbed Rascal, holding him close to her. He squirmed.

"Please, put the gun away. He thinks you are going to harm me. He's not dangerous, except to criminals." Laura held tightly, fighting her fear and anger and a struggling cat.

"Put the gun away, Miller," said the judge.

The man holstered his gun, but stood by for further orders. Laura released Rascal who sat between her and the guard, ears back, eyes narrowed as if daring the man to move.

"Now, ma'am," the judge turned to Laura, "I'll give you about three minutes to explain who you are and what gives you the right to barge into my office with an unleashed wild animal." He spoke evenly, keeping his eyes on Laura.

Laura took a deep breath, returned his gaze, and answered, "I'm Reverend Laura Kenzel and the only right I have for barging in is that my friends are being torn apart by some order that you *supposedly* signed. A man, who says he's from the Prosecuting Attorney's office, even went to the school and managed to turn my ten-year old grandson and his best friend against each other. I haven't met you, Judge Walker, but from what I've heard, you are a just and honorable man. I can't believe you would do such a thing, but you're the only one who can stop it."

Laura struggled to keep the anger from her voice. She wasn't stating her case very well, and it was her only chance.

"Shall I throw her out?" The security guard waited by the door, his hand near the gun, itching to use it. Rascal growled and stood his ground.

"Thank you, Miller, for being alert, but I think I want to hear what Reverend Kenzel has to say. I'll have Pauline call if I need you."

The security guard and secretary scowled at Laura and Rascal as they left the room. Judge Walker looked at Laura. "You know, Reverend Kenzel, I could have you put in jail for barging in like that."

"I know, but it seems another judge in another time told someone greater than I the same thing. And my answer is the same as His, 'you would have no power except that God gives it to you.'"

Judge Walker laughed. The young woman looked confused.

"I'm sorry, Judge, I didn't come here to preach to you."

"I like you, Reverend Kenzel. I've heard a lot about you as well. And from what I hear, you would never barge in here without a reason. And if you had a reason, nothing would stop you, not dead bodies or even bullets. Now, please say hello to D. J. Summerfield, Prosecuting Attorney and be seated. Then I want you to start at the beginning and tell me why you're here. These friends, would they include the Cottonville's Police Chief Williams and Glenville's Homicide Detective Morgan?"

Laura sat in a leather armchair beside D.J.'s chair. Rascal jumped to a corner of the judge's desk. "Rascal, you don't get on other people's desks without asking."

Rascal turned to Judge Walker, bowed, and said, "Meow?"

Judge Walker, surprised, chuckled, and reached a hand to Rascal, who laid his paw in it as if shaking hands. The judge laughed again. "Of course, you may sit there as long as you don't chew up my papers."

Rascal said, "Meow," and covered his face with a paw as if snickering at them. D. J. and Judge Walker laughed. Rascal then sat like a sphinx guarding a tomb.

"I apologize for him, sir. He's very protective and smart, but he was trained to be a performer."

"And a very good one," said the judge. "Now, back to my question. These friends of yours?"

"Yes," answered Laura. "Todd, Steve and the others."

"And does all this involve the woman's body you found in your church?"

"Yes, again, except I didn't find her. Our organ technician did."

"Now, what is all this about your friend being accused of murder." He glanced at D. J. "Did we make an arrest on that case?"

"Not that I'm aware of. We have two suspects—the husband and a woman named Carolyn McMichaels."

"Is that the friend?" The judge peered at Laura over his square, half reading glasses.

"Yes, but she..."

"Excuse me a moment. You two get acquainted while I check with Pauline."

Laura wondered, is he going to call security back and have me put in jail after all?

Eleven

"Reverend Kenzel, do you always do things so…so…dramatically? Does your cat often open doors for you?"

Laura laughed in spite of her panic. "Please, call me Laura. I don't intend to be dramatic, but when I feel strongly about something, I simply have to act on it, regardless of the consequences. And yes, Rascal often accompanies me and sometimes opens doors. He and Mischief are two Maine Coon Cats who adopted me when Jerome McMichaels and I rescued them from my church belfry. They've saved our lives several times. Mischief is at the school right now, guarding the boys, because of this trouble."

"You would actually be willing to go to jail to help your friends?"

"They have all done so much for me. Can I do less for them?" She paused then asked, "What does D. J. stand for?"

It was D. J.'s turn to laugh. "Daisy June. Doesn't that make a nice sounding name for the Prosecuting Attorney? Daisy June Summerfield. The jerks around the courthouse would have a field day with that. I started using my initials in college. It sounds more professional."

Laura laughed and told her about her own name—Laurance Ellen. "The District Superintendent who sent me here made a point of giving the first name and middle initial to the church. They thought they were getting a man. That was fun trying to explain."

They were both laughing when the Judge returned. "Well, I am glad to see you two are getting along so well. Now, Reverend Kenzel, tell me about these orders that I was supposed to have issued."

"I had a call from Carolyn McMichaels this morning and went her house. The bank suspended her from her job because a man, who said he was from the Prosecuting Attorney's office, told the manager that he was indicting her for murder. Police Chief, Todd Williams—her fiancé—also received an order by the same man, supposedly signed by you. The man warned him not to talk to her for any reason until the case came to trial. They are to be married in less than two weeks!"

Judge Walker and D. J. scribbled notes as fast as Laura could talk. The judge nodded for her to continue.

"I called Detective Steve Morgan to see if he could give us the information. He didn't know anything, but called me back. Todd couldn't talk to Steve either. While he was on the phone with me, the man served papers to him. Neither Steve, nor I, believed the man was from the Prosecuting Attorney's office, or that you signed the papers. Because of the surprise and all that Todd and Carolyn have on their minds, they couldn't think it through. They will in time."

Laura paused, took a deep breath, and continued, "SaraBelle Cotton contacted her attorney, James Coffman, in Glenville for Carolyn. He arrived on the heels of a strange man, who claimed to be the deceased woman's brother. He was calling Carolyn everything but a lady. The cats and Mr. Coffman sent the man on his way."

Judge Walker raised his eyebrows, but nodded for her to continue.

"As I said, I think they would have realized the complete redundancy of it all and I would have laughed with them later tonight. But, it didn't end there. When I got back to the office there was a message from the school. Our boys—my grandson and Carolyn's son—had been in a fight. A man talked to Jerome at the fence. From Jerome's description, I'm sure he was the same man who claimed to be Judy Franklin's brother. I didn't see the man who talked to Todd or Steve, but I would be willing to stake my life that it was the same man in all cases. The man told Jerome he was from the Prosecuting Attorney's office and if he didn't stay away from Josh and me, his mother would go to jail for a long, long time."

Laura paused, fighting back her anger. Judge Walker gave her a minute to compose herself, then said, "Reverend Kenzel, let me assure you, you are absolutely right. Neither D. J. nor I had anything to do with those orders."

"That's right." D. J.'s eyes flashed with anger. "I don't even *have* an assistant. And I certainly would not send them on such a useless, illogical, and illegal errand if I did."

"I understand," said Laura. "I felt that all along. It was such an impossible scenario. I never heard of a restraining order to keep an investigating officer from asking questions. I knew you were the only one who could make any sense of this chaos and turn it around."

"I am in the process of doing that as we talk. I asked Pauline to contact all the parties involved, except the children, and get them here pronto."

He looked from D. J. to Laura. "Reverend Kenzel, please don't hear me accusing you of withholding information, but I have the feeling you either know, or suspect something more."

Laura dropped her gaze from his eyes for the first time. She focused on her folded hands in her lap. Rascal's fur stood on end. She lifted her eyes to meet Judge Walker's gaze once more.

"It's only a suspicion," she said, "based on gut feeling. I don't know how it's possible, but I feel certain that Colin Jacobson is behind this farce."

D. J. and Judge Walker both jerked their head around to look at each other. Rascal growled in agreement.

"Why do you think this, Reverend Kenzel? I gave Jacobson a life sentence."

"I know you did, but, somehow, someway he's responsible. I know he is."

"Laura," D. J. spoke as kindly as she could. "We have learned the man you described to us is a hired hit man from New York. We haven't learned who hired him, or why." Looking back at the Judge, she asked, "Is it possible that Jacobson could be directing things from prison?"

"Possible," he said, "but not very probable. I'll call Tom Jenkins, the Warden there and ask him. He's a friend of mine. We'll find out."

Judge Walker started to reach for the intercom when Pauline buzzed him on it.

"Yes, Pauline?"

"The people you asked to see are all here. Shall I send them in?"

"Yes, please, Pauline."

He stood and walked to the door to greet them as they entered—Carolyn, her attorney, Todd, and Steve.

Twelve

"Laura? Rascal?" Steve moved quickly to her side. "I saw your car downstairs. I might have known you would figure this out and take charge." He grinned at her. "Where's Mischief?"

"With the boys." Steve raised his eyebrow in question, but Judge Walker was beginning the introductions.

Then the judge went right to the point. "Reverend Kenzel has been telling me some fantastic tales," he said. "It seems you have all been hoodwinked by a bogus Prosecuting Attorney. Let me assure you, I knew nothing about any of this until this fearless woman of God barged into my office."

"Laura, you didn't?" Steve winked at her and squeezed her shoulder.

"You are all smart enough that once the shock wore off, you would have known better. Apparently, Reverend Kenzel was a little more objective—until the boys were involved. That was the breaking point and she came to me."

"The boys?" Carolyn turned a shade lighter than the pale she already was.

"They're all right. Mischief is with them," said Laura. "They were fighting at school. I'll explain later."

"I think you better explain now," said Judge Walker, because if what you suspect is true, this is only the beginning."

"I guess you're right. I just don't want it to be so."

"Laura, what happened to the boys?" Steve knelt beside her chair and Laura once again explained that Mrs. Ellis had called her to the school. Then she told them what Jerome had told her.

"I'm sure it was the same man who came to your house this morning, Carolyn."

"But, he said he was Judy's brother."

"He also said he was the Assistant Prosecuting Attorney." Laura answered.

"You're sure it was the same man?" asked Todd. "Did you see the man who claimed to be the Assistant Prosecutor?"

"She didn't have too," interjected D. J. "The man she described is the same man we were discussing when she…eh…barged in. He's a hit man from New York."

"What?" They all answered together.

"And if Reverend Kenzel is correct, and she sure has a talent for sniffing out the facts, the man behind it all is Colin Jacobson."

"But…he's in prison." Carolyn couldn't believe what she heard.

"Is he?" Steve asked quietly.

Laura jerked her head up to face him almost nose to nose. "Steve?" She couldn't ask what she wanted to know.

"I was on my over here to see the judge when I got the call from Todd saying he wanted to see all of us. We just got word from the FBI in Washington. Jacobson has disappeared—again. They don't know how, or when, but sometime within the last three or four days. I'm sorry, Laura, I didn't want to tell you at all, and especially not like this."

"I think you're a little late, Morgan," said Judge Walker. "She's way ahead of you. That's what she told me earlier. Now we need to put our heads together to keep you all safe."

"It's me he's after," said Laura.

"Then why is he playing games with the rest of us?" asked Todd.

"To hurt me."

"Then isn't it likely he'll do more to your friends to hurt you?" D. J. wasn't trying to be malicious. She wanted Laura to face the reality.

"What can I do?" Laura asked. "How can I stop him?"

"You can't, darling," said Steve. "All of us together have a better chance."

"He's right," added the judge. "So let's do some brainstorming. I've asked Pauline to hold all my calls and cancel all my afternoon appointments."

* * *

Laura glanced at her watch, rubbed her eyes, and said, "I don't know about the rest of you, but the boys will be coming home from school soon and I certainly don't want them coming to an empty house—not after all we've talked about today. I'm going home. I can't think anymore. My brain hurts. My nerves are stretched to the limit."

Steve put his arm around her waist and walked to the door with her, Rascal beside her.

"Are you sure you can make it?" The concern in his eyes and voice caused Laura to laugh.

"After all the stuff I've been through including wrecking your car and being shot, I think I will live through this little irritation."

He smiled at her. "You're right," he said. "I guess we're all over-stressed and over reacting. Take Shebop and Rascal home. I'll be there in a little bit."

Turning to Todd and Carolyn, he said, "Why don't you two come over for dinner," he said. "We can continue to talk. The rest of you are welcome too, if you want," he added.

"First, I need to go see Robert Franklin," said Todd. "He has some explaining to do."

"Let me know what he says," said Judge Walker. "I'll be interested to know why anyone would put out such a blatant and obvious lie. Surely he knew it was only a matter of time until we found him out."

"He probably had no choice," said Laura.

"You mean he had a gun to his head—figuratively speaking?" Judge Walker looked at her with a sense of respect and surprise.

"And probably literally. My guess is the hired gun from New York is no relative. This whole ruse was staged to buy time for Colin Jacobson to make his move—whatever that might be ...And...you'll be lucky to find Robert Franklin alive."

"Laura, aren't you being a little melodramatic?" D. J. stood to place her notes in her briefcase.

"Am I? I hope you're right—but I have known this Colin Jacobson, alias Bill Collins, too long. He may seem like an ignorant jerk, but he's smart. And he never forgives—or forgets."

"I hope you're wrong this time, Laura," said Judge Walker.

"So do I," responded Steve, "but unfortunately she has a record of being right about Jacobson. Let's make sure the boys don't come home to an empty house."

"I'll go to the school and pick up the boys while you see Robert Franklin," said Carolyn as they left the courthouse.

The phone was ringing as Laura walked into the house. She hesitated then reached for it, knowing Steve was right behind her.

"Laura, is Steve there yet?"

"Just a minute, Todd. I just walked in and he's just coming across the porch." As Steve opened the door, Laura said to Todd, "He is dead, isn't he?"

There was a silence at the other end. Todd found his voice, "I guess they got all the mileage they could from him. Laura, don't worry. We've got you covered."

"Todd, I'm not worried about me."

"I know. We've got the boys covered, too."

"Here's Steve. I think I'll go make some coffee."

Thirteen

Thursday passed without incident—no more bodies, no fighting, no sign of Jacobson or his hired killer. Everything was quiet—too quiet, except for the recurring nightmare that was back with some variation. Always, Laura was alone in a darkness that chilled her to the bone. Several times throughout the night, she wakened gasping for breath. Returning to sleep the disturbing dream would play again. But what could she do about it? When Friday dawned, promising to be another summer-like day in September, Laura crawled out of bed, trying to push aside the feeling of impending disaster.

Going to her favorite chair in the living room with her morning coffee and Bible, Laura found some peace. Still a nagging premonition made her uneasy. She had finished her devotions and was planning her day when Josh came down the stairs dressed and ready for school.

"You're up early today," she teased. Had he too experienced nightmares?

"I'm almost ready for school," he answered, then grinned.

"What do you need to do yet?"

"Eat," he answered. "I'll just get a bowl of cereal and…"

Laura tousled his hair and walked past him to the kitchen. "Josh, you don't have to make up for Wednesday's trouble. That's all over; you're forgiven. Remember?"

"Yeah, but…" He followed her to the kitchen and stood looking at the floor. "…I should have been punished, or something."

"Looks to me like you were," said Laura, placing her hand under his chin and tilting his head back so their eyes met. You'll have that black eye for some time yet."

"But, I hurt you and you should hurt me back." Tears welled up in his eyes.

"Josh, love doesn't work that way." Laura held his face between her hands. "You learned a valuable lesson. You didn't like the feeling of being mad—especially at your best friend. You didn't intend to hurt me. It was just the fallout of what happened. Sometimes we hurt people we love without even knowing it, or intending to do it. Love lets us forgive and move on. Okay?"

"Okay," said Josh with some reservation. Then his familiar grin returned.

"Speaking of moving on, we better get you some real food for breakfast. You need something to hold you until lunchtime. And you don't want to be late."

"Some French toast would be nice."

"French toast it is."

Even though Rascal and Mischief would walk to school with him, Laura watched him with a touch of uneasiness as he threw his backpack over his shoulder and started down the drive. A chill ran down her spine. She shivered and went to the kitchen.

Laura put the dishes in the sink and gathered some papers. Today was Friday. Sunday was coming. The wedding was only a week away. She tried to erase from her thoughts the strange behavior of Robert Franklin and the hired killer who passed himself off as Judy's brother. The earlier foreboding returned with a vengeance; the nightmare that intruded in her sleep now grated on her nerves while awake. She shivered and started for the door.

The phone rang and she considered ignoring it. Whoever it was could call at the church office. Sense of duty wouldn't let her leave without taking the call. It might be an emergency. Maybe Josh forgot…

"Good morning, Love. You sound tired. You need a prayer this morning." Cora didn't wait for Laura to answer, but prayed her short prayer for God's special blessing upon her friend, said, "Amen" and Laura held a buzzing phone in her hand.

Just what I need, she thought. Cora's calls usually mean more trouble than I really want to face today—or any day. In spite of her misgivings, Laura lifted her concern to her *Boss*. "Thank You, God. I have a feeling I'm going to need a lot of Cora's prayers again. Thank you for her. Whatever trouble is coming my way, I need Your help."

She glanced at the clock on the mantel and started for the door again. Rascal and Mischief should have been back by now. Maybe they decided the boys need protection today. I'll leave the church basement door open a crack so they can get in and call the school in a little bit if they don't show up.

Fourteen

Josh ran to the Square, where Jerome waited. Together they started walking toward the school, laughing and planning for the coming weekend. Suddenly, a cat was on each of their shoulders.

Giggling because the whiskers tickled his neck, Josh said, "Rascal? What are you doing?" Rascal purred and pressed his nose against Josh's cheek.

"Maybe they're tired of walking," said Jerome.

"Yeah, they got to run back home when we get to school."

The cats began to pull at the boys' backpacks. "What do you want, Rascal? If you want to ride, you're making it awful hard for me."

"Yeah,' said Jerome. "Maybe they want to ride in the backpack."

"Why would they want that?"

"Why do they want to do anything? Because they are cats and...just because."

The boys stopped walking and slid their backpacks off their shoulders. They took the books out and opened the backpacks.

"Is this what you want?" said Josh.

"Meow," the Maine Coon duet replied urgently.

The boys shook their heads and giggled as Rascal jumped into Josh's bag and Mischief jumped into Jerome's. They settled to the bottom of the bags with hardly a stir. Had the boys not known they were there, even they would have been fooled.

Laughing Josh and Jerome picked up their books and started off again. As they rounded the last corner before the school, they noticed a black Cadillac parked at the curb with its motor running. A man stood beside it.

Jerome grabbed Josh's sleeve. "Josh, that car was parked by the school Wednesday when that man came over and talked to me. That's not the same man, but... I'm scared. Let's go."

They started to run, but they had to go past the man and he, anticipating their action, moved faster. He grabbed Josh and threw him into the back seat of the car. Jerome was scared, but wouldn't leave Josh.

"You leave my friend alone," he yelled and kicked at the man, who cursed and slapped Jerome hard enough to stun him. Throwing him in beside Josh, the man got behind the wheel and took off locking the doors from the front so they boys couldn't get out. A darkened glass window between the front and the back slid shut. They could neither hear, nor see, the driver.

Josh started to say something, but Jerome cautioned him not to speak. He pantomimed that the man in the front might hear them. They glanced at their almost motionless backpacks lying at their feet. Were the cats all right? Each boy checked his backpack. When they felt a sandpaper lick across the fingers, they put their hands over their mouths to hide their grins. They'd dropped their books in the scuffle, but they had their secret weapons.

Although they couldn't see out, they could feel the car going uphill. It had to be Gopher Mountain. Jerome whispered to Josh. "Pretend you don't know where we are." Aloud, he said, "Where do you think we are Josh? What is he going to do to us?"

"I don't know, but Grandma's going to be really upset. I'm scared Jerome."

"Me too."

They didn't have to pretend that part of their conversation.

Soon the car pulled onto a bumpy, dirt road. Neither boy knew where there was a road like that on Gopher Mountain. The car stopped. The man got out and opened the door.

"Come on kids. This is the end of the line."

"What are you going to do to us?" Jerome's voice trembled.

"Yeah, what do you want with us?" Josh was afraid, but tried to be bold.

"It's not you we want kid. We want that preacher-lady. We figure this will get her attention real fast. Now, come on. We got a little walk up the mountain. And don't try anything funny. I know how to use this thing and I don't mind using it on kids." He pointed his gun at the boys. They grabbed their backpacks and started up the mountain.

"You don't need those things," the man said and reached for Jerome's backpack. Jerome pulled away.

"No, it's mine."

"What's in it?"

"What do you usually put in a backpack you take to school?" Josh asked contemptuously.

The man made a harsh sounding noise that he considered to be a laugh that reminded Jerome of Randy. He shivered in spite of his resolve to be strong.

The man reached again for the backpacks. "You don't need books where you are going. We'll toss them…"

Another man spoke from the path ahead of him. "Leave them alone, Hughie. Books will give them something to do while we wait for our instructions. We won't have to listen to them whine and complain. Come on kids, move it."

Josh and Jerome ran up the path so the men wouldn't try again to take their backpacks. The man on the path was the one Jerome had seen at school. Jerome tried to stay as far away from him as he could. They reached the top of the hill—and a cave.

"All right, kids, get in there and don't make a sound if you know what's good for you. Killer is itching to use his gun and he doesn't care who he uses it on." The man called Hughie pointed to the cave. Then he laughed and added, "Not that anyone would hear you anyway."

"You sure this place is far enough away?" asked Killer.

"Yeah, this place hasn't been used in years. No one will find us out here."

Inside the cave, Josh and Jerome sat side by side. They knew they were in the cave above Gopher Mountain Falls, where they had gone last summer when Randy shot at them.

Careful not to draw the attention of the men outside, they slowly opened their backpacks. In the dimness of the cave, lighted only by the cave's gaping mouth, two dark shadows slid behind them to await their chance.

"We got to let your mom and my Grandma know where we are," whispered Josh.

"But how?" Jerome whispered back.

"My code ring. Let's make a note and put in the ring."

"And…?"

"Rascal. We'll put it on his collar. He'll get it home somehow. We'll have to wait until it gets dark so they won't see him."

"What are you boys whispering about in there," called Hugh.

"Nothing," said Jerome.

"You told us to be quiet." Josh tried not to be to antagonistic. He added, "So we were just trying to draw some pictures."

"Yeah, you do that. Draw lots of pictures. It's going to be a long day."

Josh and Jerome drew a picture of a caveman standing by a waterfall. They thought Josh's grandmother would understand, but just in case, they added what they thought looked like a gopher. Then they folded the picture as small as they could and put it inside Josh's Code ring. He snapped it shut as Killer turned to look in the cave.

"What was that?" he asked.

"What was what?" The boys together spoke as one.

"It sounded like something snapped."

"Oh, you mean like this?" said Jerome. He snapped his own ring.

"Yeah, what is that?"

"It's a spy ring," said Jerome. "I got it as a prize. It's real neat. Want to see it?"

While Jerome was talking, Josh unfastened Rascal's collar and put his ring on it. He fastened it back and hoped it wouldn't jingle.

"Naw, I expect it's just a piece of junk."

"That's what my mom said, too," Jerome lied.

Fifteen

With a heavy uneasiness in the pit of her stomach, Laura sat at her desk, computer on, mind absent from her surroundings. Vaguely the strains of Bach drifted from the sanctuary. She hadn't heard Dorothy or Karen come in.

"Are you going fishing again this morning?"

"Fishing? No why?"

"You've been sitting there for at least the last twenty minutes watching those fish on your monitor. I thought you were trying to decide how to catch one."

Laura looked at Dorothy then glanced back at the screen. "I guess my mind is elsewhere."

"Is everything all right with Josh at school?"

"I think so, since we got Wednesday taken care of."

"You know, Pastor, I don't know why you should be so lucky to capture the attention of that gang of crooks."

"If that's luck, I could sure use a lot less of it."

"Speaking of luck, it sounds like the organ is working all right now. Course it helps to have the repair technician on hand." Dorothy laughed again. "Are the cats with them?" She nodded toward the sanctuary.

"No, they went with Josh. They weren't back yet when I left the house." Again, the prickling sent a shiver across her back. "I left the basement door open a crack for them."

Dorothy went back to her office. Laura turned her attention back to her computer, until Dorothy once again broke into her musings.

"Pastor?"

"Hmmm." Laura answered. Then she turned to her secretary. "I'm sorry, Dorothy. Did you want me?"

"Pastor, is something else bothering you? I know the last couple of days have been unsettling, but they are over. Aren't they?"

Laura stared for a minute—as if she was trying to focus on a far off scene. "I don't know, Dorothy. I wish I knew. I can't shake the feeling of a second shoe about to drop." She tried to laugh, but failed. "It's unusual for the cats not to return home after taking the boys to school. I don't know if they went to school with the boys, or if they are just being cats. I'm concerned about them, I guess, but more concerned about the boys…I just feel uneasy."

"Maybe we should call the school, you know, just to check if the cats are there and if the boys are in trouble."

"Maybe you're right. Mrs. Ellison would understand my concern. Why don't you get her on the phone for me?"

The phone rang before Dorothy could reply. She stepped back into her office to answer it. Sticking her head back in Laura's office she said, "It's for you—Mrs. Ellison."

"Good morning, Mrs. Ellison. This is Reverend Kenzel. No more trouble, I hope." She tried to sound cheerful. It didn't quite come across that way.

Dorothy waited to make sure Laura didn't need her and saw the color drain from the pastor's face.

"Reverend Kenzel," said Mrs. Ellison, "I am truly sorry to call you again so soon, but the boys didn't show up at school today and I wondered if they were ill and maybe you and Mrs. Dugal forgot to call."

"Did you call Carolyn, or Sophia?"

"No, I thought it would be better to check with you first."

"I understand. Josh left at his usual time to meet Jerome at the Square. Let me call Sophia and check it out. Maybe Jerome forgot something and they went to his house to get it. I'll get back to you. Thank you for calling me."

"Reverend Kenzel, I'm not an alarmist, but after Wednesday, I was concerned. You will get back to me this morning?"

"Yes…in a few minutes—with whatever I find out."

"Thank you Reverend Kenzel. I hope it's nothing to be concerned about, but well, you understand. I'll let you make your calls. Bye."

"Goodbye, Mrs. Ellison."

"Pastor? Are you all right?"

Laura raised her eyes to meet Dorothy's concerned look. She spoke to Dorothy, but reached for the phone and began dialing at the same time. "The boys didn't show up at school this morning," she whispered.

"Maybe they went fishing," said Dorothy.

Laura shook her head. "After Wednesday they wouldn't do that to us. They...Sophia," she turned her attention to the phone. "Laura here. Did the boys forget something and come back there for it?"

"No, Laura. Why? Is there a problem?"

"I don't know, Sophia. Mrs. Ellison just called. They didn't show up at school today."

"Jerome left at his usual time. He should have met Josh at the Square just a few minutes before time for school. Do you suppose they decided to go fishing?" Sophia asked trying to keep the panic out of her voice.

"Dorothy asked the same question. Maybe they did. Why don't I call Todd? He knows where Jerome likes to go. He can send someone out to see. In the meantime, I'll run over to the house and make sure they didn't come back there for something."

Laura had a difficult time keeping her own panic under wraps. She didn't replace the phone, but pushed the button to get a dial tone, then dialed 911. Todd answered.

"Todd, the boys didn't make it to school today. Can you send someone to the fishing spot to check it out? I'll run home. Maybe Josh forgot something and returned to get it."

"Sure, Laura. If they did go fishing I will personally whale the daylights out of my soon-to-be-son."

"Todd, there was something else unusual that you should know. I've worried about it all morning. Now, I'm scared."

"What is it Laura?" Todd knew when Laura Kenzel admitted to being scared there was a reason for it.

"The cats. They've been walking to school with Josh then returning in time to come to the office with me. They haven't returned yet."

"You think...?"

"I don't know what to think. I'm too scared to think. Please send..."

"I'm on my way. I'll stop by your house when I've checked out the fishing spot."

"Thanks, Todd." Her voice faltered to a whisper.

"Oh, Pastor," Dorothy was in tears.

"Dorothy, call Mrs. Ellison back. Tell her Chief Williams is checking it out. We'll keep in touch with her. I'm going home to check. I'll let you know when I find out anything."

Laura didn't wait for an answer. Dorothy would call Mrs. Ellison, as well as, Cora, SaraBelle, and Martha. Dorothy, glad to have something to do, hurried back to her office and started dialing.

Laura left the office and ran down the steps, out the door, and across the lawn. Bounding up the four steps in two leaps, she was across the porch and in the house within seconds. The house was quiet—too quiet. The boys weren't there. Neither were the cats. Needlessly, Laura went from room to room calling to all of them. Only breath-stopping silence answered her.

The back door banged. Laura ran. Todd was alone. He knocked the way he usually did as he entered. The look on the other's face, told each of them what they didn't want to hear. The boys were gone.

"The light was blinking on the answering machine when I ran through the living room," she said. "I ignored it to search for Josh and Jerome. Maybe they were calling from…somewhere." Todd followed her to the living room and she punched the play button.

"Laura, sorry I missed you. Tried to call your office. The line was busy. I'm calling from my car on my way to Columbus and the signal is fading. Got a lead on Jacobson. Be back late tonight or tomorrow morning. I'll call you later tonight. Try to stay out of trouble while I'm gone. I love you."

The dial tone replaced Steve's voice. As if her legs gave out on her, Laura dropped onto the chair by the phone, hands balled into fists, teeth clenched. She forced deep breaths of air into her lungs to chase away the anger, fear, and most of all, the tears that threatened. She would not break down like a hysterical woman who had no hope. She needed her wits. Tears fled, but fear gave way to angry words.

"Darn him! He's always off somewhere when I need him!"

Todd, surprised at her angry outburst, stared. Laura looked up at him, stricken with guilt and remorse. She threw her hand over her mouth and stared back. Todd said nothing. Finally, she said, "You know I didn't mean that, Todd. Please don't tell Steve I said it. He's doing what he has to do."

"I'm sure he understands, Laura. He's always saying the same thing—complaining because he never seems to be here when you need him most. Like you said, he's doing his job—trying to track down the Jacobsons. They seem be in charge of the problems. I won't say anything to him. That's for you two to work out. I'm sorry to have to leave you, too. I wish we could all wait together, but…we need to have both phones covered…"

"You need to be with Carolyn, Todd. I understand. I'll be all right. I just needed to vent a little frustration."

"You're right. As hard as it is, you need to be here to cover your phone. We need to have a police person on the premises so I'll send Mark over to stay with you."

"I'll be all right."

"I know you will, but…in case a ransom call should come in."

Laura nodded, at a loss for words. "I understand. Thanks, Todd."

Todd called Mark and left to get Carolyn. She had just gone back to work after they squelched the murder rumor. Now, Todd had to take her home to wait for a call that might never come.

Laura watched him drive away. She had never felt so alone—not even Rascal and Mischief were there to comfort her. She hoped with all her heart they were still with the boys. Giving into her need for companionship, she fell to her knees beside her chair and let the words of the Psalmist speak to her. *Oh, Lord, be gracious to me, for I am languishing; …My soul is sorely troubled…I am weary with my moaning…* "Please take care of the boys."

Laura slid to a sitting position with her arms resting on the chair and gave in to the only tears she would shed until this new terror was over. Deep within her memory the rest of Psalm 6 soothed her soul, *The Lord has heard my supplication; the Lord accepts my prayer.*

Not sure how long she sat there, Laura rose when she heard footsteps cross her porch. She opened the door as Sergeant Mark Goodwin raised his hand to knock.

"Pastor, I'm so sorry about all this," he said. "I'll stay out of your way as much as possible, but I do need to be here." Mark, Todd's top man on the force, was being groomed to be Assistant Police Chief.

"I understand Mark. I just wish…"

"It's all right. You don't need to explain. You have too many other things on your mind."

"Can I make you a cup of coffee or anything?" Laura felt that if she didn't do something, she was going to fly into a million pieces and would never be able to function again.

Mark must have sensed that. "Sure, coffee sounds great."

For the rest of the morning and most of the afternoon, Laura paced and prayed. Mark was willing to talk, but was comfortable with the silence when she didn't want to talk about anything. Dorothy brought a note over from Cora, who didn't want to tie up the phone in case someone called about the boys. She wanted Laura to know she was praying.

Six o'clock, the phone finally rang. Laura was afraid to answer. She felt as if ice water had replaced her blood. Mark moved toward the phone.

Sixteen

The morning slipped into afternoon and afternoon to evening. The boys would have preferred setting Rascal and Mischief on their capturers, but were afraid to because of the guns. It was a comfort just knowing the cats were there—even when it got so dark inside the cave they couldn't see them.

"Maybe we should try now," said Josh.

"Yeah."

"Rascal? Where are you?" Josh whispered. "He's gone. Sometime, somehow, he slipped out without us knowing."

"Mischief is still here," said Jerome. She cuddled between them to keep guard until Rascal returned with help.

Outside the mouth of the cave, Killer and Hugh talked and played cards until it began to get too dark to see. "We could build a small fire," said Killer.

"And have someone see it from the road, or an airplane? Can't take a chance," said Hugh.

Later Killer, not used to country living, said, "This place gives me the creeps." He lit a match and held it near his watch. It's eight o'clock. Time to take the note." Killer laughed his evil laugh. "You go," he continued, "I might get trigger happy. Big Boss wouldn't like that." He laughed again as if he had told a great funny joke.

"Just keep your cool with the kids. He'll be more upset if you hurt them before he's ready."

"Hey, pick up some beer while you're in town. A man can get mighty thirsty out here."

"You know what Boss said. No drinking until the job is done," Hugh said and started down the mountain. The car started up, the sound of the motor faded into the night.

Josh and Jerome huddled together to keep warm and to keep the fear away. Mischief draped herself across both of them.

"Where's our angel?" asked Jerome.

"Maybe he figures we don't need him with Mischief here."

"Bet he's guarding on the outside."

"Me too."

With that thought, they dozed and waited for what would happen next.

Seventeen

Trembling, Laura shook her head as Mark approached the phone. "I'd better answer it," she said. "Jacobson will hang up if he hears another voice." She reached for the phone and answered tentatively—just above a whisper. "Hello, Reverend Kenzel speaking."

"Laura?" Immediately, Steve knew something wasn't right. "What's wrong?"

"Oh, Steve." Her voice choked. She couldn't breathe…couldn't talk.

Mark took the phone from her while she struggled for control. "Steve, this is Mark. We've got big trouble here. The boys left for school and never made it. Todd's with Carolyn in case someone calls there. I'm staying here until we hear something."

Mark held the phone away from his ear. Laura couldn't hear what Steve was saying, and probably didn't want to. The yelling stopped. Steve said something to Mark, who handed the phone back to Laura. He smiled. "I think he's calmed down a little."

"Steve…"

"Don't try to explain. Darling, I'm sorry I'm so far away. I'll be on the road in five minutes or less. It's about a six-hour drive. Don't do anything rash. Don't do anything without Todd's approval. I'll put my flashing lights on all the way and be there as soon as I can."

"Steve, please don't take chances. I need you…"

"I need you too, so please…" He couldn't finish. He wanted to say, "stay out of trouble," but he knew she couldn't promise him anything.

"Steve, I love you."

"Laura, please don't… Never mind. You'll do what you have to do and I understand that. Just remember I love you and I really want us to have a life together. See you as soon as I can. Bye."

"Please, be careful. Bye."

Laura replaced the phone. With a feeling of weariness, she realized she hadn't eaten since breakfast and Mark probably hadn't either.

"Mark, I'm sorry I didn't offer sooner. Would you like something to eat? More coffee?"

"You don't need to worry about me," he answered.

"Well, I think I could use something. You will join me, won't you?"

"Sure," he said. "It might not be a bad idea to fix something for the boys. When they get home, they're going to be hungry. I guarantee that."

"Oh, Mark," she smiled briefly. "That is the most hopeful thing anyone has said to me in a long time. Why don't I put some spaghetti sauce on? I'll fix us a salad while it cooks, then we can have some spaghetti when the sauce is done. Maybe they'll be home by then."

"That sounds like a plan to me," he answered. Mark had been around long enough to know that it was a slim hope, but hope, nonetheless. And Laura needed to have a goal, something to work toward.

Laura went to the kitchen and started the sauce then cut up vegetables for a salad—doing everything with precise determination to keep her mind off what could be happening with the boys. It didn't block the fear completely, but helped somewhat. She fixed a large salad, dished up some for Mark and herself, and refrigerated the rest. Then she toasted some garlic bread. When the sauce was ready, she cooked some angel hair pasta and forced herself to eat; she knew she must. She didn't know what to expect or how long it would be before she would have to face it.

Eighteen

Hugh Jacobson drove down Gopher Mountain to Glenville. A man waited in the shadows of the trees that lined the back of the IGA parking lot. Hugh pulled into the lot, left the car running, while he strolled into the store. The man darted from the trees and slid into the backseat of the car, rolling to the floor to wait for the car to move.

Hugh returned a moment later with a small sack,—cigarettes, colas, chips—got in his car, and turned back up the mountain. Once the car was out of sight of the town lights, the man rose from the back floor and leaned against the front seat.

"Nice work, Hughie," he said. "Now, let's get to Look Out Point."

"Welcome home, brother," said Hugh and they both laughed that infamous Jacobson cackle.

"Everything okay?" Colin asked.

"Just like clockwork. As soon as I drop you off at Look Out Point, I'll deliver the message through her window." They both laughed; it was a joke. Colin knew more than he'd told either his brother or his hired killer from New York. After all, he was the Boss. He didn't have to tell them everything.

"The kids give you any trouble?"

"No. They've actually been quiet. It's almost like they know something we don't know."

"Like what?" snapped Colin.

"Now, if it's something we don't know, how would I know what it is?" Hugh snapped back. "They just don't seem to be afraid like most kids would be."

Colin Jacobson, alias Bill Collins, laughed again. "They probably think Morgan or Williams will save them, but I sent Morgan on a wild goose chase to Columbus. He won't be back until tomorrow. By then, it will be too late."

"What about Chief Williams?"

"He's too dumb to make a move without Morgan. Besides, he'll stay with his fiancée to wait for a call. The only one smart enough to figure anything out is *my* dearest wife-to-be and I'll fix her."

"I don't understand your obsession with that woman. You know she's trouble." Hugh glanced at his brother in the rearview mirror keeping his attention on the curves of Gopher Mountain Road.

"I don't really want her, my dear brother. I just don't want Morgan to have her. And there's the little business about her ruining us and sending us to prison. Oh, she'll pay, Hughie. She'll pay dearly before I'm done with her."

The coldness in his brother's voice made even Hugh Jacobson shiver involuntarily. Colin didn't miss it and snickered even more contemptuously.

"What are you going to do with Killer once we have the Kenzel dame? He did a good job on the Franklins. He's itching to take care of those kids."

"Maybe we'll let him do that before we shoot him. Again, Colin gave a manic kind of laugh that reminded Hugh of Randy, their deceased nephew. Hugh was beginning to feel a little uneasy about his brother's mental stability. He didn't dare let on so he laughed with him.

"Some day they'll find him with the kids—if the bears or cougars don't get them first."

Hugh thought it would be a good ending for a big-shot hit man from New York. He still felt uneasy, but they were at Look Out Point and he had other things to think about.

"Let me off here," said Colin, "then get down there and deliver my message. I'll wait over by the path for her to show up. Take the car back to the hidden road and leave it there. I'll honk the horn when it's time."

"Got you Boss!"

Colin Jacobson got out of the car and walked to the path off to the side of the Look Out Point that led to Gopher Falls. He found a stump to sit on, pulled out his cigarettes, and settled in for a couple hours of waiting while Hugh continued down the mountain to Cottonville. Once there, he sat in his car in the shadow of a huge oak for several minutes, gripping the steering wheel with sweaty hands. He breathed in short raspy sounds.

"Get a grip," he whispered to himself. "Colin won't let them send you back to prison, but he will punish you himself if you don't deliver this message."

Only the preacher's car is in the driveway, so she must be alone in the house. Taking a deep breath, wiping the sweat that dripped from his brow to his eyes, he left the motor running and the driver door ajar, making sure he closed it enough to extinguish the dome light. Carrying the brick with a message wrapped around it, he ran across the lawn, glancing furtively at the dark corners and shadows. That Kenzel dame is too smart. She just might have the placed surrounded by police.

Hugh hurled the brick bearing its message and didn't wait around to see if it found its mark. The minute the missile left his hand, he bolted for the safety of his car. Glass shattered behind him and he hit the gas pedal as he closed the door. He thought someone ran toward him, yelling. He didn't wait around long enough to see who it was, or even *if* someone was after him. He sped down the street and turned toward Gopher Mountain. He was home free. Now, he could take care of Killer.

Nineteen

Fred Martin, trustee of Laura's church and protector of his pastor, had been away for a two-day business trip. It was late; traffic had been heavier than usual until he reached Gopher Mountain Road. Now rain was threatening. Tired and hungry, he fought sleep. I should have stopped somewhere, he thought, but I'm too close to home. Emma will be waiting up for me. A lunchmeat sandwich with Emma is far better than a steak alone.

Had Fred been just five minutes earlier, he would have seen the black Cadillac stop at Look Out Point, long enough to leave its passenger there, and drive on to Cottonville. But Fred was only interested in getting home. The only trouble he thought he might encounter would be a deer, or smaller animal, running across the road in front of him. Listening to his favorite music station—the oldies of the previous decades—he watched not only the road ahead of him, but also the sides from which critters often darted. He'd never hit a deer, but had come close several times.

Had he glanced to the side when he passed Look Out Point, he might have seen the red glow of a cigarette. He didn't look. He just wanted to get home.

Slowing for the hairpin curve beyond Look Out, he muttered out loud just to hear his voice—to help keep him awake. "Good place to run into wild life. It's not easy to watch the sides of the road and still watch the sharp forty-five degree curve." From the corner of his eye, he caught a movement at the side of the road. "Probably the wind blowing tree limbs and brush. But...what's that?"

A dark furry form landed on the hood of his car. Two red, glowing eyes stared at him through the windshield. Fred's heart pounded as he stomped on the brake—afraid his foot would go through the floor—or that he would skid over the edge of the mountain.

He sat for a few seconds that seemed like hours, waiting for his heart to stop beating like a jackhammer. He stared at the large cat-like creature that

81

stared at him. "That is either a raccoon or one of Laura's cats. What would it be doing out here on Gopher Mountain alone? Is the pastor in trouble again?"

Fred reached for the door handle; the animal jumped off the hood. He opened the door, prepared to get out and call to it. The animal sailed over his head. From the passenger seat, Rascal licked Fred's cheek, stared at him with his green eyes, and waited for him to close the door.

"Rascal? What are you doing out here alone? Never mind, don't answer that. I take it you want a ride home?"

Rascal settled onto the seat, tucked his paws under him, and closed his eyes for a short catnap. Fred laughed aloud. "I've been having a hard time staying awake. Guess I'll make it home now. I don't know what is going on, kitty, but if you're out here alone this time of night, the pastor's in trouble again. Hang on; we won't dally."

"Meowell!"

Fred turned up the street toward the church and parsonage. A huge black car passed him doing triple the speed limit. Fred swerved, his side tires running over the curb, to keep the car from sideswiping him.

"What a night!" he muttered. "First a cat lands on my car in the middle of nowhere then I'm almost clobbered by a speeding maniac. Rascal, something isn't right with this picture. Let's get you home and find out what's going on."

As soon as he pulled into the drive, Fred was certain there was trouble. The front picture window had a hole big enough to drive a truck through it. He could see Mark Goodwin and Laura in the living room. That wasn't a good sign.

"Can you walk, or shall I carry you?" he asked as he stepped out of the car. Rascal jumped to his shoulder, growling in his ear as if urging him to hurry.

"All right, let's go."

Twenty

It was already nearing nine o'clock. Laura and Mark finished eating and were sipping their coffee when the sound of shattering glass startled them. Setting the cups on the table, they ran for the living room. The picture window had a large, gaping hole in it; glass was everywhere. The missile that had caused the destruction lay innocently on the couch in a pool of shattered glass waiting for someone to lift it out of the sparkling shards.

Laura started toward the couch to pick up the brick. Mark put out his hand in front of her. "I know you're anxious, but we need to wait for Todd—or at least make sure we don't smudge any prints."

"You're right, Mark. I just…"

Mark had his cell phone in hand dialing. "Todd, Mark here. We have action. Brick through the window with a note… No, we haven't touched it yet. Want us to wait? Okay."

"He'll be here in about two minutes. Can we wait that long?"

Laura tried to smile at him. "Do I have a choice?"

"He said if I couldn't stop you, he would understand." Mark grinned at her.

"I'll wait. I've waited all day what's a couple more minutes?"

Laura and Mark had been too absorbed by the brick through the window to hear the car pull into the drive. When they heard footsteps hurrying across the porch, they looked at each other questioningly.

"Even Todd doesn't drive that fast," said Mark, drawing his gun.

Before either of them could move toward the door, Fred Martin opened the screen and poked his head in, knocking on the door post as he did so.

"Pastor, if you wanted air conditioning, you could have asked. I'm sure the trustees would be more than willing to give it to you." Fred laughed at Laura's expression until he saw Mark's gun. "Hey! What's going on here?"

"Fred? Rascal!" Laura started toward them, but Rascal, apparently deciding he could do it faster, flew to her shoulder.

"Where did you find him?" Hugging Rascal close, Laura buried her face in his fur.

"I found this fellow—or rather, he found me—out on Gopher Mountain Road. I figured there must be something wrong here. He wouldn't be out there alone this time of night otherwise."

"Gopher Mountain Road?" Mark said, placing his gun back in its holster.

Before Fred could give them any more information, Todd ran across the porch and almost ran into him as he came through the door. "Fred? What are you doing here? Rascal? When did he…?"

"Fred just brought him home," Laura said. "He was just about to tell us where he found him."

"Fred?" Todd asked, as he reached for the brick, his hands covered with rubber surgical gloves.

"All right, I'll tell you then you tell me what's going on here. I was on my way home. Rascal jumped on the hood of my car at the hairpin curve. I just about had a heart attack. I opened the door to see if he was all right. He jumped in and said, 'Home please,' more or less. So I brought him home. Now will someone tell me what's going on? Why was he on Gopher Mountain alone? Why is there a gaping hole in your window? And why are the police here?"

"Fred, you are an angel in disguise," said Laura.

Mark filled Fred in just as quickly and succinctly as he had Steve earlier in the evening.

Laura was reading the note over Todd's shoulder while Rascal draped himself around her shoulders, purring in her ear, trying to get her attention.

Todd held the note by the corner and read it aloud: "Laura dearest, meet me at Look Out Point at midnight. Come alone—no cops, no hero church people. I don't need to remind you this is the only way you will ever see those kids alive again."

"Bill Collins," whispered Laura.

"You aren't going." Todd declared.

"Todd, I have no choice. The kids…"

"Laura, you don't know that he has the kids. You can't trust him."

"He either has the kids, or knows where they are."

"How can you be so sure?"

"Fred told me." She smiled at Fred.

"Me? I don't know anything about this!"

"You told me where you found Rascal. If he was on Gopher Mountain Road, then that's where the boys are—somewhere on Gopher Mountain."

"Laura, you might be right—but Gopher Mountain is a mighty big place. How...?"

"If he wants me to meet him at Look Out Point, then the kids must be close by and..." She stopped mid-sentence. Stroking Rascal unconsciously, she suddenly realized something was on his collar.

"Laura?" Todd knew the look. She either thought of something, or had some kind of inspiration.

"Todd, help me." Her hands began to tremble in her excitement. "There's something on Rascal's collar. I think..." she looked closer. "It is! It's Josh's secret code ring."

"Secret code ring?" asked Fred.

"The boys each got one the other day. They ordered them from somewhere a few weeks back. The stone snaps open and you can hide a message inside it." Todd explained as he removed the ring from Rascal's collar.

"This is Josh's ring all right. The stone is red. Jerome's is blue." He snapped the stone open and pulled out the tiny scroll of paper.

He grinned as he handed it to Laura. She grinned too. "They're in the cave above Gopher Mountain Falls." She handed the note to Fred, who looked confused.

Laura laughed aloud. "See," she said, "pointing to the pictures. There's the waterfall with a caveman standing beside it. And that little critter has to be a gopher."

Fred looked at the note once more and then broke into a belly laugh. "Those kids are pretty smart. But how did they manage to get the cats with them? And how did Rascal...?"

"We won't know that for sure until we get the boys back," said Todd.

"I can pretty well guess," said Laura. "The cats have been walking the boys to school. This morning they didn't return. Somehow they went with the boys when they were kidnapped."

"But how did they do that without being seen. Surely the kidnapper wouldn't have taken them..."

"No," said Todd. "He probably would have shot them first."

"Then how...?" Fred scratched his head and looked from Laura to Todd.

"Maybe the boys sensed trouble and hid the cats somewhere—maybe their backpacks."

"I think that might be close, Todd," said Laura, "but I think the cats sensed danger—as they often do—and somehow got the boys to hide them in the backpacks. Either way they were there when the boys needed them."

"Meow!" answered Rascal.

"I think he agrees with you," said Fred.

"We found their books lying on the ground about a block away from the school, just after they rounded that last corner, so it would make sense that they exchanged books for cats. Someone was waiting for them. They never had a chance, but the cats were hidden and the kidnappers never knew they were there."

"Why didn't the cats just attack the kidnapper?" asked Fred. He knew they had done that on more than one occasion.

"Probably because the men—and it would seem there were at least two of them—had guns. And how would they get the boys home? They're probably safer in that cave than they would be any place on that mountain—especially with the cats there to protect them."

"But one of them is here. And how do you know there are two men?" Fred wasn't a law officer and didn't understand how they could deduce certain things from a few facts.

"Because someone just threw a brick through the window and someone had to stay with the boys, or they might try to get home. And if Rascal was there—and we know he was—then Mischief was with him. And she's still there. She can handle the guarding until he brings help."

"Wow," was all Fred could say. Then he added, "Hey! That black Caddy that almost ran me over was heading toward the mountain."

"It looks like we're on the right track," said Todd. "Let's go."

Twenty-One

"Wait, Todd. You can't just go running up there and get the boys and Jacobson. If he sees you, he'll kill the boys. If you get the boys, he'll get away."

"We have to get the boys, Laura. You know that." Todd ran his fingers through his hair and squirmed. He also knew she was right.

"You and Mark get the boys. I'll meet Jacobson." Laura said and turned toward the stairs.

"Nothing doing," said Todd laying a hand on her arm. "We'll get the boys and we'll meet Jacobson—somehow."

"If anyone except me shows up at Look Out Point he'll signal for the others to kill the boys. Collins will get away to come back and try again." Laura's brown eyes flashed as they locked with Todd's.

"Laura, I won't let you go out there alone" Todd was determined. "I'm the police officer in charge."

"Maybe I could hide in the back seat," said Fred.

"No!" Todd and Laura both turned to face Fred and spoke together.

"We can't let you risk your life," said Todd. "Laura is not going and that is that." One glance at Laura and Todd knew he shouldn't have said it quite that way. The stubborn set of her jaw told him he was going to lose this battle.

She said nothing to Todd, but turned to Fred. "Fred, I really appreciate your offer. I know you could do it. You did before, but the first place he'll look when I drive up will be the back seat floor. You wouldn't have a chance to get out."

"How about the trunk?" Fred was not willing to give up.

Laura smiled at him.

"Oh," he said. "I forgot. Chevettes don't have trunks."

"I will have protection," she said softly. "I'm not going out there completely ignorant of the situation."

"Something we don't know about?" asked Todd skeptically.

"Rascal will go with me. He can hide under the seat when Bill looks in the car. I'll leave the window open so he can get out."

"And suppose Jacobson sees Rascal and shoots *him*." Todd didn't want to be harsh, but he had to make her think sensibly.

"Then it will be the last action he takes." Laura said through clenched teeth.

"Laura, how… Laura, there's something else you aren't telling me." Todd had that *Oh no, here we go again,* look.

"Yes." she said quietly, determinedly. She couldn't look him in the face.

"Laura, I have to know what you're planning. As a police officer, I can't let you take the risk. As a friend of Steve Morgan, I definitely can't let you take that risk." Todd almost pleaded with her.

"Todd, I…" She looked embarrassed.

"What?" He waited.

She took a deep breath and said, "I have a gun and I know how to use it." Laura turned to face him.

"What?"

"How long have you had it? Laura if you only bought it since coming here because of all the trouble…" He didn't know where to go with that line of reasoning. He knew she wouldn't know enough about it to use it properly. Going against a man like Jacobson could mean real disaster. "Laura, do you…"

"Have a permit? Yes, along with a number of sharpshooter awards. I've had the gun since I was about six."

Todd, Mark, and Fred stared, mouths open. Finally, Fred found his voice. "Pastor, why have you kept this such a secret when so much has happened?"

"Because, I hate guns. They give people a sense of power and cause them to take chances."

"Then why…? Sharpshooting awards?" Todd was bewildered.

"It's a long story that I don't have time to get into…but I will go to Look Out Point—with or without your blessing. Rascal will go with me. If you tell me to leave the gun here, I will do that."

"Let me see the gun, Laura," Todd said.

"And the permit?" She smiled.

"Yes."

"I'll get it."

Laura went upstairs and returned dressed in jeans and a navy sweatshirt. She handed the wooden gun case to Todd, who opened it and whistled. He lifted the polished, nine shot revolver from the box.

"This is a beauty. And you've obviously kept it cleaned and well oiled." He balanced it in his hand, checking it over. He scanned the permit and the certificates. "This last one was six months ago with the Chicago Police Department."

"I had special permission to go there for practice and competition—secretly. No one knew, especially not Harold."

Todd gave her a quizzical look, but didn't press the issue about her dead husband. That was between her and Steve if she chose to tell him. "I still don't like you going out there alone. I'm sure Steve wouldn't want you to go, either. But, you're right, as usual, on all counts. It's probably the only way we can rescue the boys and capture Jacobson. If Rascal is there, and you promise not to do anything rash with this..., Lord, help me if I am making the wrong choice. As soon as we get the boys safely away from there, Mark will be there to cover you."

"I can live with that," she said.

"I sure hope you can," said Todd. "Live that is."

"It's after eleven already," she said neatly tucking the gun into her jeans at the small of her back.

"I'll go see Frank. We'll get this window covered before you get back. It is supposed to rain tonight." Fred started toward the door. He turned back to Todd. "Is it all right if I call my wife and tell her where I am and what's happening? She'll be worried."

"Sure," said Todd. "Emma will be discreet. Tell her not to call any of her friends tonight. Tomorrow it should all be over."

"Thanks, Fred—for everything. Come on, Rascal, let's go catch us a crook." Laura tried to sound normal, but Todd and Mark both knew she was scared. That was good—maybe.

"Laura," said Todd as he and Mark followed her out. "Please be careful. Carolyn and I are depending on you to do a wedding next week."

She grinned at him. "Nothing is going to stop that wedding, Todd Williams. Nothing. If I don't make it back, I've left a letter to be mailed to the Bishop. He'll come and do it."

"Laura!" Todd wanted to shake her. She laughed and ran to her car, Rascal right behind her. "Give us at least a ten minute start," called Todd as he and Mark went to their cars. She opened the driver side door; Rascal jumped in and settled on the passenger seat.

"Shebop," she said to her car. "Don't let me down. This is the most important mission we've been on together. With you and Rascal to help me, how can I fail?"

Giving Todd and Mark the head start they needed, Laura waited and listened for the familiar chuckle of assurance. No chuckle—only a sense of sadness and the heaviness of heart.

"I am surrounded on every side," she whispered, "I'm scared, Lord. I'm afraid for my boys; I'm afraid for Todd and Mark; and God, I'm afraid of what Steve might think of me for keeping secrets from him. Most of all, Lord, I'm scared for me. I am about as close to hating a person as I can be. Don't let me act in the heat of passion. Don't let me kill him, if I can wound. Don't let me even use the gun if there is any other way. And most importantly, don't let me run ahead of You. Lead me. Give me Your assurance."

Then she felt it—not the familiar chuckle, but a long, groaning sigh.

"I'll be careful. I really will. I don't want to die, but I want even less for my boys to die, so I will be careful."

A soft little chuckle gave her courage. She put the car in gear and backed out of the drive.

Twenty-Two

Last week, quite by accident, Mark had learned about a dirt road that took them closer to the Gopher Mountain Falls. With no concern about the speed limit, Todd sped up the mountain road resisting the desire to put on the flashing lights and siren. Just before the hairpin curve, Mark said, "pull in here."

The dirt road was so well hidden that, had Mark not known it was there, they would have missed it. Todd pulled in behind the black Cadillac that sat like a chariot in a cornfield. Todd and Mark jumped from the car, closed the doors as quietly as possible, and started up the hill. Dark clouds, accented by rumbles of thunder and flashes of lightning, rolled across the sky hiding their ascent. At least the rain was holding off.

Meanwhile at the top of the hill outside the cave, Killer and Hugh argued. Hugh didn't bring the beer Killer had asked for. Thunder rumbled; lightning flashed. Both men were jumpy and edgy—snarling at each other like a couple of stray mongrels after the same bone.

"Was that a car stopped down there?" Killer cocked his head to one side to listen better.

"Don't be stupid," said Hugh. "No one knows where that road is. It's just the storm."

"Someone's down there," said Killer trying to see the unseeable.

"You're crazy. Who would be there? Morgan's in Columbus. Williams is waiting with his girlfriend," responded Hugh.

"What about that dame?"

"If she knows what's good for her, she'll meet Colin."

"You're the only one who's left this place," accused Killer. "Maybe someone followed you. I'm getting out of here. I ain't sticking around to get caught like a rat in a trap."

"And just how do you think you're going to go anyplace. If someone *is* down there, he's with the car. You gonna grow wings and fly or something?" Hugh laughed his Jacobson manic laugh. "I don't think you are going any place. My brother gave me orders to take you out when he gives the signal. I don't know what's happening down there, but you're saying goodbye to this world."

"What about the boys?" Killer sneered.

"Well, he did say you could kill them then I was to kill you."

"Now ain't that interesting. He told me the same thing."

"You're lying. My brother wouldn't do that to me."

"Wouldn't he? Wake up Hughie. Your brother is using you. He doesn't need you hanging around his neck like an albatross. Once he gets that dame, do you think he wants you tagging along? He knows I'll go back to New York."

"You're lying," yelled Hugh.

"Careful there Hughie. Your brother will hear you and then you'll be in even more trouble—especially if *she's* with him. It is almost midnight." Each held a gun pointed at the other—glaring in the darkness lighted only by flashes of lightning. "Why don't we take care of these kids and then get the heck out of here? We can settle our differences after we get away from whoever is coming up that path," said Killer.

"Yeah. Okay."

Josh and Jerome, knowing what Killer and Hugh intended to do, backed up as far as they could. They pressed their backs against the darkest corner of the cave. They could feel Mischief between them, back arched, hair on end, and tail three times its normal size swishing across their legs.

"She knows," said Josh his teeth chattering—not from the cold.

"Yeah," Jerome was having trouble keeping his jaws clenched. "What are we going to do?"

"I don't know, except pray like SaraBelle told us to do." Josh whispered then he began, "Dear Lord, Jerome and me are just little kids. We didn't do anything to make these men mad. Neither did Grandma, really. It will hurt her something terrible if we get killed, so please, if they shoot us, could they maybe just, sort of wound us?"

"Yeah," added Jerome. "We try awful hard to be good so we don't cause Mom and Pastor any more trouble. They have so much stuff to think about. Don't let us be the cause of more worry. And please, don't let them hurt Mischief. She has protected us and comforted us."

"Hey," called out Killer. "What's that?"

"What's what?"

"There's some kind of film or something over the cave. I can't seem to get through it." Killer's voice was shrill with panic and surprise.

"You're crazy," said Hugh. "I'll get in there. Hey, what is this? What are you trying to pull Killer?"

"It ain't me, man. This place is weird. I'm outa here. Your brother can take care of the kids himself."

"Our angel?" whispered Josh.

"Sounds like it," Jerome whispered back.

Mischief purred her agreement.

"You aren't going any place," said Hugh. "My brother said you weren't to leave here alive and I follow my brother's directions."

"If that's the case, Hughie, I have my orders too."

Lightning flashed and a loud crack of thunder boomed so close the ground vibrated. Killer and Hugh, only inches apart, each pulled a trigger. Each bullet found its mark. Two bodies toppled and fell.

Josh and Jerome put their hands over their ears and squeezed their eyes shut—even though they couldn't see anything in the inky blackness. Mischief started twining around their legs.

* * *

Todd and Mark paused in their climb. "Was that...?" Todd asked.

"Sounded like it," said Mark.

"Surely they didn't..."

Todd turned on his flashlight and began running heedless of any noise. If those shots killed the boys, no one—not even levelheaded, Mark would keep him from tearing those two men apart limb by limb. Mark ran beside him. He would back up his friend in whatever he did.

At the top of the hill, Todd stopped. It was too quiet. His flashlight and the lightning showed him what he needed to know—two bodies lying inches apart, guns still clasped in lifeless hands.

"What the...?" He moved the flashlight beam around on the ground.

"Looks like a falling out among thieves—or murderers," said Mark. "The boys...?"

* * *

"It must be safe to go out," said Josh.

"Mischief seems to think so," Jerome added.

Tentatively the boys crept toward the entrance. They heard the thunder and saw the lightning flash.

Todd stepped inside the cave, shining his light around the interior, calling softly, "Jerome? Josh? Are you in here?"

"Dad!" Jerome ran to Todd, wrapping his arms around the man's waist; Josh followed; Mischief landed on Todd's shoulder.

"Are you boys all right?" Todd asked holding both of them close to him.

"We are now," said Jerome. Josh nodded in agreement.

"They're all right, Mark," said Todd over his shoulder with a catch in his voice. "Get going and be careful."

"I'm on my way." Mark turned and headed toward the falls. He would go to Lookout Point by way of the back path, so he could protect Laura better.

"You had us pretty worried until Rascal showed up," said Todd leading the boys out of the cave.

"I knew he could do it," exclaimed Josh. "I knew he would find a way to get there."

"He hitched a ride with Fred Martin," he said. "I'll tell you about it on the way home. Now, let's get you out of here and…"

"Grandma…" said Josh. "That man wants to take her. We have to help her."

"We got that covered, Josh."

"How? She went to see him didn't she?"

"How did you know?"

"Killer and Hugh talked a lot. They talked about everything. We got it all on our tape recorder. They said they were taking a brick to throw through the window with a message from him. She was supposed to come and meet him if she wanted to see us again. She did, didn't she?"

"Josh, you're right, but the best thing we can do for your grandmother is to go home and wait. If we go down there, he will kill her for sure and maybe you also."

"I don't care if he kills me," cried Josh. "I won't let him hurt her."

"Josh, she has Rascal with her. She's not alone."

"Is Grandpa Steve there?"

Todd looked straight into Josh's brown eyes. He blinked. For a minute, he could almost believe it was Laura. He could not lie to her grandson, anymore than he could to her "No," he answered.

"They were right. They were laughing about how that man managed to send him on a wild goose chase to Columbus so he wouldn't be around to interfere," said Josh.

"Mark's already on his way down there. He knows the way down the path and how to stay hidden. He'll be there by the time we get to the car. Jerome, your mother is worried sick about you. We need to go home and wait. It's hard for me, kids. It's the hardest thing I've ever had to do. But I had to make a choice of saving my kids, who only had one cat to protect them, or taking a chance of helping a woman who has proven many times that she can take care of herself. She has Rascal and Mark will be there. Come on boys. She'll be all right."

"He's right, Josh," said Jerome. "We need to go home and wait. They waited for us all day, not knowing if we were dead or alive. Now it is our turn to wait, not knowing."

"I know you are right," sobbed Josh, "but…but…I love her. I don't want her to get hurt."

"None of us want that, Josh. Let's get out of here. There's less chance of her getting hurt if you're safe."

Todd helped the boys down the hill to the car where he opened the door for them. The thunder and lightning continued playing overhead effectively covering any noise from the car door and engine starting.

"Come on Mischief," said Josh. There was no response. He looked all around. She wasn't with them. "Mischief?" He called to her again. Still no answer. "Where is she? Where…?"

"Let's go boys," said Todd. "I think Laura's chances just improved by one more furry body."

On the way back to Cottonville, Todd picked up the car phone and called Carolyn. "I have the boys," he said. "We're on our way home. I think Laura made some spaghetti. Why don't you meet us over there? I know a couple of hungry boys and it will save time…No, she isn't there…I will try to explain later…You know Laura. How could I stop her other than by putting her in a jail cell? And I don't think even Morgan would go for that. See you in a bit."

When he was on Gopher Mountain Road and they were safely on their way home, Todd called Mark's cell phone, which Mark had put on vibration mode. As Todd pulled in Laura's drive. Fred and Frank were putting the last nail in a plywood cover over the window. Thunder rumbled and boomed overhead; lightning flashed fast and furious. Quarter sized drops of rain began to splash on the car.

"Looks like we got this window covered just in time," said Fred as he greeted Todd. "Glad to see you got the boys back safe and sound. What about…?"

"Should hear from Mark soon. I'll get the boys settled and join the wait at the foot of the mountain." He hoped and prayed that Laura could handle it and Mark was close enough to help.

"I think I'll stick around a while, if you don't mind," said Fred.

"Me, too," said Frank.

"Sure," said Todd.

The boys ran ahead and fell into loving arms, tears flowing along with incoherent expressions of fear.

"Pastor made you some spaghetti," said Sophia. "Want to give it a try?"

"Not till Grandma…"

"Josh," said Todd, "she made herself cook when she was scared for you because she believed you would be home and be hungry."

"But…"

"He means we need to make ourselves eat even if we're scared for her, because we believe she'll be home and glad she cooked for us," Jerome said.

"Okay," said Josh who reluctantly moved to the kitchen and washed his hands beside Jerome at the sink.

"Maybe Mr. Martin and Mr. Jennings would like to join us," said Jerome.

"Yeah," said Josh brightening. "Tell us how Rascal hitched a ride with you."

"Sure," said Fred. "That smells mighty good. Picking up misplaced kitties and closing up windows worked up an appetite."

"Maybe a small bite," said Frank. "I'd like to hear that story, too."

Todd gave Carolyn a quick kiss and said, "I'm going back to help Mark." Before he got to the door, however, the phone rang. Todd grabbed it. "Mark?"

"Todd? Where's Laura?"

"She's not here, Steve."

"She did something foolish, didn't she?"

"She went to meet Jacobson."

Like Mark earlier, Todd held the phone away from his ear. "Steve, Steve, cool it man. There are women and children present."

"What?"

"The boys. We got them back. They're safe and eating like horses. Carolyn and her mother are here."

"Todd, who went with her?"

"Rascal. After we rescued the boys, Mischief went with Mark to help her. I'm waiting for his call. We got cars on both sides of the mountain ready to move in when he gives the word."

"Where were the boys? Where is Laura?"

"They were in the cave at Gopher Mountain Falls. Laura is meeting Jacobson at Look Out Point."

"I am almost to Gopher Mountain Road."

"Steve, don't stop and don't use your lights or siren. He'll kill her for sure. Just past the hairpin curve, there is a dirt road to your right. It was well hidden, but has had a lot of use tonight. You should have no trouble seeing it. It's not far back to the Point from there on the main road. I wouldn't try to go through the woods in the dark and it would be dangerous for her if you used a light."

"Got it."

Todd stood holding a buzzing phone. Now he knew why Laura complained about that.

Twenty-Three

"There he is, Rascal," Laura said as she pulled into the parking area of Look Out Point. "You better get under the seat. He's moving this way. I'll leave the window down for you, but be careful. I don't want to lose you."

Rascal poured himself off the seat and slid under Laura's feet like liquid putty. Anyone watching would have thought, maybe a shadow moved. Laura rolled the window down. Jacobson was almost beside the car by the time she turned the engine off and slipped the keys in her pocket. She got out of the car as quickly as she could, hoping to hide any activity by Rascal.

Thunder rumbled and rolled around them accompanied by sharp flashes of lightning. Wind pulled the storm clouds toward Gopher Mountain and whipped Laura's hair around her face. Was Todd with the boys yet? Would they make it home before the storm hit?

"Laura, dearest, I knew you would come." Jacobson laughed his manic laugh. "But, you seem to be in a hurry to get out of your car. You wouldn't be trying to hide someone in there would you?" He moved closer to the car and shoved Laura aside.

"How would I hide a person in a Chevette? I'm not stupid."

"No, dearest, you aren't stupid. That's your problem, you know. You're too smart. If you were like most women, I would have no problems with you. Now, let me look in your car."

She backed away as he pulled the back door open on the driver side, and looked in the back seat and the hatchback. Lightning flashed so brightly that it blinded them for an instant. That was all the time Rascal needed to slide out of the front door and under the car. Even Laura didn't see him move. A loud crack of thunder covered what vaguely sounded like two gunshots further up the mountain.

"It's going to rain, Laura dearest. Don't you think we better put your window up."

"I'm not staying that long," she said.

"Oh, but I think you are." He rolled the window up.

"Glad to see you were smart enough to do as I told you. You're right about a little car. It can't hide anyone. Of course, Morgan is nowhere around. I sent him off to Columbus on a wild goose chase."

"How did you manage that?" She was amazed she could carry on a normal conversation with this man who had killed before and probably intended to kill her.

"Come, my sweet, and I'll tell you all about it."

Thunder and lightning moved closer but the rain held back. Jacobson grabbed Laura's wrist and pulled her toward the path. Laura jerked her arm free.

"Come where? You said you wanted to talk. *Here* is where we'll talk."

"As you wish, but you're being foolish my dear. It's going to rain in a little bit and we'll get soaked—unless of course I have to kill you before that. You know I have no intention of letting you leave alive, except as my wife."

"That will never happen and you know it." Laura was moving away from him, closer to the viewing spot with the mounted telescope. A single pole light with a halogen bulb lighted that area.

"We shall see. We shall see. I know a lovely waterfall where we can sit and get to know each other. And if it rains, there's a nice little cave up the mountain a ways."

"I know about the falls. We'll talk here where I can see you. She moved to the wall and stood by the telescope with her back to the wall. Jacobson followed her laughing his weird, eerie laugh.

"So, how did you manage to send Steve to Columbus? You don't have anything to do with the police department—or FBI." Laura tried to sound casual like she was talking to a friend, but she knew her voice trembled with anger and fear.

Jacobson laughed again and caressed her face with the back of his hand. She cringed; he laughed again. "Laura dearest, for someone who is so smart, you can be so naive. All I had to do was call to the FBI with an anonymous tip that Colin Jacobson had been seen in the vicinity of Columbus and follow it with a call from Detective James Martin, Columbus Police Department. He fell for it hook, line, and sinker." His laughter was almost lost in the rumble of thunder around them.

"I suppose you're the one who sent Randy here to kill us last summer, too," Laura said, her voice much calmer than she felt. She had to keep him talking as long as possible. She had to give Todd and Mark time to find the boys and get them safely out.

"That was Randy's idea." Jacobson was saying. "I sent him to scare you. That was Randy's problem. He was stupid—couldn't follow instructions. He was too dangerous to have around."

"Is that why you killed him after he killed Ed Winters?"

"Oh, you figured that one out too. How long did it take you? Five minutes? Ten? A day?"

Laura stared past him, refusing to answer him. His arm shot out, and his hand slapped her hard enough that she fell against the wall. Leaning against the wall to steady her legs and get her anger under control, she felt a slow trickle down her chin. Clenching her teeth, she refused to check it with her hand.

"Look at me when I am talking to you," he barked, jerking her around to face him. "And answer me when I ask you a question. How long did it take you to figure it out?"

"Not as long as it took for you to think it up," she said angrily.

He slapped her again. "You have a smart mouth, Laura. Just like that kid of yours."

Laura felt the crack on her lip widen. "If you've hurt my boys, Bill Collins, I won't be responsible for my actions." Laura spit the words out as if they were coated with the blood in her mouth.

"Oh my, aren't we feisty? Just what do you think you can do about it?" The sneer spread across his face as the lightning flashed again giving him the appearance of a mythical monster. Laura stared and tried to repress the shudder.

"Hugh—you remember my brother, Hugh?—and Killer—a friend of a friend from New York—are with them. They'll take *real* good care of them." He laughed again and stopped abruptly, staring at her with eyes full of lust.

"But, I didn't bring you here to talk about Morgan or those brats. I want *you*, dearest and I think we will go to that little spot by the falls where we can have some privacy." Jacobson stepped closer and wrapped his arms around her. Before she could stop him, his mouth was pressing on hers, splitting the tear in her lip further.

Laura struggled and pulled away from him. She swiped the back of her hand across her mouth as if he had poured something nasty on her. A car moved slowly up the mountain from Glenville. The driver swerved as if to stop in the parking lot then as if changing his mind, sped on toward Cottonville. Neither Laura nor Jacobson noticed.

"You don't like my kisses? Well we'll fix that. You'll respect me the way a good wife ought to before long. Now come here and let's try again."

He tried once again to embrace her, but Laura ducked away from his arms and moved to one side. He banged his hand against the wall, swore and reached for her again. She kept eluding him. If only I knew the boys were safe, I would call Rascal and make a run for the car. Todd said Mark will come here when they had the boys free. While fighting off Jacobson, Laura listened for activity on the path, hoping Bill wouldn't hear Mark and shoot him.

Jacobson swore again and pulled a gun from his pocket. "You want to do it the hard way; we'll do it the hard way. Now come here and kiss me like a proper fiancée ought to."

"I'm not your fiancée, Bill Collins. I never was and I never will be." Laura spoke between clenched teeth." She had backed up until she was in a corner of the wall. Before she could move out of it, he was there with his arms on either side of her, pressing his lips roughly against hers. She struggled, kicked him in the shins fuelling his anger. He hit her on the side of her face with the gun.

Laura closed her eyes to block out the stars dancing before them. She could feel a lump rising on her cheekbone.

"Maybe now, my dearest, you will be more willing to submit. I can see I'm going to have a time breaking you, but it will be fun. Come, now, kiss me like a proper bride-to-be. And you must begin calling me Colin, not Bill."

Twenty-Four

Mark had worked his way down to the falls then took the path to Look Out Point. He was almost there when his phone vibrated. He opened it and waited. "Boy's okay," Todd said. Mark closed the phone without a sound, no chance for Jacobson to hear anything.

He continued down the path. He could now hear Laura and Jacobson talking which filled him with a sense of relief. At least she was still alive. Reaching the end of the path, however, Mark stepped on a loose stone and slipped, sending a pocket of pebbles rolling.

"What was that?" Jacobson whirled around and fired his gun toward the path. Mark hit the ground, alive, but wounded. Mischief licked his face. Jacobson gripped Laura's wrist and turned toward the path. Mischief shot across the road on her tippy-toes with her tail bushy and standing straight up. She scooted under Laura's car. Jacobson laughed.

"Only a stupid raccoon. Must be getting jumpy—all that thunder and lightning. Now, where were we? Oh, yes…" He turned back to Laura who slowly let out the breath she had been holding. That wasn't a raccoon, she thought. It was Mischief. The boys are safe or she wouldn't be here.

Thunder rolled and rumbled louder and longer. Lightning flashed a noonday-like brilliance. Laura stared at Jacobson. "How can you hit me like that, tell me you intend to kill my boys, and then expect me to come crawling to you with any kind of feeling?"

Jacobson's high-pitched laughter was lost in the howling wind and the booming thunder. "Oh we will be a great pair, won't we dearest? You'll keep me on my toes and I'll keep you on your knees, like this," he said as he kicked out, knocking her legs out from under her. She fell to her hands and knees.

"Laura, dearest, you must learn to obey me then these silly little accidents won't keep happening. Now get up. I've played around long enough. You obviously aren't going to cooperate on your own, so we will go where we can be more comfortable." He pointed the gun at her head. She took a few seconds to gain control of her anger.

"Get up," he yelled and kicked her again, his foot pushing her off balance.

"Drop the gun, Jacobson. Touch her again and you're a dead man." The voice came from the steps at the parking lot. Lightning flashed and Colin Jacobson whirled around to see Steve Morgan standing not three feet away, gun leveled at him.

"Morgan! Where did you come from? My aren't we inventive? Well think about this my friend. You make one move toward me and she's a goner, but just to make sure, I think I'll put a hole in your head first."

"You can't kill both of us, Jacobson. I suggest you shoot me and get it over with or you'll never leave this mountain alive."

"Brave aren't we? You know of course if I shoot you first, then I'll kill her later."

"I don't think so, Bill." Laura spoke in a cold, emotionless voice. "You better drop the gun before I forget I'm a preacher." She stood with feet apart and both hands in front of her clutching a gun that she aimed at Bill's head. Her voice was controlled, her hands steady.

Once again, the lightning flashed and thunder sounded so loud it was like a small bomb exploding near them. Feline shadows moved closer.

"Laura, dearest, you *are* full of surprises. I didn't know you even knew which part of a gun to hold on to. Of course, you're good at bluffing. Now, put that toy away. I intend to kill him and then you. I would rather take you alive and have some fun with you first, but if I can't I'm not going to mourn your death. Oh, well enough of this nonsense. Morgan you're first."

He raised the gun level with Steve's head. Lightning flashed. A shot rang out at the same moment as thunder roared overhead. Power went off leaving the Look Out Point in darkness. Steve dropped to the ground. In the next flash of lightning, Colin Jacobson turned toward Laura, blood dripping from a hole in his hand. His gun fell to the ground at his feet.

"You should have killed me first, Bill," Laura said evenly. "I wouldn't have shot you to protect myself. But you know something? There *is* power in wielding a gun. It sort of takes over the senses. I want to finish the job in the worst way. I want to put the next shot right between those evil eyes." Laura's voice was cold and controlled.

Lightning flashed fast and furious, one bolt after another. Thunder rumbled and rolled and crashed around them, vibrating the very ground on which they stood. Laura had the gun leveled at Colin Jacobson's head and understood the meaning of the heavenly sound effects, but she didn't want to listen.

Jacobson pleaded with her. "Laura, for God's sake don't do it. Look, I'm bleeding. I'm going to bleed to death."

Steve, holding his own gun on Jacobson, kicked Jacobson's dropped gun out of the way. He wasn't sure what Laura was going to do. According to the code of the street, she had every right to hate Colin Jacobson and want to kill him, but according to her code of life, she had no right to take a life—especially a now unarmed man. Mark watched from the path as Jacobson pleaded with her for his life.

Steve eased over beside her and spoke softly. "Laura, give me the gun."

"Mark was hit. Check him. I'll hold Bill."

"Mark?"

"By the path."

"Laura…?"

"I won't kill him—much as I want to—unless he makes a move. Call Todd."

"Already did," called Mark as Steve went to him. Sirens were already screaming from both sides of Gopher Mountain. Flashing red and blue lights joined the heavenly fireworks. Police vehicles and ambulances screeched to a stop—headlights illuminating the scene before them.

"You know you can't kill me," said Jacobson and began moving toward the wall. Laura knew he would disappear over it and escape again, but as much as she wanted to, she couldn't kill an unarmed man.

"Sorry, Bill," she said. "You asked for this." He laughed and reached his hands toward the wall to throw himself over it. Laura, keeping her gun steady, said quietly, "All right, guys. He's all yours."

Jacobson's hand was inches from the wall. Rascal and Mischief flew from each side and knocked him to the ground. With claws extended, they kept him in place like an insect tacked to a board.

Thunder boomed. Lightning sizzled and crackled. Dark clouds rolled and tumbled around the mountaintop like ocean waves in a hurricane. Still Laura stood, holding the gun—now pointing toward the ground. Feeling detached and numb, she couldn't put it away, nor could she move. For a brief moment, she thought she would pass out. How did Steve get here? Where did all the flashing lights come from? Where are the boys? Electricity once again ran through the wires to the pole light, offering more light.

Todd's voice floated from somewhere. Footsteps crunched on stone. An ambulance door slammed shut. Tires squealed as it took off for Cottonville. Mark? Was he alive?

Todd and Steve moved closer to her—no, they were after Jacobson. Rascal and Mischief let them have him and darted to her, twining around her legs. Maybe I should sit down, but where? Maybe I should go home, but how?

Todd's voice sounded from a distance. "Laura? Laura, you all right?"

What is he yelling about? Of course, I'm all right—I think. She nodded. Maybe that would stop the yelling.

"Better get in the car," he yelled again. The wind whipped the words this way and that. Car? Why?

"Okay," she heard herself saying. If he would just go away. She needed to scream—to cry—to…die.

Apparently, he understood. Pushing Jacobson ahead of him, he put him in a cruiser along with three other officers. They were all gone—all except Steve. Why was he standing there looking at her like that—angry? Did she scream? Did she embarrass him? Did she forget who she was?

More lightning—ziz-zagged across the sky. Thunder so loud her head ached. And why was it so cold. Her bones hurt they were so cold. Her hands began to tremble then her arms, her whole body felt like she was on a treadmill that had gone berserk.

"Laura, give me that gun and get in the car before you hurt yourself or someone else." The words were compassionate—the tone was angry. Like Harold. But…Harold was dead, wasn't he? Steve reached for the gun. She backed away from him.

"Laura, give me that gun." He reached for it again. "You're bleeding. You need to…"

Laura stared into his eyes. No twinkle. With determination, she removed the cartridge container, dropped it in her pocket then slid the gun back into waist of her jeans. All the while, she stared at Steve, never blinking, never saying a word.

"Laura…" Steve reached out and took her arm. She jerked away from him.

"Laura, why are you being so pig-headed and stubborn? What in the name of common sense were you thinking? Coming out here against Jacobson with a gun that…"

"That what? That I don't know anything about? That I don't know how to use?"

"You got a lucky shot. He could have killed you."

"He would have killed you first. But that's all right, I suppose. It's all right for me to watch him kill you, but not all right for you to watch him kill me. Just who do you think you are anyway to tell me what I can do and can't do? I didn't see you here when the boys disappeared—when I had to wait all day for word—when a brick flew through my window with a message—when…"

Words dissolved, swallowed up in a choked sob, blown away by the wind. Laura turned and ran for her car while thunder rolled and lightning flashed. The swirling clouds opened and rain fell in torrents. She knew God was trying to get her attention, but she was too exhausted and near shock to care. She had spent her energy. She hoped there was enough to get her home. She hoped she knew the way home.

She opened her car door and felt flying feline fur sail over her head. She started the car and drove off, leaving Steve standing at Look Out Point in the pouring rain.

Twenty-Five

Laura pulled into her driveway, having no idea how she got there. She was on Gopher Mountain Road; now she was home. Shaking her head, she got out of the car, closed the door, barely missing a furry tail, and walked slowly to the house. She was soaked. She didn't care. Something seemed urgent, but what?

Rascal ran ahead and opened the screen door, waiting against it for her to enter. Josh and Jerome, hearing the door open, jumped up from the table and ran to meet her. Laura slipped to her knees and would have fallen had the boys not surrounded her with their arms.

"Grandma, you're all right," cried Josh, "…but you're bleeding."

"We were scared for you," said Jerome. "He hurt you."

"I was scared for you, too," she answered and held them while they released their fear in torrents of tears. Tears—a luxury she still couldn't afford. She had to be strong for her boys. She had to give them comfort. "I'm all right."

"Laura?" Carolyn gently pulled Jerome away.

Without looking up at them, Laura answered, "I'm fine. Just a couple of scratches and…tired."

"Tired? You look exhausted," said Fred. "Did Detective Morgan make it back? He should be…"

"He…got soaked…went to…change."

"I see," said Fred. "Well, everyone's accounted for, so I'm heading home. Emma's waiting."

"Yeah, me too," said Frank. "You want me to send Martha over to stay with you tonight?"

Laura stood, keeping her hands on Josh's shoulder. "Thanks for all your help," she said. "I'll be all right. I appreciate your offer, but I don't think any of us will have any trouble sleeping."

"We'll be back in the morning to take care of that window properly," Frank said and he and Fred left.

"We better get this fellow home to bed, too," said Carolyn with her arm around Jerome.

"See you tomorrow, Josh," said Jerome.

"Yeah," said Josh.

"You better get a hot shower," said Sophia. "You're shivering. We don't want you to get pneumonia before that wedding next week. Sure you don't want someone to stay…?"

"Thanks, but I'll get Josh to bed and go soak in a hot tub of water." Laura tried to smile. Why don't they just leave? I'm going to start screaming if they don't.

They left and she turned to Josh who was already heading up the stairs. "I can put myself to bed," he said indignantly.

Laura smiled—or tried to. "I know you can," she said. "It was just an expression."

"Oh. Come on kitties." Rascal sailed to the steps and ran around Josh. "Hey, where's Mischief? Didn't she come home with you? She's not still lost out there…Grandma we gotta go find her. She saved my life…she went to help you…" Panic was rising in his voice.

"She's all right, Josh. She did come to help me. She…she's with Grandpa Steve."

"You sure? Why…?"

"She'll be here when you wake up in the morning. Rascal's not concerned."

"You sure she's okay, Rascal?"

Rascal blinked, and ran up the steps. Josh followed. Laura was trembling so violently she wasn't sure she could make it up the steps. She heard Josh's door close and crawled up the stairs. Leaning against the wall, she made it to the bathroom, where she turned on the hot shower, laid the gun still in two pieces on the counter, and struggled out of her wet clothes.

Stepping under the flow of hot water, Laura felt the warmth slowly begin to penetrate her cold, clammy skin. Gradually the trembling stopped; the chill in her bones didn't give up so easily. Only when the hot water turned lukewarm did she turn it off.

Wrapping her giant bath towel around her, Laura picked up her gun and went to the bedroom where she slipped on her red sweat suit and slippers. She would tend to her cuts and scrapes later.

Twenty-Six

Steve, fists clenched at his side, teeth clamped so tight his jaws ached, stood in the rain, watching the retreating taillights of Laura's Chevette. *How could I ever have thought I was falling in love with that stubborn, pig-headed, woman? What ever possessed me to throw caution to the wind and ask her to marry me? What kind of life would we have when she ignores my feelings, driving off leaving me in the middle of nowhere getting soaked? At least I haven't given her the ring yet. I will just return it and take a long vacation— maybe go to Alaska, or the Antarctic.*

Wind whipped around him, rain washed across his face, thunder rumbled, lightning lighted the road ahead of him. "She's the one who needs Your help," he said absently as he began slowly walking back down the road to his car. *I may as well go back to Glenville to my apartment, get a hot shower and go to bed. I'm drained after racing across two thirds of the state to get to her to keep her from doing something stupid, only to be minutes too late.*

Steve opened the car door and was surprised when a wet feline sailed over his head to the passenger seat.

"Mischief? What are you…? Laura will be worried."

Mischief began purring and grooming the rain off her fur. "All right," he said, "I guess I'm going to Cottonville after all. I'll go to Todd's. He probably would appreciate some help with the paper work."

As he drove into Cottonville, he glanced over at his passenger who was still licking wet fur. "Would you like for me to take you home? Are you going with me to Todd's? Or do you want to walk the rest of the way in the rain?"

Mischief narrowed her eyes, laid back her ears, and hissed.

Steve laughed. "All right, forget the walk in the rain. I'll take you home then go to Todd's."

Mischief slid off the seat and under it. "You don't want to go home?" Mischief returned to the seat and resumed her grooming. Steve lifted his eyebrows in question, but of course, she didn't answer him.

The apartment was dark. Todd was either at Carolyn's or finishing paper work at the office. Steve pulled out his key and let himself in, going to the guest room where he'd spent a good deal of time lately. He already had arrangements to rent the apartment after Todd's wedding, so he could be closer to Laura. Maybe he would give that a second thought, now. She didn't want him and he wasn't all that keen on seeing her again. He would be civil for Todd's sake until after the wedding then it was back to Glenville and his life of singleness.

Mischief followed him and made herself at home on the couch while he got out of his wet clothes and into a hot shower. When he returned Todd was there talking to Mischief.

"Does Laura know she's here?"

"I doubt if Laura even cares where she is." Steve couldn't keep the bitterness out of his voice.

"Whoa there," said Todd. "Sounds like something happened besides the boys being kidnapped. Carolyn said she looked like she had taken quite a beating and was more like a zombie than a person. They thought she was exhausted and left so she could go to bed."

Steve didn't say anything. He sat beside Mischief and began absently stroking her fur. She moved closer to him and purred loudly.

"I'm not sure why Mischief is here," said Steve. "Laura got in her car and took off. Maybe she didn't have time to get in the car. When I opened the door to mine, she flew over my head. She didn't want to go home, so I brought her with me. Hope you don't mind."

"She didn't want to go home?"

"She made it very clear. If Laura treated her like she did me…"

"Steve, what's the problem. Laura is not a vindictive person—to people or animals."

"That's what I thought too, but she was very curt, angry, stubborn, secretive, and…"

"Secretive? The gun?"

"You knew she was taking a gun? And you *let* her?"

"Steve, Laura said she would leave it home if I said she should. She wouldn't have ignored my warning. I weighed all the facts and let her go. Laura can take care of herself. She knew the odds."

"Todd I can't believe you just let her go."

110

"You know as well as I do that I couldn't stop her from going. Rascal was with her. The gun gave her a little more protection—and as it turned out, saved your life."

"I wouldn't have needed her to save my life if she hadn't been so stubborn in the first place and gone off to do what we are trained to do."

"Sounds like professional jealously and bruised ego, to me," said Todd. "I'm going to bed. You and Mischief can work it out. But I would suggest you talk to Laura and get all your facts straight before you go off the deep end."

Mischief looked up at him and said, "Meow!"

Todd laughed. "See, she agrees." He went into his room still laughing, which made Steve's anger flare again.

"If you want to go home," he snarled at Mischief, "there's the door. I think the rain has stopped, so you won't get wet again. Although, why you would want to go back there, when she went off and left you, I don't know. I certainly don't want to go."

Mischief butted against him, purring, trying to push him off the couch. Then she jumped to the floor and sat staring at the door. Steve opened it. She sat with ears laid back, tail slapping the floor.

"Go," he snarled.

She turned around and hissed at him.

"All right," he said, reaching for his keys. "I'll take you home. I figured you would desert me too. Guess that's why I didn't dress for bed after my shower."

Mischief waited for him to go out the door then she followed down the stairs. "Let's walk," he said. "You can ride if you want. I need to walk."

Mischief leaped to his shoulders and curled around his neck as he walked the three blocks to Laura's house. He had a key to her house, so he would deposit Mischief inside and leave.

As he walked up the driveway, the house was dark except for a light from the kitchen which sent a soft glow into the dining room fading to a mere sliver in the living room. It's highly unlikely Laura would go to bed and leave the lights burning, he thought. She's probably still up. He glanced at his watch. Two a.m. If she was so exhausted, she should be in bed.

He started to the front door. Mischief would make enough noise Rascal would let her in, even if Laura didn't. Mischief nibbled his ear and pointed her paw to the left. "You want to go in the kitchen door? Fine. Be that way."

111

Twenty-Seven

Knowing she couldn't sleep yet, Laura checked on Josh who was turning and tossing in his sleep. She took the gun with its box downstairs. Rascal followed her to the kitchen where they both began pacing. Laura had to do something. She felt as if her nerves were all shooting out sparks like an electric pole struck by lightning.

She cleaned the kitchen, then spread out newspapers on the table and began cleaning her gun to put it away. Rascal sat on a chair watching. Suddenly, his ears perked up, his tail swished, he ran to the front window then back to the kitchen where he sat staring at the back door, waiting.

"Mischief?" Laura asked.

"Meow."

She got up and filled the coffee pot.

* * *

Steve carried Mischief to the back porch. He would set her inside and leave. The aroma of coffee reached out to him and he remembered he hadn't eaten since lunch. He'd go back and see what Todd had in the fridge. He opened the back porch door, but Mischief refused to get down, even digging in her claws into his shoulder when he tried to remove her. Exasperated, he opened the kitchen door. Rascal greeted Mischief, who still refused to get off his shoulders until he stepped completely into the kitchen. Then she jumped down, bumped noses with Rascal and went to her food dish. Laura handed Steve a cup of coffee.

"Peace offering?"

She glanced briefly at him then lowered her gaze. "Rascal said you were coming. I thought…" Laura's hand began shaking. She clamped her teeth together and breathed deeply, but all to no avail. She was falling apart. Soon there would be pieces of her flying all over the kitchen.

Steve had every intention of refusing the cup and leaving, but that brief glance that told him something was wrong. As if a bolt of lightning returned and

112

hit him, he realized, she was not only exhausted, but also, near shock on top of it. She was about to crash.

He took the cup and set it on the table. "Laura, you're exhausted. You should be in bed." He had her in his arms before he could stop himself. She could no more stop the tears that cascaded down her face than she could stop the trembling of her body. Had she become an erupting volcano?

Steve held her, letting her cry on his shoulder until the trembling stopped and she could talk. She had experienced trauma after trauma and had almost killed a man. He felt her struggles. He should have realized sooner.

Between gulps of air, still clinging to him, she said, "That's the second time I wanted to kill him. How can I preach love and feel that kind of hate? How can God ever forgive me for what I wanted to do? How can you forgive me for whatever I said? I don't even know."

"Laura, you're the preacher, but somehow I don't think God will hold it against you for being human. You didn't kill the man. Wanting to, and doing it, are two different things."

"The boys…I was so scared…had no one…"

"Laura, I'm sorry. I wanted to be here. I thought I was doing the right thing—going after Jacobson."

"I know. I don't blame you. It was just so much…"

"Mark was here. He's a good man—a good cop."

"He said the boys would be hungry and I should fix something for them. He knew I needed to be busy doing something." Laura paused. Neither said anything, just clung to each other for a minute.

"I waited for Mark to let me know the boys were safe. I was going to let Rascal and Mischief take care of Bill and get back in the car. But Mark slipped and Bill whirled around and shot at the path. He didn't see Mark, but I knew he must have hit him. Bill only heard the noise and was going to go investigate when Mischief made herself look like a raccoon and ran across the parking lot. He assumed that's what he heard and didn't go look. I knew Mark was hurt. I don't know how…"

"He's going to be all right—shoulder wound."

"Then you came and he was going to kill you and…" Again her tears flowed. She started to pull away. He reached for a tissue to wipe her face, carefully caressing the lump on her cheek, dabbing at the cracked, swollen lip. He continued to hold her.

"Laura, why didn't you tell me about the gun?"

"I never told anyone. My grandfather gave it to me when I was six. He taught me all about it—how to use it; how to clean it; how to respect it. We practiced every day—shooting and cleaning. When he died, my uncle took over. They made me promise to keep it hidden and tell no one about it. I promised to practice, keep it oiled and cleaned and never use it unless I had to—if someone I love was in danger. Harold never knew. He would have destroyed it."

"Would you have told me?"

She didn't hesitate. "Yes, you would understand. I guess there just was never an opportunity—or the right time. It isn't something I'm proud of, but neither am I ashamed."

Steve looked deep into those pools of brown eyes. "Do you have any more surprises up your sleeve to cause me heart failure?"

"I don't think so, but I've lived fifty years and I've only known you a few months. How could I tell you everything?"

"You're right, of course. I really don't expect that. Like Todd said, I had an ego problem. I rushed home to save you only to have you save my life."

"I'm sorry—that I wounded your ego, not that I saved your life. I'm not sure what happened or what I said. I don't even know how I got home."

"You were in shock. I would have recognized the signs if I hadn't been so wrapped up in my own anger. You're still on the edge and need to rest."

"I will. Did you eat? It's been a long twenty-four hours, or more." She moved out of his arms to freshen his coffee that had gotten cold.

"No, but…"

"There's still spaghetti and salad."

"Well, maybe…if you join me."

"I think I am hungry all of a sudden." She turned to the refrigerator and began to gather their impromptu midnight snack.

Steve moved to the table and looked at gun lying in parts on the table. His fingers itched to put it together, but he would wait, let her show him. "Looks like you have it ready to reassemble," he said. "Mind if I watch?"

Laura grinned, grimaced at the tug on her spilt lip and put the spaghetti in the microwave. She picked up the pieces of the gun and like working a well-rehearsed puzzle, she handed it to him completely assembled before the microwave beeped.

"What a beauty. And you really know how to care for it. When did you practice last?"

"Before I left Chicago last spring." She grinned again and handed him a folder full of sharpshooter awards—the last from Chicago Police Department in April.

Steve whistled. "Care to practice with me at the Glenville range?"

"What if I...?"

"Show me up?" She nodded and he laughed. "Then I'll have to practice more."

"I'd love to do that—practice with you, that is."

Laura turned to dish up their snack. Rascal ran for the stairs, Mischief right behind him. Laura turned pale and moved to follow them. Steve held her back. "It's Josh," he said.

"Mischief, you're home," Josh cried from the stairs. "Did Grandpa Steve bring you home?"

Steve slid his arm around Laura and together they went to the stairs. "She brought me home, Josh," he said.

"Grandpa Steve! I was afraid that man killed you. Grandma was real quiet and they said he shot someone..."

"Josh, I'm sorry, sweetheart. I guess I was too...too...tired to think. That was Mark who was shot and he's doing fine. Did we wake you?"

"No, I had a bad dream and Rascal wasn't there. Then I heard voices and came to see if you were okay."

"I'm fine now," said Laura. "Want to stay up with us a while. We were going to have a snack."

"No, I'm ready to sleep some more if Rascal and Mischief come with me." The cats twined around his ankles then ran up the steps. Steve went to him.

"I know you're a big boy, Josh, but can I carry you up to bed?"

Josh giggled. "If you want to."

Steve returned a few minutes later to eat the meal Laura prepared for him. He picked up the dishes and set them in the sink. "Do you think you can sleep now?" he asked as he once again took her in his arms again.

"I think so. You?"

He kissed her in answer. They turned off the kitchen light and he walked with her to the stairs. He kissed her again and went out the front door whistling.

Laura collapsed in bed. The cats were with Josh. She was alone, but fell into sleep, the prayer of the Psalmist giving her peace—*in You my soul takes refuge; I will both lie down and sleep in peace.*

Twenty-Eight

Morning came much too soon, but weary or not it was Saturday and certain routines had to be followed. Rascal and Mischief gave Laura an extra hour and Josh still slept.

Finishing her morning devotions, Laura started to the kitchen for another cup of coffee when she heard footsteps on her front porch. Since the window had a board instead of the missing pane, she couldn't see who was there. She and Steve almost collided as he opened the screen door at the same time she opened the inside door.

"I didn't know you would be so anxious to see me," he teased.

"You're out early after such a late night. Doesn't your hotel offer room service?" She smiled at him, knowing he had stayed with Todd what was left of the night before.

"No," he said. "I'm on my own. Todd is sleeping in. He knew I could get a good cup of coffee at the Methodist preacher's house, so here I am."

Laura laughed and started for the kitchen.

"I was just trying to decide if I wanted a shower first, or breakfast first."

"Why don't I fix breakfast while you get your shower?

"Thanks. I feel like I'm a mess after last night." Her hand went involuntarily to her bruised face. Her clothes hid the other bruises. "At least I didn't end up in the hospital this time."

Steve placed a hand over the bruise and said through clenched teeth. "When I drove by the Point, I wanted to stop. If I had realized how much he hurt you…"

"I know," she said. "I better get my shower before we get carried away," she said removing herself from his embrace.

He kissed her bruised cheek. "I'll have breakfast ready by the time you're through. Is Josh up yet?"

"No, he's still sleeping. He was exhausted last night. That was quite an experience for a ten year old. And…"

"And...?" He prompted, sensing she needed to get something off her chest.

"And I can't even let his parents know. Steve, I'm so angry with my daughter. We haven't heard from her in weeks. Norman said they were having problems. I don't even know if they are still together. I have no phone number or address. If Josh had been..." she couldn't even bring herself to finish her thought.

"You want me to find them?"

"Would you?"

He grinned at her. "Laura, that's my business. Remember? I hunt people for a living—when I'm not saving damsels in distress."

Her eyes lit up. "We'll talk about it over breakfast. Cook whatever you can find. You cook it; I'll eat it. I'll only be a few minutes."

Steve went to the kitchen, poured a cup of coffee, and began rummaging to see what was there. Settling on scrambled eggs and sausage, he began whistling while he cooked. Laura was dressed in jeans and a T-shirt and back downstairs by the time Steve was putting breakfast on the table.

"Laura, we do need to talk," he said as they finished eating.

"We've been talking throughout our breakfast," she said. She knew where this was heading and wasn't sure she was ready to deal with it.

"You know what I mean." He tried to scowl at her but got lost in her brown, trusting eyes. "We need to talk serious talk—not just about Susan and Norman, but about us."

"About last night?" she asked.

"Yes, about last night for starters." He reached across the table and took her hand. "I'm not angry, darling. I'm scared. I'm scared I will lose you before I—we—can have time together as husband and wife. I don't want to wait until next spring. Actually, it will be almost summer if we wait for Susan."

"Steve, I want..."

She didn't finish. The phone interrupted. He started to tell her to let it ring, but knew she was too dedicated to her profession to do that. It might be someone needing her help. He smiled and said, "Saved by the bell?"

"Maybe. Come with me." She took his hand and pulled him with her. When she reached the phone, she pushed the speakerphone button. She could not have explained if he had asked why she did that, but for some reason she wanted him to hear—to be a part of this portion of her life—no more secrets of any kind.

"Good morning, Reverend Kenzel speaking."

"Mother?"

"Susan! What a lovely surprise. How are you dear?"

"I'm fine, mother."

"That's good to hear, Susan. I was sure you and Norman had been in a terrible accident or something and were all bundled up in casts and IV's and stuff in some far off hospital."

"*Moth*-er, sarcasm doesn't become you," Susan said sourly. "Do you have the speaker phone on? It sounds kind of hollow."

"Yes, as a matter of fact I do."

"Is Joshua there?"

"He isn't up yet. I'll have Steve go wake him."

"No, not yet… Why is that man in your house this early in the morning?" She asked with a note of accusation in her voice.

"Not that it's any of your business; he dropped in to fix breakfast for me while I took my shower." She squeezed Steve's hand. He had started to leave, but she needed his presence and support to keep her from saying things she would regret. Steve understood and placed his other arm around her shoulder as he listened to their conversation.

"Don't you think you're a little old to be playing house with a man you hardly know?"

"I'm sure you didn't call me to give advice about my love life."

"*Moth*-er!"

"Susan, do you realize that neither you, nor Norman, have written to Josh since you left him with me in May? Josh has written to you every single day and has no place to send his letters. They are in a nice neat little stack on his desk—dated on the outside of the envelope. You haven't even called since sometime in August—and that was hardly worth the effort. What was it—about a three minute call, if that?"

"I'm not a little girl. You don't have to scold me like I was Joshua's age." Susan sounded miffed.

"If you *are* an adult, then don't you think it's time for you to *act* like one? Accept your responsibility? Give your son some of your love and attention?" Laura didn't realize she was squeezing Steve's hand in her attempt to keep the anger out of her voice. It didn't help. While she didn't raise her voice, the anger came through loud and clear.

"Oh for heaven's sake. I called to share some good news, but all you want to do is complain. If Joshua is that much trouble, I'll find a boarding school for him."

"You know I would never allow you to do that to him. What's really eating at you?"

"Norman and I are separated."

Even though she had expected it, Laura felt as if Susan was in the room with her and had punched her in the stomach. Steve squeezed her hand and shoulder reminding her he was there.

"Are you still there?"

"I'm still here, Susan. What happened?"

"I found someone I like better—someone more exciting. I want to bring Jean Paul home to meet you." Susan sounded more excited. Then she added, "But, you'll have to get rid of that policeman and those cats. Jean Paul is allergic to both."

Laura took a deep breath, clenched her teeth, gripped Steve's hand harder before she answered with a cold, controlled voice. "Susan, listen very carefully to what I am going to say. I will only say it once and then I am going to hang up."

"Mother, don't be so melodramatic!"

"And don't interrupt. I want an address with a phone number where we can reach you *and* Norman. If I do not receive a letter, or a post card, within seven days, I will see my friend Judge Walker and have him begin paper work to take Josh away from you on the grounds of abandonment and neglect. If you want to come home while you and Norman work out your problems, you may do so for a limited time. You may not now, or ever, bring another man into my house until that day you and Norman are legally divorced and you are legally remarried. Have I made myself clear?"

"Quite clear, Mother." Susan's voice was cold and distant.

"One more thing your mother neglected to say to you." Steve spoke from behind Laura.

"I don't need to listen to you," said Susan.

"I think you better," he said. "It concerns your son. You can either listen to me, or I can have legal authorities over there come to see you."

"Why would I need to see the authorities either here or there?" Her voice had a sneer, almost a snarl to it.

"Then you aren't interested in the fact that Josh and his friend, Jerome, were kidnapped yesterday?"

They heard Susan catch her breath, but Steve didn't give her a chance to say anything. He continued, "If it hadn't been for the boys' quick thinking and the special devotion of those cats you don't like, they both might be dead right now. Your mother risked her life in order to free them. She, too, could be lying in the morgue. And that doesn't even take into account the fact that she was shot and in the hospital for almost a week in August. If something like this happens again, where shall I send my condolences?"

"Mother, he's lying. Isn't he?"

"No, Susan, he's not. One more thing, then I'm through. I'm calling Bishop Giles this morning. The first date he has free, Steve and I are going to be married. I wanted to wait for you and Norman to come home next spring, but it looks like that is no longer in the picture. I expect to hear from you in written form within seven days. Goodbye Susan."

Laura didn't wait for Susan's answer. She pushed the disconnect button, then turned and buried her face in Steve's chest. He wrapped her in his arms while she got her anger under control.

Twenty-Nine

Dry eyed and determined, Laura took a deep breath and looked up at Steve who still had his arms around her after Susan's call. "I have never felt so angry at my daughter in my life. How can she…?

"Call that bishop," he said. "We'll work out something. She'll not take Josh off to who knows where with some…" The phone rang again.

"Susan calling back?" Steve questioned.

"Maybe, but I doubt it." Laura pushed the speakerphone button. "Good morning, Reverend Kenzel speaking."

"Laura, this is Norman."

"Norman! How good to hear from you."

"Laura, Susan just called. Said she talked to you—or rather you talked to her." He tried to laugh but Laura could hear the pain in his voice.

"Norman, I'm so sorry. Sometimes—often, I should say—I just don't understand my daughter."

"That makes two of us, but Josh…how is he? She said something about kidnapping and you taking him away from us."

"Susan heard what she wanted to hear and repeated even less of it to you. Josh is tired, but fine. Hugh Jacobson and a hired killer kidnapped the boys on their way to school yesterday, but Police Chief Williams got them home, unharmed. The cats were with them, so they were well covered. I did tell Susan that I will do all in my power to take Josh if she continues to ignore him with what I consider neglect and abandonment. Norman, why haven't you written to him, or called him?"

"Laura, I don't understand what's happened to us. I have written to Josh every day and thought Susan had too. She was supposed to mail the letters. I just learned she didn't. Every time I asked her if we'd heard from him, she would say,'You know how boys are about writing.' I tried to call several times. She had given me a wrong number."

"Norman, are you sure about that?" Laura had a hard time believing her daughter was that cold and callous.

"The phone always rang but there was never an answer. I assumed you were out. I should have realized the answering machine would pick up…I guess I was too wrapped up in my own self-pity and wasn't thinking too clearly."

"I understand that, but…"

"I'm sorry, Laura. She's your daughter, but…well I sure wish she were more like you."

"Sorry, pal," said Steve, "but Laura is one of a kind. There *is* no one else like her."

"Steve! Hey, congratulations. Susan said you two are getting married. She thought it was scandalous. I think it's great. I wish I could be there."

"When do you have a break, Norman? We haven't talked to the bishop yet about a date."

"Not until December. This quarter is over the end of November, but…well…I don't think I could swing the airfare. I'll be with you in spirit."

"Dad, please try to come." Josh had slipped down the stairs unnoticed. Laura's heart sank. How much had he heard?

"Josh!" Norman's voice broke. "It's good to hear your voice, son. I miss you Josh."

"I miss you too, Dad."

"Hey, I'll be there if I have to walk to work and eat peanut butter sandwiches three times a day." They heard the resolve in his voice. "Do you suppose I could be an usher, or something?"

"Norman, would you walk me down the aisle?"

"You mean that? Really?" Again, his voice broke with emotion.

"Of course she means it," said Steve. "Have you ever known her to lie to you?"

"What if Susan and I…?"

"Norman, this has nothing to do with Susan. I want you. Period. Susan will be a bridesmaid or maid-of-honor if she wants to. Whatever happens between you two has nothing to do with our wedding. After all, you are the father of my favorite grandson."

"I'm your *only* grandson." Josh covered his mouth and giggled.

"And, don't worry about the airfare," said Steve. "We'll take care of that." Steve looked to Laura for approval. She smiled and nodded.

"Steve, Laura, I don't know what to say. I don't want to accept your help, but I want to be there."

"Just say yes, Dad. Grandma will do it anyway."

"Josh!" Laura exclaimed.

"Well, he's right, at least about this," Steve nodded, laughed and got a high five from Josh.

"What can I say then except..." Norman paused a second, "make it a one-way ticket. I'm not coming back here. I'll find something over there."

"Maybe you can live in Cottonville so I can see Grandma everyday and still go to school with Jerome." Josh was excited.

"I don't know, Son. We'll work out something."

"Me and Jerome will pray about it like Aunt SaraBelle taught us. Maybe our angel will help   only he just shows up when we're in trouble."

"Angels? Trouble? Josh, I really want to hear all about it, but I sense it will take more time and money than I have this morning."

"I know. It costs a lot of money to talk long distance. Tell you what. Give me your address and I'll send you all my letters."

"You got a pencil and paper?"

"Sure do. Grandma always keeps it by the phone."

"All right, I'll look forward to reading them. And I'll get yours in the mail today."

He gave Josh his address and phone number, making sure he had everything spelled right and numbers in the right place.

"Goodbye, Josh. I love you."

"I love you too, Dad."

"We'll be in touch, Norman," said Laura.

"Thanks again. Oh, by the way, forgive me for not saying it before, but happy birthday, Laura. Bye." Reluctantly he broke the connection. Laura pushed the off button on her phone.

"Birthday?" Steve asked.

She ignored him and turned to Josh.

"Josh?"

"I heard everything," he answered before she could ask.

"Your mom...?"

"Yeah, that too. I heard the phone, as I started downstairs. I shouldn't have listened, but I didn't think I shouldn't not listen either. Don't worry Grandma. God will work it out. At least Dad will be home. What's to eat?"

Laura glanced at Steve surprised by her grandson's quiet acceptance.

"Chip off the old block?" asked Steve with a grin.

She shook her head unable to understand the wisdom of children at times. But the soft chuckle in the depth of her soul told her Josh was on the right track—where she ought to be.

"Maybe Steve will fix you something while I call Bishop Giles."

Laura paused with the phone in her hand. It dawned on her this was Steve's wedding too. She seemed to be just barging ahead. "Is December all right with you, Steve? I'm sorry I haven't thought things through very well."

He kissed her on the forehead. "I really wanted next week," he said as seriously as he could then laughed at the stricken look on her face. "But, I can handle December. It's better than June. You'll make a beautiful December bride. Now call that bishop while I go scramble more eggs."

She did. They set the date for the Sunday before Christmas. The bishop planned to go to his daughter's in South Carolina for Christmas. They could stop and spend a few days, do the wedding and then move on. Laura and Steve could go for their honeymoon after Christmas.

That taken care of, Laura had to turn her attention to tomorrow's worship and next week's wedding for Todd and Carolyn.

Thirty

Laura and Steve sipped their coffee while Josh ate his breakfast. They heard someone cross the front porch. A knock followed. Steve glanced at Laura with raised eyebrows.

"Are you expecting someone else for breakfast?"

"Todd, Maybe?"

"Meow?" Rascal didn't wait for an answer, but trotted to the living room, Mischief right behind him.

"Jerome comes in without knocking," said Josh as he swiped a napkin across his mouth, giggled and jumped up from the table. "Guess we won't know unless we go see," he said and ran to the living room. "Grandma, Mr. Jennings and Mr. Martin are here."

Laura and Steve had followed Josh. Rascal had already opened the door and *invited* the men in. "Good morning, Fred, Frank."

Josh and the cats continued up the stairs while Laura motioned for the men to sit down. "You're here to fix the window?"

"We're here to discuss it," said Frank reaching out to shake Steve's hand. "Hope you don't mind if we have a quick, unplanned trustee meeting here."

"I don't mind," answered Laura, "but, isn't that a little over-kill just to replace a window?"

"It's not just the window, Laura," said Fred. "We've been sitting on these building plans and dragging our feet too long. Frank and I decided last night we need to make a decision one way or another and do something about it."

Laura's expression clearly said she didn't understand, but before she could ask any questions, the rest of the committee arrived.

"Would you like coffee?" asked Laura.

"We don't want to be any trouble," said Fred, "but if you have some made, I for one, wouldn't turn it down."

"I was just going to make a fresh pot," said Steve. "Laura and I have a lot of talking to do today."

"Uh-oh," said Fred. "Not more trouble I hope."

Laura laughed. "No trouble this time, unless you consider agreeing on wedding plans as trouble."

"Wedding plans? Really? When?"

"December 22."

"December? I thought maybe you would make it a double wedding next week." Fred winked at Steve and grinned broadly. "That's great, Pastor. I'm really happy for both of you."

The rest of the trustees found a seat and accepted the cup of coffee from Steve then Frank explained why there was a board on the window—although they all had heard about it through the proverbial grapevine by now. They shook their heads, commented about it being terrible, but "What can we do about it?"

"Well," said Fred, "one thing we can do about it is get off our duffs and start moving on these projects we've been planning all summer. We've all agreed that we need a new parsonage as well as a new garage. The contractor is ready whenever we give the word, so what are we waiting for?"

"It's difficult to tear down a house and build another in its place while people are still living in that house," said Jack Durham, looking embarrassed.

"Well, we *have* to do something." Fred was determined. "I think it would be wonderful if we could have a new house for our pastor and her new husband."

"Husband?" They all asked at once and turned to Steve.

"Well, not yet," continued Fred, "but by Christmas they will be married. We ought to be able to have a new house up by then."

"I'm sure we can do that, but what do we do with the pastor in the meantime?"

"She could live in the belfry," said Fred and winked at Laura.

Rascal and Mischief had been watching them from the stairs. They growled and chattered, going through what Steve called their *swearing tone.*

Laura looked at them in alarm; their fur wasn't bushy, but…Steve started for the door to check it out—just in case Jacobson had somehow escaped.

Josh started down the steps and stopped to pet the cats. "They don't think living in the belfry is a good idea at all," he said and went into a fit of giggles. Steve laughed and returned to his seat beside Laura.

"Sorry, kitties," said Fred. "Guess some species just don't understand my humor. Don't worry, we'll find a good place for *all* of you."

"She can stay with us," said Frank. "We have plenty of room."

"That's a great idea, Frank" said Irvine, "but the pastor should have her own place for privacy and all."

"You got a better idea, Irv?"

"As a matter of fact, I think I do," he answered. "Sue Beth and I just moved into our new home. We were going to put our old house up for sale, but it can wait until spring. She could live there for the next few months. It's almost the size of this one—four bedrooms, two baths, kitchen, dining room, living room, double car garage and basement. We can all get together Monday—or today for that matter—and move her over there. It's only a couple of houses from Carolyn McMichaels—the blue house on the corner."

The trustees were speechless. No one had ever heard Irving Markley give such a long speech about anything.

"What are you asking for rent, Irv?" Frank always thought about the finances.

"Nothing. It will be good for the house to have people in it. The only thing I would ask is that we be allowed to show it if we get any inquiries with the understanding that if it sells, the buyer can't have the house until we are finished with the new parsonage."

"What do you think, Pastor?" asked Frank.

"What can I say? It sounds like a perfect solution to me. I can live with that decision. But…today? Couldn't…?"

"We're all free today. The weather's perfect."

"Then let's get started," she said with a sigh. "What do we do first?"

"We probably ought to call Conrad Movers and see if they can come over and help us move the big stuff."

Ideas began to flow; excited chatter filled the room until Frank quieted them so he could call Conrad Movers.

"They can be here this afternoon," he said. "In the mean time we can begin packing and moving as much of the smaller stuff that we can. I'll call Martha. She'll know how to organize the women to get things packed."

Within half an hour, the house was overflowing with women packing and men with trucks loading and moving things to the new house. By late afternoon, everyone was tired. The women left to get supper for their families. Laura grumbled as she emptied a box.

"You say something, Laura?" asked Steve.

"No," she said irritably.

He stopped what he was doing and approached her with his arms out. "Come on. You need a break. Let's take a walk."

"I don't have time to take a walk," she snapped. "They could have chosen a better time to do this. Today is Saturday and tomorrow is Sunday and I have to be prepared even if I get shot at, knocked around, or moved out of my home. And don't you dare laugh or I'll...I'll..."

"You'll what? Kick me? Beat me? Throw something at me? Go ahead if it will help get you out of that pit of self-pity you're drowning in."

Laura had a pillow in her hand and before she thought about what she was doing, it was flying across the room. Steve laughed as he caught it and threw it back at her. She couldn't stay mad as she caught it and started laughing.

"Can I play?" Josh ran down the steps.

"Meow?" The Maine Coon duet added their plea.

That did it. Laura collapsed on the floor in a round of laugher. She threw the pillow to Josh who threw it to Steve. They played catch for a couple of minutes while Rascal and Mischief jumped to catch the pillow in mid-air.

"Feel better?" Steve asked as he helped her to her feet.

She nodded. "Still want to take that walk? I think I need some fresh air—although, I should start some supper of some kind."

"I think Martha is taking care of that."

"Bless her. If they don't come through, we'll go to Charlie's. I'm not cooking." She declared. "Now let's take that walk before I change my mind. Josh we'll be back in a little bit. Stick around in case someone calls, all right?"

"Sure, Jerome is coming over anyway. He's going to help me set up my room if you don't mind."

"That's fine. Just don't try to move heavy stuff until we get back to help."

"Okay."

Thirty-One

Steve and Laura walked down the street hand in hand toward the park. "I suppose we should head back," said Laura after they had walked about a half hour. "If Martha is bringing dinner to the house…"

"I think she said it would be a covered dish dinner at the church," said Steve. "Want to walk over?"

"What about Josh?"

"I'll call him," said Steve pulling out his cell phone. "He can come with Jerome."

Steve took her hand and they walked the rest of the way to the church, enjoying the twilight sounds of crickets, cicadas, whippoorwills, and children who were still playing outside. An awareness that fall was in the air—crunching leaves, wood burning in fireplaces, warm days dissolving into cool evenings—gave Laura a sense of well being. Cottonville was a peaceful place to live once again. She breathed a prayer of thanksgiving for being there. For now she would put her concerns on hold.

"We may as well go around back and into the fellowship hall. That's where they'll be."

"Steve?"

"Um?"

"Are you up to something?"

"Why would you ask that?"

"Because you…you seem…expectant. Like something is going to happen and you can't wait to be a part of it."

Steve laughed. "Laura, you should go into parapsychology." He opened the door and waited for her to go ahead of him. "You're right," he said. "I'll tell you about it later."

Assuming it had something to do with his work she accepted that answer. Happy sounds of chatter from the fellowship hall ceased as soon as she walked through the door. George Melody sat at the old upright and struck a chord. Everyone began singing, "Happy Birthday." Rascal and Mischief sat on top of the piano, blending their Maine Coon voices with the humans, which sent them all into peals of laugher until tears streamed down faces.

"I told you they're tone deaf," said Karen wiping tears of mirth from her face.

Rascal and Mischief, show cats that they were, took advantage of the situation to perform for *their* audience. They covered their mouths with a paw and *snickered*, which brought more laughter, then jumped from the piano in synchronized flight and landed on the floor, rolled into balls and went into five minutes of their trained routine. They bowed to the applause then marched to the table laden with food and sat as if waiting to be at the head of the line.

Martha took their vacated place and said, "I didn't plan on entertainment—only food, but thank you Rascal and Mischief."

Rascal and Mischief turned and bowed. The congregation broke into laughter and applause then Martha took control again.

"We're here to celebrate the trustee's decision to build a new parsonage and our pastor's decision to be married in December, but most of all we are here to celebrate her birthday today. Happy Birthday, Reverend. Now, I've asked Cora to give the blessing then you can help yourselves—down both sides of the table. Someone might want to carry plates for the performers."

Cora in her bright red dress beamed. "I'm glad I could come out tonight. The Lord told me our pastor needed a special prayer of blessing for all she's been through." With no pause or hesitation, Cora continued with her prayer asking God's blessing not only on the food, but also on Laura and her family and her church.

Martha sent Laura, Steve, and Josh to the head of the line behind Rascal and Mischief. Laura and Steve, with plates filled, sat at the end of a long table. Rascal and Mischief had their plates off to the side where they wouldn't get stepped on.

Laura turned to Steve. "Is this what you were expecting?"

Steve smiled, but neither denied nor confirmed. "I didn't know it was your birthday until this morning when Norman said something. Remember?"

"Then how...Josh?"

Josh started giggling and ducked his head. He set his fork down and ran out of the room, returning with a crystal vase filled with roses. "Happy Birthday,

130

Grandma," he said, setting them on the table in front of her. "I hope you don't mind. I called Dad back when I went upstairs this morning and asked him if it was really your birthday. He told me to get you some roses from him and me. Then Jerome and me told Mrs. Jennings and she did the rest. And Grandpa Steve isn't as innocent as he acts. He knew what we were doing. That's why he took you for a walk." Josh laughed—his kidnapping of the night before seemingly a forgotten event.

"You have a smart grandson," said Steve, "and a thoughtful one. He loves you and he wanted you to have a special day once he found out. He felt bad that he didn't know about it earlier until I told him I didn't know either. Another secret you kept from me," he accused teasingly.

"You never asked and the subject never came up. Birthdays have never been a big deal. Most came and went without me even remembering. This one would have too if Norman hadn't said something. I'd even forgotten. When is your birthday? You never told me either." She returned the accusation.

"Touché," he said. "Mine's not until December—the twenty-second to be exact."

"You're teasing me," she challenged.

"No, I'm not. It really is my birthday. And I will be getting the best birthday present I have ever gotten in my entire life. It couldn't have worked out better if you had planned it that way. Thank you."

"I don't believe you."

"Do you want to see my birth certificate?"

"No, but..."

Martha rapped on a table to get their attention. "We can't have a birthday party without cake, now can we? I know some of you are still eating, but we do need to cut the cake now so those who have to leave early can do so." She nodded toward the kitchen and Fred and Frank carried in a sheet cake decorated with roses and flaming candles. "Make a wish and blow them out," said Fred as they held the cake before Laura.

"Can we help?" Josh and Jerome ran around the table.

"You better," said Laura. "I'm not sure I can. All this attention takes my breath away."

"Better this attention, than the kind you've been getting," said Frank.

Laura nodded and they all blew out the candles.

"Now," said Martha, "just a few gifts of appreciation."

Two other men carried out another table laden with gifts—everything from small gag gifts to produce from gardens to canned goods to flowers and cards with cash.

Laura looked at Steve and bit her lip to hold back the tears that begged released. "I've never had a birthday party before," she whispered. "I'm speechless."

"There's one more gift that's not on that table," he said. He cleared his throat and glanced at Todd and Carolyn then around the room. "I think everyone here knows that Laura and I have set the date for our wedding—December 22. I think it's time I made it official and public."

He laughed nervously at Laura's expression and pulled the box from his pocket. Opening it, he took the simple gold band with a heart shaped solitaire diamond and placed it on her finger.

Laura stared at the ring. This time tears of joy would not stay hidden. "It's the most beautiful ring I've ever seen. It's what I would have picked out. How did you know?"

"It had Laura written on it," he smiled.

"You'll never get me to part with it." She held it out for her congregation to see the sparkle. Steve kissed her and the congregation exploded into applause again. Rascal and Mischief covered their eyes with their paws and Josh and Jerome giggled.

Thirty-Two

Unpacking boxes, hanging pictures, arranging furniture and kitchen cabinets for the second time in four months had its advantages—but not many. Time flew, however, and Laura, not sure if that was help or hindrance, felt a small twinge of panic. Friday already. Rehearsal tonight—tomorrow the biggest wedding in Cottonville for many years—her *first* wedding.

"You nervous, Grandma?" Had Josh learned mind reading from the cats? She turned and smiled at him.

"A little," she said. "Are you?"

"I only have to light the candles. You got the most important part. Jerome's mom and Chief Todd can't get married if you flub up."

"Thanks, Josh," she said, "I *really* needed to hear that!" He giggled at her sarcasm.

Laura turned her head to listen. Footsteps on the front porch. "Is that Jerome already?"

Rascal and Mischief went to investigate and Josh started to get up from the table. "Finish your milk and don't forget your books."

"Okay," he gulped down the last swallow and ran for the front door. "I'm glad Jerome only lives two doors away, now. We can start out together and don't have to meet at the square." Rascal and Mischief waited at the door. Even though Jacobson was behind bars again, the cats continued to walk to school with the boys, return home, then go back to meet them after school. Laura was glad. There should be no reason for fear or caution, but a nagging foreboding lingered.

"Hi," said Josh as he pulled the door open. Instead of Jerome, Carolyn stood ready to knock. "Are you going to school for Jerome today?" He giggled and called over his shoulder, "Grandma, Mrs. McMichaels is here."

Carolyn smiled at Josh and nodded toward the sidewalk. "Jerome is waiting outside for you. I want to talk to your grandmother before I go to work."

133

"Okay. Bye Grandma. See you later." He ran back to give Laura a quick hug and kiss on the cheek then hurried out to meet Jerome.

"Bye, Josh; come on in, Carolyn. Have time for a cup of coffee?"

"If it's made," she answered.

"I think there are still a couple of cups in the pot. You want to sit in the kitchen, or out here? Is this a serious, last minute jitters talk, or just a friendly chat?"

"I don't know," said Carolyn on the verge of tears.

"Sounds like the former. Get comfortable and I'll bring the coffee in here." Laura returned with two cups of coffee, sat across from Carolyn, and said, "Now, what's the problem?"

"Oh, Pastor." Tears began running down Carolyn's face. "I…I…" She buried her face in her hands.

"You don't know if you can get married? You aren't sure you're in love with Todd?" Laura sipped her coffee and looked over the rim of her cup at her friend.

"How did you know? Is it that obvious? How can I tell him? Why can't he see it?"

"Carolyn, what is obvious to me, is that you are a bride-to-be about to commit your life to another person. You are about to give up your freedom of being a single person—a single mom—and take on the responsibility of a husband and father for your son. You're scared, because it's a scary undertaking. Unless you and Todd have changed drastically in the last twenty-four hours, what is obvious to anyone who sees the two of you together is that you are totally, hopelessly in love with one another. What you're feeling is plain old everyday fear—fear of the unknown future."

"Do you think so?"

"Yes, I think so."

"But, what if I'm not a good wife? What if he and Jerome don't get along? What if…what if…" Tears started to flow again.

"What if he gets killed in the line of duty and you become a widow?" Laura finished for her.

"Are you a mind-reader or something?" Carolyn looked up at Laura in amazement.

"No, but remember I'm in love with a police officer too. That fear is constantly with me, but it's a fear I can live with because I know we will love each other for all the time we have together—whether that is one day, one year, or many years. I have been close to death too many times while watching Steve work. I understand there is danger, but Steve doesn't take unnecessary chances. He's careful. That's all I can ask. It's the same with Todd. He loves you. He won't put himself in harm's way without good cause. You have given him more reason to be careful—to live."

Carolyn was quiet for a few minutes, sipping her coffee and absorbing what Laura had said. Finally, she set her cup down, sighed deeply and said, "I guess Mom was right." She laughed. "She likes to give me those old clichés like, *don't trouble trouble until trouble troubles you* and…well, you know how she is."

"Listen to your mother, Carolyn. She's a bright woman who loves her daughter very much."

"Laura, do all brides act this way, or is it just because I am older and have a ten year old son?"

"They all have moments of doubt, but ultimately, love is a decision. You decide to love one another for the rest of your lives. The feeling may fade, but the decision remains. Of one thing I am sure, Todd loves you very much. And he couldn't love Jerome any more if he were his own son. You can't ask for much more than that."

"What if I get sick going down the aisle?" Carolyn was serious but Laura couldn't keep from laughing.

"You sound like Jerome and Josh. Carolyn, I've never heard of a bride getting sick, passing out, or dying during her wedding. You'll be fine. We'll go through it as many times as we need to tonight to make you feel comfortable. All you have to worry about is getting down the aisle. I'll tell you where to stand, what to say, and when to say it. Trust me. You'll be fine."

"I just wish I had my dad…or my brother…someone to lean on." Again, her eyes misted.

"Do you want Steve to walk down with you? Todd can get someone else to stand with him. Or Steve can walk down with you and then stand with Todd."

"I've never seen that before. Wouldn't it look odd?"

"Do you care?"

Carolyn laughed. "I don't know."

"How about Mark? Steve can walk down with you and Mark can stand with Todd."

"Why does Todd need anyone to stand with him? I'm not having anyone."

"Well, that's a point. So Steve can walk you down the aisle and then sit with Jerome, or Jerome can walk you down."

"Do you think? Would that be all right? He's not too young? That's what I really would like."

"Then we'll work it out tonight."

"Steve can stand with Todd and…"

"You have another idea, Carolyn. I can see it in your eyes."

"Could…could my mother stand with me as my matron of honor? Does she have to sit alone?"

"Carolyn, it's your wedding. If you want your mother and she doesn't mind, I have no objections."

"Can I call her and see what she says?"

"Sure. You know where the phone is. Shall I make us some more coffee?"

"No, thanks, I have to get to work."

Laura returned from taking the cups to the kitchen as Carolyn hung up the phone. "She thought I was nuts, but she was crying. I know she was. Thank you, Laura, for being a friend as well as a pastor." She gave Laura a hug then left for work.

* * *

The phone rang. Laura was walking toward the door. Why does that phone always ring when I have my hands full and I'm ready to leave the house? They could call the office, but maybe it's Steve.

Giving in to her sense of curiosity, as well as responsibility, she dropped her briefcase on the couch and grabbed the receiver on the third ring.

"Good morning, Love."

"Cora, how are you?"

"Still recuperating from the party last week. Are you all unpacked and settled?"

"Almost."

Cora hardly ever wasted time with what she called small talk. She went to the heart of the matter. "The Lord told me you need special prayers today with the big wedding and everything." She prayed her prayer asking for special strength and courage for Laura then left her holding the buzzing phone.

Laura shook her head and closed the door. Rascal and Mischief, back from walking the boys to school, waited on the porch. "Well, kitties, Cora just called.

136

Wonder what we're in for this time? The wedding? The boys?" A chill slid down her spine. "Surely not Bill Collins. He's in prison for life—again. Isn't he?"

Rascal and Mischief began to fluff up at the mention of his name—even his alias. They shook themselves and ran to the car waiting for Laura to open the door for them.

Thirty-Three

Back home for the afternoon, Laura worked on last minute details before the rehearsal. Rascal and Mischief had gone to meet the boys and Steve was still in Glenville where he'd had time-consuming meetings with the FBI all week. She wondered if he would be able to make it for the rehearsal. He often worked with the FBI, but usually he was undercover or consulting in Washington. Must be something important, she thought, since he hasn't even been over here for several days. Is it possible that Jacobson is…? No, I won't let my thoughts go that route!

The boys will be home soon. I better get their snack ready. Sophia has her hands full with the wedding. Laura smiled to herself. I do too, but it's different when your only daughter is getting married. Cookies on a plate, glasses out for milk, Laura glanced at the clock and frowned.

They should be here by now. Wonder if I should go look for them. The ringing phone stopped her at the door. Maybe they're calling to say they're staying after school to help their teacher or went to a friend's house. Her nagging subconscious threw in an added thought—they wouldn't go anywhere with the big rehearsal tonight.

"Hello, Reverend Kenzel speaking."

"Mother?"

"Susan? What's wrong?"

"What makes you think something is wrong?" She sounded defensive, but also on the verge of tears.

"I'm sorry, Susan, I shouldn't jump to conclusions. You just sound like you're hurting."

Susan tried to laugh, but the sound that escaped was more sob than laugh. "You always could tell when I was down. Oh, Mom, I've made such a shamble of my life. I have no right to even call you…"

"Susan, where are you?" Susan hadn't called Laura *Mom* since she was a little girl.

"I'm in Glenville. I just got off the bus."

"Are you calling from a pay phone?"

"Yes, and my time is about up."

"Give me the number and sit tight. I'll call you back in a minute or two. All right?"

"All right." She gave Laura the number of the pay phone and hung up.

Laura heard the boys and cats on the front porch as she glanced out the window. She breathed a sigh of relief, but wondered how she had missed seeing them coming down the street. She had dialed the first three digits of Steve's number when Josh and Jerome burst into the house. Each had a cat draped around his shoulders. They were so pale and their eyes wide with fear that Laura replaced the phone and dropped to her knees to enfold both boys in her arms.

"Josh? Jerome? What is it?"

"It's *him.*" Josh's voice trembled.

"It's who, Josh?" Laura asked, afraid she would get an answer she didn't want to hear.

"*Him.*" Josh could never bring himself to give Colin Jacobson alias Bill Collins a name of any kind.

"Yeah, it was him all right," said Jerome. His lower lip trembled.

"Where?" Laura forced herself to use a natural tone of voice. She didn't need to add to their already wide-eyed fear.

"At the school," Josh said.

"He was just standing there, leaning against his big ugly car, staring at us when we came out of the school," said Jerome.

"We ran back in the building and told the teacher, but he was gone when she got there. She thought we were mistaken." Josh was beginning to get the color back in his face.

"The teacher said it couldn't be him 'cause he's in prison."

"But, he isn't, Grandma. He was there. We saw him. *You* believe us, don't you?"

"Of course I do, Josh."

"Rascal and Mischief were at the school. They were all bushy. We ran the other way—toward our old home. Then we circled round the back way so he wouldn't know we moved." Both boys were gaining a little color in their pallid cheeks.

"That was a good idea, boys." She turned to the cats. "Good job, Rascal and Mischief. Thank you. Now, you boys go have your cookies and milk and give Rascal and Mischief a treat. I have to make a phone call."

"You going to call Grandpa Steve?" asked Josh.

"Yes, I was going to call him anyway, when you came in. Now I really need to call him." She picked up the phone and dialed the familiar number.

"Glenville Police Department."

"Joe, this is Laura. Is Steve there?"

"He's here, Laura, but he's been in the conference room all day with some big-shots from the FBI. Do you need to talk to him, or can I give him a message when he's done?"

"I think I need to talk to him, Joe. I wouldn't interrupt if it wasn't important. It's about Colin Jacobson."

"Hold on, I'll get him."

She waited for a minute or two listening to the noises in the background of a busy police department. "Laura? What's this about Jacobson?" Concern and strain were evident in Steve's voice.

"He's out of prison and he's in this area. That's what your meetings have been about the last few days, isn't it?" She wasn't angry or accusatory, simply stating a fact. There was a slight pause at the other end.

"How did you know?" He almost whispered, sounding perplexed. "Todd and I have done our best to keep it from you and Carolyn, at least until after the wedding."

"No secrets, huh?" Anger did creep into her voice unbidden.

"I'm sorry Laura. I should know better by now. You are usually one-step ahead of me—where Jacobson is concerned anyway. How did you find out?"

"The boys saw him at school today."

"What?" She held the phone away from her ear while he ranted.

"Steve, does that make you feel better?" she asked when he came back on the line.

"No," he said. "Did he try to…?"

"They only saw him standing at a distance, beside his car, staring at them. By the time they got back with the teacher, he was gone. She thought they were mistaken. But, they weren't."

"How can you be so sure?"

"Steve, how can you even ask that? They, of all people, know who he is and what he looks like. They were both so pale I was concerned. Rascal and

Mischief met them at the school with their fur bushy like it is when he's around. They came home by a round about route in case he was watching. They didn't want him to know we had moved and where."

"Smart boys and you're right. That is why we have been meeting. We knew he escaped—killed the guard who was transporting him to Chillicothe. We were certain eventually he would be back in this area—just not so soon. Now that we know he is in the area for sure, the meetings will be over. I should be able to leave here within a half hour. Keep the boys close and please don't do anything foolish. You have a wedding to do."

"Steve, there's one other thing. I was about to call you anyway when the boys came in. Susan is in Glenville at the bus terminal. Could you...?" She wasn't sure she should ask him considering how Susan felt about him.

"Could I bring her home?"

"Maybe I shouldn't ask."

"You shouldn't have to ask. Just tell me. Be glad to. Give us a chance to get better acquainted."

"I'll call her back and tell her. Thanks. I love you."

"Because I am willing to transport your spoiled kid for you?" he teased.

"Yes." She wasn't teasing.

"Get the guest room ready for her. If we don't kill each other before we get there, we should be home in about an hour."

Laura got the dial tone again and dialed the number Susan had given her.

"Hello." Susan answered.

"Susan, Steve will pick you up in about twenty minutes. You can wait at Marie's across the street. Tell the station master where you're going and who you're waiting for."

"I'll just wait here."

"Susan, do you have money for coffee?"

There was a long pause. "No."

"Did you have lunch? Breakfast?"

"No."

"Go to Marie's and get something to eat. Steve will pay for it when he picks you up."

"Mother, I can't accept charity from a man I hardly know."

"Susan, it isn't charity; it's love. And that man you hardly know will soon be your stepfather, so get to know him. Please, Susan, let him do this for you."

"All right, mother. And, thanks."

"We'll see you in a little bit, darling."

As Laura replaced the phone, the small voice beside her startled her.

"Was that my mom?"

"Yes, it was." Laura smiled. "She's in Glenville and Steve's going to bring her home. Is that all right with you?"

Josh looked as serious as a ten-year old could. "As long as she doesn't try to put Rascal and Mischief outside and chase Grandpa Steve away." Then he broke into the familiar giggles Laura had learned to love.

"Is she here to stay? Did she bring that other jerk with her? Is she…?"

"Josh, you don't know the man. Don't call him a jerk—even if he is one. I don't know what she's doing. If he's with her, Steve won't bring them, or at least not him. I think she's alone—and hurting."

"Like you did when Grandpa Steve didn't come back and that man…?"

"Yes, like that Josh. Now, why don't you and Jerome go play with the kitties while I call Sophia and tell her you're going to stay here until we leave for the rehearsal."

"Because of that man?" asked Jerome.

"Yes." Laura saw no reason to try to hide any fear. They were too smart and had been through too much.

"Okay. We'll go do our homework."

They ran up the steps; the cats passed them half way up. Laura lifted her eyes heavenward. "Is this what Cora called about this morning? I don't want to complain about all I've been through, because the gain has been so much more than the loss. But, I don't want to lose what I have gained—Josh and Steve and all my friends. Please take care of them—and now, Susan. What's going on here anyway? Is it sock-it-to-Laura time or something?"

Before Laura could complain any more, she felt the soft chuckle in her soul. Then it turned to a full-fledged laugh.

"All right. You know what's going on. I do trust You, but it would be nice to know before hand what I should say and do."

Words suddenly pushed forward in her mind. *Take no thought what you will say. I will give you the right words and actions when the time comes. But you will have to face a difficult obstacle before you can find the happiness you seek.*

"Oh great. More obstacles."

Once more the chuckle was there, tinted with a note of sadness.

Thirty-Four

Josh and Jerome had seemingly forgotten their near encounter with Jacobson after school. Excitement over Susan's arrival and the coming wedding rehearsal took precedence over fear. The wedding was a first for both boys, but Josh was more excited about seeing his mother after almost four months. Every time a car drove down the street, Josh ran to the window.

Finally, Steve pulled into the driveway and Josh ran out of his room, down the steps, and out the door. Before Steve even turned the motor off, he was pulling on the passenger door handle. When the door flew open, he flung himself at his mother. Susan, not used to such a display of emotion, fumbled with her seatbelt and stiffened. Josh started to back away. Feeling Steve's eyes on her back, Susan reached for Josh's hand and pulled him back.

"Help me get untangled from the seatbelt," she said. When she was free, they wrapped their arms around each other.

"Mom, oh Mom. I missed you and I love you so much."

"Joshua?" She held him at arms' length to see him more clearly. "Is this the same Joshua I left with Grandma four months ago?"

"No," said Josh seriously. Tears clung to his eyelashes. "I'm not the same. I'm not Joshua any more. I'm Josh. I'm not that quiet, little mouse that studied in the corner all the time. I'm alive and run and climb and..." He stopped, gave her a searching look and asked, "Is that stupid? Is it all right that I've changed? I'll try to go back to being Joshua if that's what you want."

Steve, not intending to eavesdrop, was retrieving Susan's bags from the trunk. He couldn't miss the exchange. He held his breath, praying she wouldn't kill the spirit in that little boy he had grown to love as much as his grandmother—well almost as much.

"Joshua..." Susan started, smiled through her own tears, and started again, "*Josh*, I think you are the only one who has benefited from these months of separation. The change is...is...wonderful. I'm sorry so much has happened to you, but I'm glad if it's made you happy. You are happy, aren't you Josh?"

143

"I sure am." He beamed at her and threw his arms around her again. "I'm happy you're here and Dad will be here in December for Grandma's wedding. Tomorrow Jerome's mom and Chief Todd are getting married. We're going to practice tonight. Did you…?"

Steve, let out the breath he had been holding, as he closed the trunk. "Josh, don't you think maybe your mother would like to get out of the car?" He smiled and winked at Josh, who grinned.

"Oh, yeah. Come on. What are you waiting for? Grandma fixed a room for you upstairs beside mine. I'll tell Rascal and Mischief to stay out of your way." He took her hand and started pulling her toward the house where Laura met them at the door. Rascal and Mischief sat on either side of her—ears back, tails thumping, eyeing the newcomer.

"Welcome home, Susan," said Laura.

"Oh, Mom!" Susan threw her arms around Laura and sobbed. Steve waited while Laura and Susan greeted one another. He marveled how much they looked alike and yet they were so different in appearance. Both were slim and fit but Susan a little taller and almost too thin. She pulled her blondish brown hair into a ponytail the way she used to wear it as a teenager. He had noticed her hazel eyes on the drive over from Glenville, much harsher than Laura's soft brown ones. Mother and daughter held each other until Steve cleared his throat.

"Would you two like to move aside so we men can get these bags in the house?" He winked at Josh who had picked up one of the bags.

Susan and Laura laughed and moved inside to let them pass. "Come and sit with me for a few minutes. The rehearsal is in about an hour, with dinner afterward at the church, so we won't have much time to talk. We'll stay up all night if we need to."

Laura pulled Susan toward the couch. Rascal and Mischief followed Steve and Josh as they carried suitcases up the stairs. Josh and Steve returned. Josh plopped down beside his mother, taking her hand in his.

"Thanks, Steve," said Laura holding her hand out for him to take it, which he did. He leaned over and kissed her then sat in a chair across from them.

Susan watched the exchange with a strange look on her face which Laura couldn't interpret—almost a look of envy?

"Steve told me all that's happened since you came here. Mother, I have a hard time believing it. Murder? Kidnapping? And you were shot? Tell me it wasn't true."

"I'm sorry, dear, I don't know what Steve told you, but I am sure every word of it was true."

"Why didn't you tell us? We never would have left Josh here if we had known." Susan sounded almost angry.

"Most of it happened after you left," said Laura. She didn't add that Susan had given her no way of notifying her. "When you brought Josh here last spring I thought it was all over—until we found that body in the garden. Then it was too late. What could you have done? Send him to a boarding school? In the summer? I don't think so. Not while I'm alive and well anyway…and no comment from you two," she said to Steve and Josh.

Josh giggled and Steve said, "Would I say anything to contradict you? Not on my life."

Josh remembered Jerome who was upstairs in his room. He yelled up the stairs, "Hey, Jerome, come on down."

"Just a minute," yelled Jerome back. Then he appeared at the top of the steps. "I had to turn off the computer. You don't want to let it run all night do you?" Rascal and Mischief raced down the stairs ahead of him and stopped once again to stare at Susan.

"My mom will be here for a long time. Her and your mom can be good friends like we are."

"If you say so," said Jerome, following the cats' example and eying her with suspicion. "I think maybe they'll have to work that out for themselves if they want to be friends. We can't make it happen."

"Good point, Jerome," said Laura. She glanced at the cats who sat like mechanical toys—tails thumping in synchronized taps. She reached a hand toward them. "Susan, I think Rascal and Mischief are waiting to greet you," she said.

Susan glanced at them with as much suspicion as they seemed to have for her. "Meet me, or eat me?" she said.

"You didn't give them a chance before," reminded Laura.

"Yeah, Mom," said Josh. "They are mine and Jerome's best friends. They saved our lives when we got tied up in the school and when we got kidnapped and when…"

Susan's face reflected the horror of his word. "Josh…"

"It's okay," said Josh. "It's all over—mostly. Rascal and Mischief help us cope."

"Cope?"

"Yeah," said Jerome. "That means they help us when we don't understand."

"Then I guess I owe you kitties my apologies and my gratitude," she said stretching her hand for the cats to sniff. "Truce?"

Rascal and Mischief stared as if reading her mind, slowly moved to sniff her fingers, then turned and chattered to each other. Apparently deciding they would give her a chance, they each placed a paw in Susan's hands. Surprised, she laughed then said, "Thanks. It's a start. We'll work on friendship in time."

"Speaking of time," said Laura, "I need to change and get over to the church. Can you folks find your way without getting into trouble or getting lost?"

"Can I stay here with Mom?" asked Josh.

"You're going to be an acolyte, so I need to show you what to do. Besides, I thought your mother would come with us since we're going to have dinner afterwards at the church."

"Oh, I couldn't do that." Susan was hesitant. "I don't know these folks."

"You will," said Josh. "They're my best friend's parents—or at least one of them is and the other one will be, or something like that." He giggled the way he had done so often in sheer enjoyment of life.

"It will be all right, Susan. You remember Carolyn from the Memorial Day picnic and fireworks. She'll be glad to have someone to talk to. I'm her friend, but I'm also her Pastor. I can't be everywhere."

"If you're sure she won't mind. I really don't want to be alone tonight."

"Do you want me to wait and bring you over, or would you rather bring the boys in Laura's car?" asked Steve.

"I think I'll just come with the boys. I'll drive them over unless Jerome's mother wants to do it."

"I think she would be glad to have one less thing to think about," laughed Laura. "Jerome, why don't you call her and tell her she won't have to pick you up."

"Okay."

Thirty-Five

Sounds of *O Promise Me* drifted from the sanctuary as Laura and Steve started in. They stopped to listen. Laura always got a lump in her throat when Jody sang. Steve understood.

"Jody has a beautiful voice," he said. "She will sing for our wedding."

It was the first time he had offered any ideas for their wedding. Actually, there had been no time for them to even begin thinking about it. Laura turned to face him. "The Lord's Prayer?" she asked. "During the service?"

"More if you want it, but at least that," he said smiling at her. He hesitated and then kissed her just as the door to the sanctuary opened from inside.

"Ah ha! Caught the preacher in the act of stealing." George Melody laughed. "Sorry, didn't mean to interrupt. Please continue. I was just going out to get some music Karen forgot. Pretend you didn't see me."

"Shall we kick him out and continue?" said Steve.

"Maybe we better not. He might take Karen with him. I can't have that."

They all laughed and George continued to his car while Steve and Laura entered the sanctuary. There were always last minute things to do. Laura ran through the service mentally as she walked around the sanctuary, looking for stray bulletins or other debris from Sunday that the custodian might have missed. Of course, there wasn't any. He always did a superb job.

Voices drifting from the stairs told her the rest had arrived. Already she could smell the aroma of coffee and other good things coming from the kitchen. They could depend on Martha and her crew to serve a memorable rehearsal dinner. Josh and Jerome tumbled through the doors giggling with excitement and nervousness. Neither had even been to a wedding, much less participated in one.

Susan, Carolyn and Sophia came in with Todd. Laura was about to gather them in the front of the sanctuary to give instructions for the rehearsal when two felines bounced down the aisle and plopped themselves on the organ.

"Josh…?" Laura started toward the organ to remove them.

"They just came," he said. "We thought we closed them in the house, but when we opened the car door they flew over the seat and refused to get out."

"Refused to get out?"

"I reached for Rascal and he smacked my hand."

"He what?" Rascal had never been violent with the boys.

"He didn't hurt me. Didn't even have his claws out. But…"

"He made it very clear they would not be left behind," laughed Susan. "I think they believe they should be here."

Laura frowned. Did that mean they were into their protection mode? Was Jacobson nearby? She shivered slightly.

Karen called from the organ. "It's all right with me, as long as they don't try to sing."

Laura laughed, remembering when they found Judy Franklin's body and her impromptu birthday party last week. "All right, we'll see how it goes. You two sit tight and no singing." She shook her finger at the cats.

"Yowell," they answered in their Maine Coon duet, then blinked their eyes and settled on the organ top with front paws tucked under them. Eyes almost closed, Rascal and Mischief watched for any trouble through narrow slits in their dark faces.

Thirty-Six

It was close to eleven by the time they got home. Josh was tired, but wanted to be with his mother. Susan slumped on the couch looking lost and lonely—not quite sure of herself.

"Josh," said Steve, "I think your mom and grandmother need to have some woman talk. What do you say you get your things and come with me to Todd's tonight? He's taking Jerome."

"Really? Can I Grandma? Or, Mom? Or... Who do I ask for permission for anything now?" Josh looked confused.

Laura and Susan laughed together. Laura looked to Susan. "He's your son. I'm only in charge when you aren't here."

Susan looked at Steve, then Laura, then back to Josh. "I don't see any reason why not, but don't stay up all night. You have a big wedding tomorrow."

"Thanks, Mom. We'll talk later. You will be here won't you?" Josh was almost afraid to ask.

"I'll be here for at least a couple of weeks if Grandma doesn't mind," she said.

"Good," said Josh. "Then we'll have lots of time to catch up." He ran to get his stuff and was back in a flash. "Is this a bachelor party?" he asked.

"Josh, what do you know about things like that?" Steve glanced at Laura who shrugged. She hadn't said anything to him.

"Matt, one of the kids in our class, said when his brother got married, they had a bachelor party and the men were so drunk the next day they had to postpone the wedding for a couple of hours."

Susan looked horrified.

Laura laughed. "Josh, it is a bachelor party because you are all guys, but no one will get drunk. You can't get drunk on coffee."

"Coffee?" asked Steve. "You mean I have to pour out..."

"Steve!"

He laughed and kissed her. "See you tomorrow. Don't worry. We won't drink anything the kids can't drink."

He and Josh left laughing. Laura and Susan heard the car drive away as they went to the kitchen. "Want a cup of tea, or hot chocolate?"

"I haven't had any of your special hot chocolate in years," said Susan.

"Then hot chocolate it is," said Laura as she pulled out the cocoa, sugar and milk. "Want to sit in here or go to the living room?"

"Let's stay here," she said.

Susan sat at the table and watched her mother preparing the drink, breathing the aroma of chocolate seasoned with a touch of vanilla. "Josh has changed," she said.

"He's a good boy, Susan. I'm going to hate to lose him."

"I can see that. You've been better for him in four months than I have in ten years. Maybe we *should* give you custody."

Laura started to laugh, but noticed the serious look on her daughter's face. "Susan, I would never do that as long as you and Norman are alive. Josh loves you."

"But...he loves you better," said Susan biting her lower lip.

"Not better, just differently."

Laura set the cups on the table and poured in the hot chocolate. Susan waited until Laura sat across from her then took a deep breath and asked, "Mother, how can you love Steve the way you do? I know you do. I see it in your eyes. I see it in the way you look at him, the way you say his name—oh, in everything. And he loves you with the same kind of love. But..."

Laura waited, sipping her chocolate. Susan was troubled about something and she needed to express it in her own way, in her own time.

Finally, Susan finished her thought. "What about Daddy? You never looked at him that way or..."

"Susan, people change. Look at the change in Josh in just a few short months. I'm not the woman I was when your father and I were married. Harold and I had an emotionless marriage. He needed a woman to be a showpiece for him. I needed security. But I took my marriage vows seriously. I was committed until "death do us part." It did. That commitment was canceled."

"What about Steve?"

"What about him?"

"Wasn't he committed to his marriage?"

"Circumstances were different for him and that was thirty years ago. His marriage lasted less than a year."

"But...oh, never mind." Susan said.

"Come on, Susan get it out in the open. You'll never find peace until you do."

"Daddy told me once...I think I was about ten...that he wasn't my father...that you..."

Laura drew in her breath and exhaled slowly to dissipate the anger that boiled up within her—anger at Harold, anger at herself for not being more honest with her daughter. "Why didn't you tell me?"

"He said he would send me away to an orphanage if I did."

"Oh, Susan." Laura's hands clenched into fists and her jaw set in anger.

"I'm sorry, Mom. Please don't be angry with me."

"Susan, I am very angry, but not at you. I'm angry with your father and I'm angry with myself. I should have realized, but I guess I was too busy trying to keep up my own façade to notice. I thought he loved you. He always seemed to dote on you."

"He did when anyone was near."

"Susan, I kept the truth from you all these years because I didn't want to destroy your belief in your father. Had you told me...but we can't go back and undo the past. You need to know the truth, however."

"Mom, it's all right if..."

"Susan, Harold was your father, but he had no sense of humor. My uncle teased me about having a *shotgun wedding*. Your father assumed I was pregnant. He rushed me off to the judge for a quick marriage after which he took me to a dingy motel for consummation. When we returned to my uncle's house, my uncle was in the midst of a heart attack. I stayed through his sickness, death and the settling of his estate. Harold returned to his appointment in Ohio. I was three and a half months pregnant when I returned to Ohio. Your father never believed you were his child."

"And you stayed with him all those years for me?"

"I thought he at least loved you. I didn't know..."

They sat in silence for a time trying to absorb the truth of past heartaches. Then Susan said, "Obviously you and Steve were drawn to each other from the start. That's what Steve told me."

"Yes," said Laura waiting for Susan to say more.

"What if Daddy had been sent here and you had met Steve. The attraction would still be there. Would you have left Daddy for him?"

"Ahhhh," said Laura as comprehension dawned. Susan was trying to sort out her own misadventure. "No, Susan. Our marriage was not the best, but I was committed to making it work. That doesn't mean I wouldn't have been attracted to Steve in those circumstances. It does mean I would not have acted on that attraction. He would never have known and Steve would never have pursued his feelings for a married woman. The flame would simply have died for lack of fuel."

"How can you be so sure?" Susan wasn't being argumentative. She was searching for answers and Laura realized she was asking more for her sake than for knowledge.

"The answer still is in the sense of commitment, Susan. When you promise to stay together for life, you honor that commitment as far as possible. Obviously, there are circumstances when that can't happen, but you do all in your power to make it work then leave the results in God's hands. Steve's marriage couldn't work for a lot of reasons. He's certainly different today than he was thirty years ago. I'm not the same as I was even four years ago. People change. If you can change together, you will be better off. If one changes and the other doesn't, then you find yourself living with a stranger."

"Mother, I don't know if I can love Norman that way anymore."

"Susan, did you love him once?"

"I thought I did, but…"

"Susan, I don't want to hear your side of the story until I can hear Norman's. I'm sure it wasn't either/or, but both/and. Just take some time to really think about the good times and what you can do to make them happen again. Norman will be home in December. He's quitting his job over there and moving back permanently. He misses his son, too."

"Oh, Mother, have I messed up my life so completely?"

"You're asking the wrong person, Susan."

"You mean I need to talk to Norman." She answered flatly.

"No, I think there's Someone higher than Norman, who has a stake in your life."

"Mother, God doesn't care about me."

"Did He tell you that?"

"Of course not. God doesn't talk to people."

"He doesn't? Could have fooled me."

"Well, most people," Susan grinned that little girl grin Laura hadn't seen for a long, long time, "present company excepted."

"Susan, God loves you for who you are. He cares about you. He cares about Josh. Have Josh tell you about his angel. He cares about Norman. What more can I say? Listen to your heart. Give it some time."

"Do you really think God could, or would, help me get it all together again?"

"Of course."

"Easily?"

"No."

"I didn't think so." Susan tried to laugh but tears got in her way. "Mother, I want to believe. I really do, but it hurts so much to even think."

"Give it some time, Susan. Don't put barriers in the way. Let God work in His own special way. Can you do that?"

"I think so, with your help. And Josh's. And Steve's."

"Meow?" The Maine Coon duet surprised them Rascal and Mischief sat like statues near the table.

Laura and Susan laughed. "And, yes, with your help too," said Susan, reaching tentatively to touch their soft fur. They moved closer and let her touch them, even giving her a short purr.

"That's all we ask, sweetheart," said Laura. "Now, how about some sleep? I've got to work tomorrow and the next day."

Susan threw her arms around Laura and cried. "I love you, Mom. Please forgive me for being such a bad daughter."

"Susan, you're not a bad daughter. You made some bad decisions, as we all do. Of course, I forgive you."

* * *

Unable to sleep right away, Laura sat by her window, sorting out the day's activities, praying, softly singing hymns. Finally, deciding she needed to get some sleep, she moved to the bed.

"Bed time kitties?"

Where are they? Now that I think about it, they haven't been on the bed or the windowsill since I came in here. Did they go with Josh? No, they were here earlier. I'd better check on them. It's not like them to disappear without a reason. Rascal can open the door and go out if he chooses to do so, but surely, Josh or Steve would have called me if they showed up at Todd's apartment.

Laura started toward the steps to see if they were downstairs. Susan's door was ajar. She paused to look inside. Rascal and Mischief were stretched on either side of Susan, giving her comfort that only cats can give.

Laura smiled to herself, went to bed and slept easily.

Thirty-Seven

Saturday. The big wedding day. Red, orange, and magenta clouds overcast the morning sky. Birds sang outside Laura's window doing their best to chase them away. Rascal and Mischief pushed Laura's door open and leaped to her bed in one giant coordinated leap.

"Oh, you decided to give me a little attention?" Laura stroked their soft fur. "Could it have something to do with food? Well, come on. We have a big day ahead of us," she said. "You were good kitties at the rehearsal last night, but you don't need to go to the wedding, you know."

Two sets of crossed, green eyes stared at her. Laura laughed, but felt uneasy. Their crossed-eyes usually meant they were upset about something—or something was going on that they didn't like.

Her morning routine completed, Laura was relaxing with a second cup of coffee when Susan joined her. "Good morning," said Laura moving toward the cupboard. "Did you sleep well?" She chose a cup with a smiling cat on it and poured Susan's coffee.

"Thanks," said Susan, reaching for the cup. "I slept better than I have in months. I think I had a couple of fur blankets on me." She laughed as she glanced down at Rascal and Mischief who stared at her.

"I know," said Laura. "I missed them last night and was afraid they might have gone over to Todd's to be with the boys."

"Do they go with you very often?"

"They were on the pulpit beside my notes my first Sunday here. Since then, they accompany either me, or the boys. They like to be a part of the action and seem to know where and when they will be needed. I've learned to trust their instincts. They're trained as show cats and like to be around people, especially when they can show off, but they're usually well mannered in public."

"It was funny—odd really—to see them sleeping on the organ during the rehearsal."

"I doubt they were really sleeping. They were alert to everything going on."

"Will they go to the wedding?"

Rascal and Mischief had been sitting quietly near Laura turning their heads from one to the other as mother and daughter exchanged thoughts. In their Maine Coon duet, they emitted a sound that could have been interpreted as, "Of, course!"

"I guess that's your answer," said Laura. "What shall we have for breakfast? Unless I miss my guess, we should have two men and two boys in about fifteen minutes."

"Here? Won't they…"

"Cook there? Not unless they have to. They won't go to Carolyn's; Todd will want to keep her as free from responsibility as he can today. And Steve and Josh belong here."

"Mother, you *have* changed. You are more…more…oh, I don't know. Relaxed? Alive? Yes, I think that's it. You are more alive."

"After so many brushes with death, maybe I am glad to be alive. Except for the Jacobsons and their obsession with getting me out of their way, this is a wonderful community for healing of the spirit, for learning to love—really love. And I'm not just talking about Steve, but all the people who have become a part of my life here."

"I envy you." Susan said wistfully.

"You don't need to envy me, Susan. Open your heart. You'll feel it too."

"I wish I could, but I can't stay here forever. I need to go where I can find a job and…"

"Susan, I just had a marvelous idea."

"Really mother?" Susan answered in mock sarcasm. "Do you need a resident artist in your church?"

"No," said Laura, "but close. I just remembered a letter I got from the school board the day before yesterday. They wanted me to post a notice on our bulletin board. They need an art teacher for Cottonville High School immediately—like next week. Irv Markley, the school board president is a member of my church. Actually, this is his house we're living in temporarily. He wants to sell it when the parsonage if finished—but that's beside the point," Laura waved her hand as if pushing aside an unimportant fact. "If you're interested in teaching, I'll call and set up an appointment for you."

"I don't know. Where would I live?"

"Here, at least for as long as you need to get yourself together. If you decide you like it and want to stay, well, like I said, this house is going on the market by the first of the year."

"Do you really think I could? Teach, that is?"

"You're an excellent artist. You have a degree in art. Why couldn't you?"

"I've never taught before. I'm not very…"

"Talk to Irv. Let him decide."

"Well, all right, but…"

"But what? You want to get the job without my influence? You want it to be your choice?"

Susan laughed. "You always could read my mind."

"Don't worry, darling. I'll call and set up an appointment, beyond that you're on your own." Laura paused for a minute then added as an afterthought. "For that matter, why don't I give you his name and number? You call. I won't get involved at all. You don't even have to tell him you're my daughter if you don't want to."

"I'm not ashamed of being your daughter."

"I know that, but I understand your need to make it on your own. If you take the job, you have to feel it's because you are qualified, not because of who you know. That's all right."

"Who is he? When can I call?"

Laura caught her breath at the excitement and hope on her daughter's face. "His name is Irvine Markley and I would wait until after nine o'clock. His number is on the rolodex by the phone."

"Today?"

"Why not?"

Before Susan could answer, they heard the front door open. In a flash of fur, the cats disappeared and soon boys and cats were rolling on the floor and laughing.

Susan laughed so hard tears streamed down her face. "Those cats act more like dogs than they do cats," she said, brushing a tissue across her cheeks.

"I know. Sometimes I think *they* think they're dogs—but don't let them know I said that. Sometimes they even think they are human."

Breakfast over, the boys and cats went to Jerome's house. Steve and Todd helped Laura clean up the dishes. Susan excused herself and went upstairs, returning in a few minutes.

156

"Mother," she called excitedly as she ran down the steps.

"Susan?"

"He wants me to start Monday. He said I can be a sub until the board meets with me, then we'll go from there. I've got a job! A real Job! Oh, Mom, I'm so excited and...I'm scared. What if..."

"You'll do fine. No what ifs. They only muddy the waters."

"Can I call...?" She stopped remembering she had left Norman.

"Call him, Susan. He'll be happy for you."

"Oh, I couldn't...could I?"

"Do it. That's an order." Steve spoke from behind Laura.

Susan looked at him beginning to bristle then saw the twinkle in his eye.

"Thanks," she whispered and ran back up the stairs.

"Thank you," Laura whispered as she turned to Steve who had his arms around her and a kiss upon her lips before she could finish her sentence.

"All right, you two, break it up. Are you sure you don't want to join us at the altar this afternoon?" Todd interrupted them with a smile.

"We *will* be there." Laura laughed. "If I'm not, you're going to have a hard time getting through a wedding."

"That's right," said Steve. "And if I'm not there you might try to run away and then Carolyn will be upset with all of us."

They all laughed. Todd was getting nervous and needed all the distractions he could find. He was glad the wedding was set for four o'clock and not seven or eight. It was already ten so he didn't have too much longer to wait.

Thirty-Eight

Karen was arranging her music and the stops on the organ. Rascal and Mischief, who made it very clear they would be there with or without their human's permission, gave the impression of sleeping on the organ. Suddenly, both heads raised, eyes wide, fur fluffing. Their ears twitched. Then as if Karen had struck a discord on the organ, they shot to the floor and became two blurs of orange/brown stripes pouring down the aisle toward Laura's office. She had her hand on the door, ready to go in and put on her vestments. The cats streaked past her, pushed the door open and ran into Dorothy's office.

"What was that all about?" asked Steve.

"You got me," said Laura perplexed.

Yowling, spitting and hissing along with a cry of pain and cursing gave them the answer. A door slammed and someone ran down the fire escape. Steve had his gun in his hand and was in the office before he remembered he was in the church. The cats, still bushy-tailed, jumped at the panic bar to open the door. Steve pushed it open and ran down the stairs. Laura, right behind him, started to follow. Rascal and Mischief sat before her refusing to let her to move toward the door. Tires squealed. Steve returned, placing his gun back in its shoulder holster.

"Jacobson?" It was really more a statement of fact than a question. "They knew," Laura said nodding to the cats. "Look at them."

The cats trotted to Laura's office and sat down in the middle of the floor chattering in angry sounds and shaking their heads. They hissed and spat as if trying to rid themselves of a nasty taste in their mouths. Finally, they finished grooming themselves and each other. Once they were presentable, they returned to their organ perch.

"Laura…" Steve started.

"Don't say it, Steve. None of us could have known he would try anything like that."

158

"How did he get in the office?"

"Probably came in the front entrance with other guests and slipped into Dorothy's office from the hall."

"If you had gone in your office…"

"But, I didn't, did I? My protectors took care of it. Do you suppose we'll have to take them with us on our honeymoon when we're married?"

Laura teased, but Steve said between clenched teeth, "I hope we're rid of Jacobson for good by then, but, if not… Well, we'll see."

"Go get Todd and get in *your* place. The Wedding March will begin in about ten minutes."

Laura was more shaken than she wanted to admit—even to herself, much less to Steve. The whole episode took less than five minutes and the congregation never knew. But she knew. She had to sit for a couple of minutes before getting her vestments out of the closet.

"Lord, am I going to have to face him again? Please say I won't."

There was no answer. No familiar chuckle. Just a feeling of a warm blanket wrapping around her.

"All right," she sighed. "I can accept that. As long as I know You are holding me in Your arms, I will face him when, and if, I have to. Now, help us get through this wedding without further incident, please."

Minutes later Laura led Todd and Steve from the side entrance where they waited, facing the congregation. Laura signaled for Sophia, as Matron of Honor to begin her walk down the aisle.

Regally, Sophia marched to the music as if she were presenting her daughter for a coronation. Her radiant smile, seemed to light the path to the altar. Wearing a soft, autumn rust, wool suit, she was almost as beautiful as her daughter. When she was in place, Karen began the Wedding March.

Everyone stood. Carolyn in her white linen suit, walked beside Jerome in his black tuxedo. A perfect gentleman, Jerome held his arm at an angle so his mother could rest her hand on it until they reached the altar. He glanced up at his mother and smiled then placed her hand in Todd's and stepped back. Laura asked, "Who presents this woman for the blessing of this marriage?"

Jerome answered in a clear, proud voice, "My grandmother and I do." Then he grinned at Todd and stepped over to stand beside his grandmother. No more disturbances ensued—from cats or Jacobson. As the service ended, Todd looked deep into Carolyn's eyes for a few seconds then kissed her a little longer than was necessary. Laura smiled and signaled for Karen to begin the recessional. Rascal and Mischief sat on their haunches on top of the organ, smiling their Maine Coon smiles as the wedding party departed from the sanctuary and formed the receiving line in the Alpha Room.

Following the reception Susan asked, "Do you want me to take the cats with us?"

"You can try," said Laura. They both laughed, but Laura couldn't shake her uneasy feeling. The cats had been so competent that the encounter with Jacobson was over quickly and few people knew there had been potential trouble. Steve told Todd; they decided Todd could tell Carolyn later.

"Come on Rascal and Mischief," called Josh and Jerome. "We'll race you to the car."

Cats and boys zipped out of the church in a race against time. By the time the boys—as fast as they were—reached the car, the cats were sitting on the hood waiting for them, grinning, making their cat sounds—a combination of chatter, and chuckling.

Thirty-Nine

Rascal and Mischief jumped onto the bed. Laura groaned and turned over. She was tired—more tired than she had been when she turned off the light the night before. Two nights of sleepless turning and tossing were taking their toll.

"It's not time to get up," she snapped at the cats.

They hissed and smacked her arm.

"Sorry kitties. It's not your fault that I'm tired. Come on let's get food in us. Maybe that will help."

Sipping her second—or third—cup of coffee, Laura glanced at the kitchen calendar.

Only days away from November. She gazed out the window at the clear blue sky behind the reds and yellows adorning the maples and oaks. Susan and Josh had already left for school. Now that Susan had a fulltime teaching position, and a car, she took the boys to school. Rascal and Mischief no longer needed to walk with them. Today, however, Rascal deserted her and Mischief to go to school with the boys. Mischief sat on the chair beside her, watching her every move.

Laura was so out of sorts and tired that she didn't stop to wonder why Rascal had chosen to accompany the boys that morning. She glanced at Mischief and said, "Rascal deserted you too, didn't he? What is it with men? They...never mind. It's not men. It's tension and pressure and...Mischief, I'm rambling, but he *could* call me...or I suppose I could call him. It's only been two days...he's been gone for longer periods of time. But this is different. This time it's anger—on both our parts."

Even though the day promised to be a very warm Indian summer day Laura felt cold and...lonely.

"You know, Lord, this love business is for the young. Why did You let me fall in love with such a stubborn mule? Well, they will be selling snowshoes in Kenya before I call to apologize for something I didn't do." The familiar chuckle irritated her even more.

"I may as well go to the office. I have plenty to do. If he wants to be so childish, then let him. Maybe it's a good thing I found out now. Maybe I should call the bishop and…"

The annoying peal of the phone interrupted her tirade to her Boss. Laura's heart skipped a beat. So sure Steve was calling to apologize, she rushed to answer, not even identifying herself.

"Hello." She tried not to sound too smug.

"Good morning, Love."

"Cora." She tried not to sound too disappointed.

"I know you're busy with the big wedding coming up and the holidays fast approaching, but the Lord was insistent that I call. Wedding jitters, maybe. Anyway, let me pray, Lord, you know my precious friend's need. Keep her and her loved ones safe from harm. Give them joy. Amen."

Laura slammed the phone down. "Doesn't that woman ever say goodbye? I'm always left with a buzzing phone in my hand. And what kind of trouble am I in for now?"

Mischief sat on the floor, ears laid back, eyes crossed. Laura glared at her. "Don't *you* start on me too," she said. Mischief turned her back on Laura.

"Are you coming with me or staying here and ignoring me?" Laura picked up her briefcase and started out the door. Mischief, not as adept as Rascal at opening doors, flew out between Laura's legs before she could close the door.

Still irritated with herself, with Steve, with Cora, and with anyone else who happened to cross her mind, Laura went to her office. Wedding or not, she still had a church to run—Stewardship Campaign, building a new parsonage, renovating the church, Charge Conference, Thanksgiving and Advent/Christmas. Things were piling up and time was speeding to December.

Laura was still mumbling to herself when Dorothy checked in with her, "Why did I ever agree to a wedding in the first place, and December of all times?"

"You could always go see Judge Walker and forget the wedding," said Dorothy who was up to her ears in her own problems. "Or you could just call it off and forget it all together."

"You know I can't do that!"

"Then, excuse me for being direct, but why don't you just quit your belly-aching and live with it."

Laura jerked around from her computer. Anger flashed in her eyes. "Dorothy Jean Barker, I don't have to take that kind of talk from you or anyone else. It's really none of your…"

Laura stopped mid-sentence. She covered her flaming face with her hands and sat in stunned silence for what seemed hours. When she finally looked up, Dorothy was staring at her in disbelief. No matter what they had been through, Laura had never raised her voice to her friend.

"Dorothy," she whispered, "Please, forgive me. I can't believe I yelled at you like that—and over nothing! I am so sorry."

Dorothy started laughing. "Forgive me for laughing," she said, "but it's good to know my pastor is human after all. I was beginning to worry that I was working for an angel in disguise, or something."

"Dorothy, believe me, I am very much human, and I had no right to speak to you that way."

"You didn't speak to me as a pastor. That was the scared bride-to-be speaking and it'll happen again unless I miss my guess. You counsel others all the time about such things. Who is your counselor? The bishop is a couple hundred miles away."

Laura tried to smile at Dorothy's insight. "No one. I usually talk things out with Steve, but he…"

Dorothy laughed again. "He's having jitters of his own."

"Do you think so? Is that why…?"

"Ahhhh," said Dorothy with a very wise look on her face. "So there is trouble in paradise."

"Not trouble, exactly, it's just that we…that he…that I…I don't even know what *is* wrong."

"Let me see," Dorothy tapped her temple with her forefinger and pretended to think. "You don't feel as close as you once did. He isn't as attentive as he once was. He doesn't call you as much. He complains about Josh and Susan being around all the time and never having you to himself. He thinks he needs to be your protector and you don't have a brain in your head. Shall I go on?"

"Dorothy, how do you…? I haven't even talked to Susan about my problems."

"Maybe that's your problem. You don't talk to *any*one, including Steve. Just because you are a preacher and he's a homicide detective who understands people, that doesn't mean you understand each other completely—especially when you both have such high charged occupations. And more especially since you have only known each other less than a year."

"Do you think I'm marrying him too soon? Maybe I should wait."

"Maybe you should talk to him. He's not a mind reader. You could drive over to Glenville and take him to lunch. You've hardly taken a day off since Todd and Carolyn's wedding in September and it's almost November."

"You're probably right. But, there's so much to do."

"You know something Pastor, this church kept itself together for almost two years without a pastor at all. I really think we can do it for a half a day."

Laura stared at Dorothy then a smile slowly spread across her face.

"Dorothy, you're an angel. I don't know what I would do without you. Thank you. With your help I might make it to that wedding after all."

"Oh, great, I haven't got enough responsibilities, now I'm a marriage counselor, too. That'll cost you extra. I think…" Dorothy paused and screwed up her face as if she was trying to figure something in her head. "…I think about two weeks of peace and quiet around here after Christmas ought to just about do it."

"I'll do even better. How about two weeks off with full pay—after Christmas, of course"

"Sounds great, but if we are both gone, this old church just might fall apart. I'll stick around until you get back and then if you can keep your feet on the ground long enough to run the church, I'll take a little vacation."

"Dorothy, you are truly a friend. Thanks for helping me through this. I'm going to Glenville and begin a little Christmas shopping. If anyone calls, I'll return their call later."

"Shall I call and tell him you are coming?"

"No," Laura hesitated. "I think I'll just drop in. If he's not there, or busy, I still have shopping to do."

"That bad, huh?"

"We parted very angrily two days ago."

"Get going. It will be all right. Trust me. I have never seen two people more in love. Don't throw it away with stubborn pride."

Forty

Laura opened the car door and Mischief jumped to the passenger seat. "Sure you don't want to stay home, or go to school with Rascal?"

"Meow." Laura could have sworn she said, "No."

Mischief sat sideways in the seat, front paws tucked under her, wide green eyes staring at Laura.

"I don't know, Mischief. Everything seems to be going well—Norman and Susan are talking on the phone and writing letters; the church is growing and thriving; even Bill Collins hasn't caused any major trouble recently. So why are Steve and I quarreling, and why did Cora call me this morning, and why do I have this dreaded sense that something is about to happen?"

Mischief blinked and purred, except at the mention of Bill Collins. Then she growled and spit.

"I know, sweetie. I feel the same way. I know he's out there somewhere. As much as I try to forget him, he's always there—nagging at the perimeter of my consciousness."

Again, Mischief hissed and shook her paw as if to rid her world of a pesky bug. Laura agreed and changed the subject. "It's not even November yet— a little early for Christmas shopping, but with so much to do before Christmas, it isn't a bad idea to start early."

She reached for the radio and pulled back her hand. "It's too early for Christmas Carols on the radio, so let's sing our own." She began singing and laughed as Mischief joined her. Karen was right; the cats were certainly tone deaf when it came to music, but Mischief *sang* with all the gusto of a music lover and Laura continued with one carol after another.

When they neared Look Out Point, Laura tried not to look that way, but found herself glancing out of the corner of her eye. She saw a large black car parked there and a shiver found its way up her spine. Mischief puffed up as if Jacobson were sitting next to her.

"Let's see if we can get some music to accompany our singing," Laura said and leaned forward to turn on the radio. Mischief growled. The glass shattered at Laura's side and at the same moment, something stung the back of her neck. She reached back to rub it and brought back a red, wet, sticky hand. She was bleeding.

"Oh dear Lord, not again. Please, my little Chevette can't take going over the mountain the way Steve's Buick did. Help me get through this. Don't let me die without telling Steve I'm sorry."

She reached for her phone. "Maybe we can make it to Glenville, but I better try to call Steve." She opened the phone and glanced in the rearview mirror. The black car was behind her—speeding up. She hit the pre-programmed number and hoped Steve was there—or would answer if he was.

It rang several times while she frantically drove as fast as she dared. "He's not going to answer, Mischief. He doesn't want to talk to me."

"Meow," Mischief jumped to the back seat and peered out the back window. Laura heard the ring switch over to either another phone or a recorder—which would do her no good.

Surely, Joe would...

"Joe, here, Steve is tied up. Can I help you?"

"Joe...it's Collins...he's..."

"Laura?"

"Gopher Mountain Road... He's..."

Another shot whizzed past her from behind, shattering the back window and making a hole in the front windshield surrounded by spider-web like cracks. Mischief flew back to the front seat.

"Laura that sounded like..."

"It was. Collins...going to run me off...can't outrun him. Tell Steve... I'm sorry and... I love him."

The Cadillac increased speed and moved as if to pass her, but rammed into the side of her car instead, jamming the doors. Then he dropped back behind her and began ramming her from behind, nudging her toward the edge of the road. Laura dropped the phone and tried to swerve toward the wall of mountain, but Jacobson pushed the little Chevette over to the edge like it was a toy. Laura felt the front wheels go off the road.

"Steve!" Laura screamed as the rest of the car followed the front tires. The car careened down the side of the mountain. Laura pressed the brake to the floor and pulled the emergency brake. They both gave way and began smoking.

"Mischief…jump…door…stuck…please sweetie…jump."

Laura tried to force Mischief out the shattered window. She squirmed loose and leaped back to Laura's side where she chewed at the seat belt. Laura released it—not that it would do any good with the door jammed. Maybe she could crawl over to the passenger side. With the center console, she knew she would never make it in time.

Mischief jumped back to Laura's lap and together they pushed once more at the door. Still stuck. Laura hugged Mischief close and prayed, "O God please let them catch him. Don't let him hurt the boys."

Laura and Mischief screamed together as the car hit a bump. Laura bounced then fell forward, hitting her head on the steering wheel. Her world became gray and fuzzy. Everything felt so far away—Mischief's yowling, metal crunching, wind around her, ground under her and the pain in her head. Somewhere she thought she heard a crash of metal against stone, an explosion. She felt waves of heat. Gray faded to black. Sound drifted to silence.

Forty-One

Rascal had jumped into the car with the boys when Susan was ready to leave for school. Mischief watched from the window as they drove away. That wasn't unusual. One or the other of the cats often accompanied them. It had been so long—at least six weeks—since they'd seen, or heard from Jacobson, and being kids, Jerome and Josh had simply pushed the possibility of danger out of their minds.

At the school, Rascal trotted into the building and down the hall with Josh and Jerome. Miss Campbell, busy at her desk, looked up and smiled at the boys.

"Looks like we have a visitor again this morning. This is… Rascal?"

"Yes, ma'am," said Jerome. "We don't know why he decided to come with us."

"He'll be quiet," said Josh. "I'll call my grandmother to come and get him if you don't want him here today."

Miss Campbell, like everyone else in town, was well aware of Reverend Kenzel's cats and their uncanny way of sniffing out trouble. She also understood they generally had a reason for what they did. "We have a math test this morning," she said, "so he'll have to sit quietly." She smiled again and winked at Rascal who gave her his Maine Coon grin then slid under Josh's seat.

Class began. Miss Campbell was explaining the procedure for the test when, fur on end and tail bushy, Rascal suddenly ran for the door. He had his paws around the doorknob and the door flew open before anyone hardly knew he had moved. Josh and Jerome jumped to run after him. Jerome paused long enough to speak to Miss Campbell.

"I have to call my dad," he said with a tremble in his voice. "Pastor's in trouble and he knows it."

Miss Campbell nodded, knowing it would do no good to tell him he couldn't go to the office. She also knew Chief Williams would know if it was a legitimate call and he would discipline the boys if they were only trying to get out of a test.

She laid the test back on her desk. "We'll do this tomorrow," she said, to the class. "Get out your math books and work on Practice Set number three on page thirty-six.

Josh and Jerome ran down the hall to the office. Rascal had already opened the door and waited, on the corner of Miss Richard's desk, tail thumping impatiently. Jerome, breathing hard, said, "Please, Miss Richards, I have to call my dad. Pastor's in trouble."

Mrs. Ellison stepped out of her office in time to hear the exchange. She nodded to the secretary who dialed and handed the receiver to Jerome who was blinking back tears. It had to be bad trouble for Rascal to disturb class.

"Chief Williams here." Jerome held the receiver like a hot potato.

"Dad, Pastor's in trouble. Rascal's setting up a ruckus."

Todd didn't question Jerome. With as much control as he could command, because he too, knew when Rascal said there was trouble, it was likely to be big trouble, he said, "Wait with him at the door until you see the cruiser. Then let him out to meet me. Thanks, son."

Todd hung up and dialed Laura's office on his cell phone as he ran out the door. Dorothy answered on the first ring, as he knew she would. "Dorothy, this is Todd. Is Laura there?"

"She left about ten minutes ago for Glenville. Can I give her a message?"

"No, but I think she might be in trouble again. Call your prayer chain ladies. I'll talk to you later."

He pushed the off button and motioned for Mark who was just walking toward the door. "Mark, better come with me. We might have trouble and I'll need a good back up. I'll fill you in on the way."

Mark got in the cruiser and listened with a sober expression as Todd repeated his calls. Todd pushed the buttons to lower the back windows as he drove near the school. He slowed, but didn't stop. Jerome and Josh opened the school door and Rascal darted toward the curb. The cat leaped for the car and sailed through the open window. Todd hit the siren, the lights, and the gas pedal.

* * *

Joe had been working at his desk when Steve's phone switched Laura's call to his phone. Steve was at his desk, but Joe knew something had happened between Laura and Steve. He had been moping about like a sick puppy for the last two days. The last thing Joe wanted was to get in the middle of a lover's quarrel, but he had to answer the phone. He wouldn't lie for Steve, but neither would he try to play Cupid.

From the sound of her voice, Joe knew immediately something was terribly wrong. He motioned for Steve to get over there as he switched to speakerphone mode. Steve, knowing it was Laura from the caller ID, approached his desk cautiously. He had no intention of talking to her—at least not yet. Let her stew a while longer. When he heard her voice, he too knew something was wrong. His face went pale as he listened to her. "Laura, hold on, we're on the way," he yelled into the phone, but it was dead. He would not assume the worst. She wasn't hit by that shot. She couldn't have been.

Steve ran out the door; Joe right behind him. They each took a car, switched on the flashers and sirens. Joe grabbed his CB and ordered an ambulance to Gopher Mountain Road on the double. Then grabbed his cell and called Todd. Mark answered.

Mark listened as Joe explained the situation. "We're on our way up the other side of the mountain. We'll meet you there. Rascal already alerted us." He pushed the off button and reiterated the message to Todd, who hit the gas pedal a little harder, but on Gopher Mountain Road, it was dangerous even for a police cruiser to go over the speed limit.

They were nearing the top of the mountain when flames shot skyward from the valley. Todd turned pale and almost lost control of the car. Mark laid a hand on his arm. "Steady, there pal. We can't help her if we go off the road."

"Mark, do you really think there's any chance she can survive that explosion?" His voice choked and tears clouded his eyes.

"If she's in that car, Todd, there's no way she can survive, but maybe she got out. The other cat is with her and Laura's resourceful and smart. God is with her." Mark sounded hopeful, but if he'd been pushed, he would've had to admit there was little chance of survival. Rascal meowed and hissed as if he wanted Todd to drive faster.

"I'm going as fast as I dare, fellow," said Todd. "Hold on. We're almost there. I see the flashing lights from the Glenville cruisers." Todd screeched to a stop inches from Steve's car.

* * *

Steve and Joe were almost at the point near Bethel Boulder where Laura had gone off the road in Steve's Buick. Maybe she would hit it again, but then her Chevette wouldn't fare as well as the Buick. They passed the boulder. She didn't go off there. A sound like a bomb exploding in the valley sent flames licking the clouds. The sky filled with black smoke.

A black Cadillac passed them heading for Glenville. Joe radioed back to set up a roadblock and stop it. Neither he nor Steve dared stop, although Joe knew if Laura was in that car there was no way she could possibly survive.

Steve's car screeched to a halt inches from the tracks where Laura's car went off the road. Joe, only nanoseconds behind him, ran after Steve as he started down the mountain. "Steve, don't go down there. If she was in that car, there is no way you're going to get close enough to even see her."

Steve turned and punched his friend in the jaw and bounded down the mountain like a wild animal running *from* a fire. Fear and anger fueled his adrenalin, making him numb to his own danger. He couldn't —wouldn't— believe she was in that pile of rubble that was settling down to a slow, steady glow.

Todd hit the automatic window button as he screeched to a halt. Rascal flew out before he and Mark could open their doors. "Yowl," he screamed sounding like a bobcat cornered up a tree. He waited a half a second and cried out once more.

"He knows," said Todd reaching for him, but Rascal lifted his head, perked his ears. Was that his echo?

He yowled again. "Yowl." The reply came from halfway down the mountain. Rascal called out again. Once again, the echo came to him. Todd and Mark watched with mouths open.

"That has to be Mischief answering him," said Todd. Before he could call to Joe or Steve, Rascal leaped over the heads of the men watching the smoldering car at the bottom of the ravine. Loping down the path the careening car had left, he continued to call and follow the response.

Rascal caught up with Steve, landed on his shoulders, and yowled again. Steve heard the reply and knew it was no echo. "Mischief?"

"Yowl," answered Rascal.

"Keep talking to her. Laura has to be with her. She just has to be." He couldn't even think about the possibility of the cat leaving Laura.

Following the path of broken weeds, saplings, and tire tracks, Steve and Rascal moved as quickly as Steve could without slipping. He watched for signs of Laura. Rascal watched for Mischief.

"Laura," he called, but got no answer except Mischief's excited response. They were getting closer. The weeds parted beside them, and there was Mischief jumping up and down, chattering and meowing. Rascal flew to the ground like a flying squirrel. They followed her back the way she had come. Laura was lying on the ground near a tree, so still and lifeless Steve's own heart almost stopped.

"Get that stretcher down here," he called to Todd and Joe who were behind him. "Somehow, she got out of the car, but she's hurt." He turned to the cats, "Rascal, help them find us." Rascal loped up the path and waited for Todd, Joe, and the paramedics.

Forty-Two

Sounds—sirens, cats screaming, men yelling, tires squealing—faded in and out of Laura's numbed, aching mind. Where was she? She tried to move and groaned. She tried to sit up. Dizziness overcame her with such force she began heaving. Her head throbbed. She tried to sit again, threw up and lay back to stop the pounding in her head and the retching in her stomach.

"Laura?"

Laura's eyes opened partially, but she couldn't focus on the blurred figure beside her. "Steve?" she whispered and tried to sit up sending another round of nausea. She turned aside to heave, stomach muscles pushing against its emptiness.

"Don't try to talk. Dizziness is making you sick. We'll get something in you in a minute to stop it."

She was safe. She could sleep. No more sound. No more pounding hammers in her head. No more retching to unburden an already empty stomach. She was unconscious.

The paramedics, guided by Todd and Joe, made their way as quickly and carefully as they could. Rascal and Mischief bounced up and down in the weeds until the men saw them then they started across to Laura and Steve.

Joe Parkerson and Burt Miller, paramedics from Cottonville, dropped to their knees on either side of Laura and began checking her vital signs. Burt was still in training, but Joe watched him carefully and double-checked everything he did. "Looks like a concussion," said Burt. "Possible internal injuries. Better immobilize her on the board."

"Right," said Joe, "Good diagnosis. She was conscious?" He looked at Steve when he asked the question.

"Briefly. Started throwing up when she moved."

"We'll get something in her when we get to the vehicle. Let's get her strapped on here."

Carefully Burt and Joe with Steve's help got her on the stretcher making sure her neck and head would not move in case of crushed or broken vertebrae. The three of them with Joe Baldwin and Mark lifted the stretcher and started the slow ascent.

"This terrain is steep, so we'll take it easy," said Burt. "One slip and we could be at the bottom of the slope with that smoldering car."

Todd watched from the sideline, feeling helpless, but knowing Laura was getting the best care. He made a mental note to add paramedic training to his continuing education classes. He knew Steve was a certified paramedic and could help him. He followed the stretcher up the slope.

Mischief and Rascal stopped in front of him on the trampled path. "You want something?" He smiled, not really expecting an answer, but with these cats, he never knew what to expect.

They blinked and started through the weeds, stopped, turned to him and said, "Meow?"

"I guess they do want something," he said to himself as he followed through the tall weeds.

Todd hurried to catch up to the cats. They led him to the door from the car. Todd looked around for evidence of someone having pulled the door open, wondering why they didn't stay around to help Laura after getting her out of the car. A shiver slid down his spine. "No tracks," he said. "Looks as if the door was pulled off the frame and thrown aside."

"Meow!" answered the duet.

Todd hurried up the slope.

Steve was running toward his car. He stopped long enough to turn to Joe. "I'm sorry, Joe. I guess I sort of lost my head."

"Not your head, your heart. Call me when you find out anything. I'll go see if we snagged Jacobson. I radioed for a road block."

Todd ran to the side of Steve's car as he opened the door. "Give me your keys. You go with the ambulance. I'll bring your car. Mark will take the cruiser. We'll talk later."

"Thanks," he said and ran back to the ambulance. He threw himself into the back, as the attendant was ready to close the door. The driver took off, siren wailing, lights flashing, slowing only for the hairpin curve.

"Joe," Todd called to him as the ambulance pulled away. "You and Mark might want to check out that door." He showed him where it was. "Something's strange. See what you think."

* * *

Fifteen minutes later, the ambulance pulled up to the ER door where Doctor Cornelius waited. "Take her to Room Three," he said to the paramedics then turned to Steve. "What happened to her this time?" They followed the gurney to the examination room. "You know, Detective Morgan, Reverend Kenzel is a pretty strong woman—to say nothing of being one lucky lady—but there are limits. How much more must she endure?"

"I wish I had an answer Doctor. Jacobson is obsessed with killing her. Until we capture him—again…" Steve's voice broke. He couldn't begin to say what he knew to be the truth.

"I understand. Well, let's see what kind of damage we have this time. There is blood on the back of her neck. Was she shot again?"

"She was shot at. I wasn't with her, so I'm not sure." He then related the phone message to the doctor who was checking for broken bones and concussion.

Laura opened her eyes, tried to move, and closed them again.

"Reverend Kenzel, can you hear me?" Doctor Cornelius touched her arm and she tried to nod but her head wouldn't move.

"Do you have any pain besides the nausea?"

"My head—aches terribly. Dizzy when I move."

"No other pain? Arms? Legs? Internal?"

"No."

"Initially she looks good, though I can't for the life of me understand why she isn't dead. I want to get some X-rays and would like to keep her overnight but you know how stubborn she can be."

Steve grimaced. "How well I know."

"I'm not deaf," said Laura, which brought a chuckle from both men. The orderly came to wheel Laura to X-ray. They didn't discuss it further.

Forty-Three

Steve walked to the waiting room, where Susan was already waiting with the boys.

"I called ahead and went to the school to pick them up." Todd answered Steve's unasked question. "I hope they don't throw us out because of the cats, but they wouldn't stay out." He shrugged and chuckled. Rascal and Mischief sat on chairs beside Josh and Jerome like two stuffed toys.

Susan, pale and near panic, approached Steve. "Todd told us what happened. How is she? When can we see her?"

"She's in X-ray. There doesn't seem to be any serious breaks or punctures. Doctor Cornelius is with her. He'll let us know as soon as he can."

"He shot her again, didn't he?" said Josh.

"Josh…" Susan didn't know how to deal with this kind of problem. She looked to Steve, who had learned the only way to deal with Josh and Jerome was to be straightforward. They might be only ten years old, but they had wisdom and experience far beyond their chronological age.

Kneeling before the boys, he placed a hand on each of them. "He shot at her. She has a small graze on the back of her neck, either from the bullet or the shattered glass."

"Did he get away again?" Jerome asked.

"I don't know," said Steve as he stood. "Joe radioed back to Glenville to set up a roadblock. I haven't talked to Joe."

"He did. I know he did." There was no panic or even anger, just resignation.

"How can you be so sure, Josh?" asked Susan.

"Rascal and Mischief know. When Jerome and I got in the car, I felt Mischief say our angel jerked the door off and pulled them out. Rascal said they had a roadblock but it wouldn't do any good."

"What do you mean *felt her say*?" Susan looked confused—horrified. "Cat's don't talk to humans."

"They don't *talk* like we talk, but sometimes Jerome and me can *feel* their thoughts—kind of like ESP."

"He's probably right, Susan. Rascal and Mischief seem to have a special rapport with kids—maybe because they are more open than adults are." Steve smiled at Susan's open mouth.

"Grandpa Steve, will he ever stop chasing Grandma?"

"I wish I could say he would, Josh, but the truth is he's obsessed for some reason. I wish I knew why. It has to be more than just turning down his offer of marriage…" Steve sensed the doctor's approach even before Susan started toward him.

"She's going to be all right," said Doctor Cornelius before they could ask.

"Doctor Cornelius, I think you've probably met Susan Stewart, Laura's daughter," said Steve.

The doctor smiled at Susan. "Yes, we've met. Your mother is one lucky woman. Only a miracle could have gotten her out of that car. I don't know how she managed it without any broken bones or internal injuries. I don't even pretend to understand miracles, but I accept them willingly."

"She's not seriously hurt?" Susan was still pale.

"She said she hit her head on the steering wheel," said Doctor Jonathan. "She has a slight concussion, dizziness, and headache. She'll need a couple of stitches in the back of her neck. I know she doesn't like hospitals and usually refuses to stay, but if you folks can talk her into staying the overnight, I would appreciate it."

"Can we see her?" asked Susan, her eyes moist, lips trembling.

"Give me a couple of minutes to stitch her up and I'll have one of the nurses come and get you."

A few minutes later, the nurse approached the waiting area. "Kenzel family?" They all started toward her. "You can see her now. The doctor gave her a shot for pain and nausea, so she's a little groggy. You can all come back—except the fur-covered ones." She smiled and glanced at Rascal and Mischief. "It really would be better if they waited here."

"Rascal, Mischief, will you wait here? Do you want me to stay with you?" Jerome spoke to the cats. He really wanted to see his pastor, but Josh needed to see her more.

Rascal and Mischief settled back on the seats. They would stay. "Thanks, guys," he said and followed the others. The nurse led them back to Room 3 where Laura was half-asleep.

"Mom?" Susan's voice cracked. She'd never seen her mother unable to care for herself and others.

"Grandma?" Josh had seen her like that before—and worse, but he was still unnerved.

Laura tried to open her eyes. Things seemed blurred. Focusing was too much effort, so she closed her eyes again.

"Mom, I was so scared…"

"I'm sorry," Laura managed. "Looks like I did it again."

"No," said Steve quietly taking her hand. "Jacobson did it again."

"Steve? I…"

"Don't even try to talk," he said. "And, Laura, you need to stay here tonight."

"I…know…too dizzy."

Steve squeezed her hand. "I'm glad you're thinking rationally…"

Laura opened her eyes and smiled at him. "Maybe…knocked some sense into me." Steve laughed, but Josh spoke before he could comment.

"Mischief said our angel got you out of the car."

Jerome eased up beside Josh.

Laura lay so quiet they thought she had slipped back into sleep. She opened her eyes again and looked at the wide-eyed boys. "I'm not sure what happened. I told Mischief to jump. She wouldn't. The door wouldn't open. He sideswiped me, jamming the door before forcing me off the road. We hit a bump and my head hit the steering wheel. The door fell off. I had Mischief in my arms and we sailed across the mountainside. I heard an explosion, felt the heat and passed out until I felt Mischief licking my face and heard sirens."

Josh and Jerome grinned. "That's what we thought Mischief said too." Susan looked perplexed. Todd and Steve just shook their heads.

"I think we better leave so they can get her in a room where she can rest." Todd put his arm around Jerome.

"Mom…?"

"I'll be all right, Susan. Take care of Josh and the kitties. I'll be home tomorrow."

"But, you're my mother. I wasn't here for you before, now I should…"

"She'll be all right," said Steve. "I'll spend the night here."

"Will they let you?"

"I did before, I'll do it again."

"Do you think they can stop him?" Jerome covered his mouth to hide the giggle.

"Besides," said Josh, "you need to take care of me and Rascal and Mischief. Grandpa Steve can keep that man away from her."

Steve, who had started out, turned abruptly. Josh was serious. How did he know that was one of his reasons for staying? He certainly had inherited his grandmother's sense of perception. He quietly left to get Laura admitted.

* * *

When Laura woke sometime later in a darkened room, she sensed someone was there. Who? Had Bill Collins somehow gotten past the nurses' station? Panic seized her. She was afraid to move.

"Steve?" She thought it was a scream, but her voice sounded hollow, only slightly more than a whisper. Before she could try again, his hand held hers.

"I'm here, darling."

"I was afraid he was…"

"Not while I'm here."

"Where is *here*?"

"You're in the hospital."

"Oh, I remember now."

"How's the headache?"

"Still hurts but not so much. Nausea seems to be gone."

"You had quite a trauma—and not just the bump on the head."

"My car?"

"It's gone… I'm sorry, sweetheart. I know how much you loved that car. If you hadn't gotten out when you did, you would be gone too. Laura, when will I ever learn? It was stupid of me to get so upset over such trivial things—so trivial that I don't even remember why we quarreled. When I thought I had lost you in that fire, I…"

"Steve," she said squeezing his hand, "I was just as wrong as you were. I was on my way to ask you to lunch and beg you to forgive me. Steve, why are we acting like such children? Dorothy says all lovers act this way the closer they get to the wedding day. She suggested we go see Judge Walker and forget the wedding. I yelled at her. I've never raised my voice to Dorothy. I'm so tired of being such a juvenile."

He looked her in the eyes. "But, if you give up part of being juvenile, then you might lose the rest—you know the wonder of falling in love, the enjoyment of simple things. We'll get through this. We have one thing going for us. We may act childish at times, but we have enough years behind us to survive."

"I love you so much. I can't stand being angry with you."

"Ask Joe what a jackass I've been the last couple of days." He grinned. "I even socked him when he tried to keep me from going down the mountain to look for you."

"You didn't?"

"I did. But, he's like Dorothy. He's an understanding friend."

"Steve…, did they catch him?"

The pause was too long. He didn't need to answer. She knew. Jacobson had eluded them once more. He would be back to try again, and again, and again, until he either succeeded or one of them was killed in the process.

Forty-Four

"Good morning Dorothy," called Laura from her office. Doctor Cornelius told her to rest for a couple of days and she didn't argue. She'd had such a terrific headache that she was glad to stay put. The headache was almost gone; she felt alive and well.

"Pastor!" Dorothy got up from her desk and went to give Laura a hug. "When I suggested you go have lunch with your detective, I didn't intend for you to lure him to your room for the night by careening down a mountainside."

Laura laughed with her.

"Seriously," said Dorothy, "are you all right? I heard your car was totaled."

"Not only totaled; burned to a crisp." Laura bit her lip to keep it from trembling. "My car felt like a friend, when I had no other friends."

"I'm so sorry, but I am glad you got out in time. Rumor has it that an angel saved you."

"I don't know for sure how I got out. The boys say that Mischief told them their angel got us out. Who am I to argue with a smart cat?" She grinned at Mischief who curled around her ankles. Rascal sat on the edge of Dorothy's desk, turning his head from one speaker to the other. All I know is it was a close call and apparently I've still got work to do here."

"Is it ever going to stop—these pot-shots at you, I mean?"

"I wish I could say for certain they would, but I have a feeling they won't stop until either Jacobson, or I, or both, are dead."

"Oh, Pastor, don't say such things." Dorothy looked horrified.

"I don't want to think about it any more than you do, but the fact is he's obsessed with killing me and he won't rest until he succeeds. I just wish I knew why. I can't believe it's simply because of my part in destroying their drug ring. Others were involved with that, but it's me he's obsessed with."

"Maybe it's not you, but someone you love," said Dorothy.

"Steve?"

181

"Didn't you say the Jacobson's went to school in Glenville? Surely, some of them knew Steve, even if he didn't know them. He was into sports. Maybe Jacobson doesn't want you as much as he wants to keep Steve Morgan from having you?"

"Dorothy, you might just have a point there. Get Steve on the line for me. I think I'll throw that out for him to worry with for a while. It just might be a key."

Dorothy went back to her office and began dialing. Rascal and Mischief took a corner of the couch and curled together for their morning nap. At her desk, Laura started to work on some plans for the coming months. She smiled when Dorothy efficiently put through her call. Dorothy loved to sound professional.

"Just a minute Detective Morgan," she said, "Reverend Kenzel would like to speak to you."

Laura picked up the phone. "Steve, sorry to bother you at work, but this is about your work."

"Laura, you can call me anytime. I'll never refuse to take a call from you again—even if you call a hundred times a day just to say, 'I love you.'"

"Well, I do, but that's not why I called. Dorothy and I were talking and she came up with another angle that we haven't—at least I haven't—thought about. She wondered if it's possible that Jacobson is not so much interested in harming *me* as he is in hurting *you*. I just happened to be the tool that would hurt you most. Did you know them in school? Is there some reason he would have a grudge or jealousy against you—say from high school days?"

"I don't know Laura. Right off hand I can't say that I know of anything, but anything is worth a look-see. I'll check it out. Tell Dorothy when she is through playing church secretary we'll train her to be a homicide detective secretary."

"Over my dead body, you will." Laura paused then added, "Maybe I ought to rephrase that."

"Maybe. Are the cats with you?"

"Yes, they're sleeping on the couch."

"Good. I'm glad they're there."

"Like I've said before, they have minds of their own. If they want to come, I can't stop them. If they don't want to come, I can't make them. One thing I've learned, if they sense danger, they let me know. They probably knew they could help more if one was with the boys and one was with me when my car went down the mountain."

"Just be careful, I can't handle too many more near misses."

"You think I can?"

"Laura, get your work done, and let me start checking this out. I love you."

"I love you too. Goodbye and good luck."

* * *

Wanting to catch up with her planning, Laura had brought a sandwich with her and continued to work after Dorothy left. A knock at the side, fire escape door sent a current of panic through her. The fire door was heavy with no window and couldn't be opened from outside. She glanced at Rascal and Mischief. Their fur stood up. They raced to the door and stared.

Knowing they could easily hit the panic bar and open the door, Laura said, "Wait kitties. Don't open it until Todd comes." They sat and waited while Laura picked up the phone and dialed Todd.

"Chief Williams here."

"Todd, this is Laura. Someone is trying to get in Dorothy's office by the fire escape door. She's gone and no one should be using that door. The cats are having a fit. Can you…?"

"I'm on my way."

It would take Todd three minutes if he walked from his office to the church, less if he ran. About a minute later, whoever was there ran down the metal stairs. Laura heard shouting and gunshots. Squealing tires told her he got away—again.

Todd knocked at the door and identified himself. Rascal and Mischief shook themselves and went back to the couch.

Laura opened the door a crack, saw Todd standing there alone, and opened it all the way. "I'm sorry, Todd. I guess I panicked. Sometimes parishioners come to this door, but only when they call ahead and Dorothy knows they're coming. Not knowing who was there scared me. I've got to get over that, but Rascal and Mischief…"

"Listen to them, Laura, and don't get over being scared—not until we catch that jerk anyway. It was him all right, but damn it he got away again—excuse my language. I know better, but I just don't know how he does it. How can he hide such a big car and get back to it and away so fast? If you had opened the door…" He didn't finish the sentence. He didn't have to. They both knew he would've shot her before she could say or do anything.

"Todd, what am I going to do? I can't call you every time someone knocks at my door. Next he'll probably harass me by phone."

"Don't give him ideas." Todd grinned. "Did you walk this morning?"

"Susan dropped me off on her way to school. I planned to walk home."

"If you're about ready to go, I'll wait and take you. Or you can call me, but I don't think you need to be out alone with him driving around."

Laura bristled, but relaxed. He was right. "Just let me put my papers in my brief case and turn off the computer," she said.

"You do that and I'll get the car and meet you at the front door."

* * *

Todd pulled into Laura's driveway and as soon as a door was open, Rascal and Mischief raced across the yard to the porch. Rascal had the front door open for them by the time Laura and Todd walked across the porch.

"Care for coffee?" Laura asked

"I'll pass on the coffee for now, but I want to check out the house—just in case."

"Thanks Todd," Laura said as she slipped her jacket off. Before she could hang it up the phone rang. Remembering her flippant words about Jacobson harassing her by phone, she grinned at Todd and reached for the receiver. She changed her mind and punched the speakerphone.

"Hello, Reverend Kenzel speaking."

"Some day your luck is going to run out, Laura dearest."

The buzzing dial tone replaced the voice. Laura stood for a minute staring at the phone then she dropped onto the chair by the table on which the phone rested. Todd hurried to her side and punched the off button on the still buzzing phone.

"Are you all right, Laura? I'll get you some water."

"No. Thank you, Todd. I'm all right. I guess I was just overcome by the coincidence of my words coming back to haunt me."

Footsteps crossed the porch. "It's not time for Susan or Josh," she said.

Todd pulled his gun, moved toward the door, and jerked it open as Steve pushed from the other side.

"Todd? Laura? What's going on? I thought I would come over and have lunch with you and I saw Todd's cruiser in the driveway." He looked at Todd's gun. "You were expecting someone?"

Laura moved into his arms. Todd put away his gun and filled him in on the visit at the church and the phone call. Steve held her tighter. She felt his heart beating as fast as hers was. He was as scared as she was. That was a comfort, and a worry.

"Did you find out anything from your high school days?" asked Laura.

"High school?" asked Todd.

Steve explained Dorothy's idea.

"She might have a point," said Todd.

"I haven't come up with anything yet. And even if we do, how is it going to help us? It might give us the motive for attempted murder." He couldn't bring himself to even think about it being murder.

"We won't know until we try. If I'm going to be pursued at every turn and maybe even die at the hands of that maniac, I would like to know why."

Todd and Steve both stared at Laura as if she had lost her senses then started laughing.

"What is so funny?" she asked easing away from Steve.

"You are darling," he answered. "You have a way of putting the most horrible thoughts in the context of the mundane. What was it you said once? Something about our minds can only stand so much horror so we have to dwell on the mundane, or we would go crazy."

"Well…"

"You're right. We have to stay focused and not let panic send us running scared. We have to live for the moment."

Seizing the moment, Steve drew her back into his arms and kissed her as if he may never see her again.

"Bye," said Todd knowing they didn't even miss him.

Forty-Five

Laura had been half joking, about Collins harassing her by phone. However, two days later at midnight the phone rang. Although the other bedrooms had no phones, Laura, half asleep, grabbed it. Susan and Josh needed their sleep.

"Laura, dearest, are you thinking about me?"

Laura slammed the phone down and lay back on the bed, her heart pounding too fast to immediately sleep again. Forcing herself to relax, she finally began to drift. Again, the phone rang. Again, she grabbed it only to hear the Jacobson weird, manic laughter. Every fifteen to twenty minutes she grabbed the phone. She was afraid to answer; afraid not to answer. Suppose one of her parishioners needed her. Cora's heart had been acting up again.

Somehow, she managed to make it through the day without seeming too tired. She didn't want to worry Susan and Josh. Steve would be over later. She would have her second wind by then.

November dragged her toward the holidays. Between midnight and four a.m. each night, the phone interrupted her sleep several times. Putting on a good front for the family took as much toll on Laura as the nocturnal harassments. Every nerve ending in her body felt raw and so sensitive that it hurt to think—to move—to laugh.

"You okay, Grandma?" Josh slid behind the table and waited for breakfast.

"Sure, Josh—just tired. Big service tonight."

"Is it okay if me and Jerome walk today? Rascal and Mischief will go with us."

Susan set the toast on the table. "I suppose it's all right, but why?"

"It's the last day before the holiday and we just want to walk."

"All right, but don't dally and be late."

"We won't," said Josh. He finished his milk as Jerome opened the door and called to him, "You ready?"

"I'm coming," said Josh. He jumped up, gave his mom and Laura a hug, and grabbed his backpack off the living room chair. "Coming kitties?" He called

186

to them as he ran out the door with Jerome. Rascal and Mischief romped along beside them.

"Did you ask her?" Jerome leaned over to stroke Rascal and Mischief as they walked.

"Yeah, but she's hiding it. She don't want to worry us. Grandpa Steve will know what to do."

The boys ran to the apartment behind the Police Department where Steve had been living since Todd's marriage. They took the steps two at a time, knocked on the door and held their breath until it opened.

"Josh? Jerome?" Steve was pulling on his jacket. "Trouble, or didn't your grandmother give you breakfast this morning?" Steve smiled at the boys, but expected a serious answer. He knew they wouldn't risk being late for school for anything trivial.

"I'm not sure," said Josh, "but we need to talk to someone."

"Sure. Want to come in, or would you rather talk as I drive you to school?"

Josh and Jerome both looked relieved. "If you don't mind, we'd rather talk on the way," said Josh.

"Yeah, so we won't be late," added Jerome.

"Okay, now tell me what's bothering you." Steve started the car while the boys fastened their seat belts.

"It's Grandma," said Josh, who took the front passenger seat. Jerome shared the back seat with Rascal and Mischief. "She's so tired all the time—hardly ever smiles anymore."

"I've noticed. Any ideas?"

"Yeah," both boys answered together. Jerome leaned forward resting his elbows on the back of Josh's seat.

"Rascal and Mischief woke me a couple of times and I'm sure I heard the phone ring. Sometimes it rings again before I get back to sleep. I think Grandma gets so many phone calls every night that she can't sleep." Josh looked up at Steve with his brown eyes wide and fearful.

"We think it's *him*," said Jerome.

"She pretends nothing is wrong," Josh said.

"But, we know she's hurting," finished Jerome.

"You might be right, boys—probably are. Thank you for telling me. I'll take care of it this morning."

"You won't get in trouble, will you?"

Steve laughed. "Maybe, but I can handle it."

"We'll tell her it was our fault if she gets mad at you," said Jerome.

"Here's the school. Don't you worry. I'll stop by the house before I go to Glenville. She'll be all right. I'll see to that."

Forty-Six

Susan left shortly after the boys and Laura straightened the kitchen then started to the living room. She'd told Susan she was going to work at home and wouldn't need a ride. She really needed to get another car, but just couldn't think about it yet.

Tomorrow is Thanksgiving, thought Laura. I have to speak at the community Thanksgiving Service tonight, but why does my mind feel as if I just received a shot of Novocain at the base of my skull?

Glancing around the room, Laura suddenly felt as if she was in a stranger's home. Nothing looked familiar. Dizziness began to envelope her almost as bad as the day her car went over the mountain. Was she having some kind of flashback? Tears began to cascade, unbidden down her face. She wanted to run, but felt like a frozen statue, not even sure she was breathing. Why am I having a panic attack?

The door opened and Rascal and Mischief wrapped themselves around her ankles. Steve saw the tears and the look of panic in her eyes. With two long strides, he had her in his arms.

"Laura?"

Laura heard his voice as if in the distance but couldn't focus on who was talking or what he wanted. She began shivering and he slipped out of his jacket, put it around her shoulders and led her back to the kitchen where he sat her on a chair.

"Sit here while I get a cup of hot tea for you."

As much as she wanted to protest, Laura couldn't even nod. Thanks to the microwave, Steve soon had a cup of hot tea loaded with sugar in her hands. He cupped his own hands around hers so she wouldn't drop the cup and held it to her lips so she could sip the warm, sweet brew. She shivered again.

Finally, she managed to speak. "I'm all right," she said, "I felt dizzy for a minute and I was afraid…" She didn't have to finish. He had been there.

"Laura, what's going on? Why are you so tired? This isn't the first time I've noticed. Maybe you better go see Doctor Jonathan."

"I'm all right," she said again as if trying to convince someone—maybe herself. She got up and put her cup in the sink. But she wasn't all right. She wanted to scream at him to leave her alone, but she didn't have even enough energy to be angry. "I just haven't been sleeping well lately," she said with her back to him.

Steve turned her around and lifted her chin so she had to look into his eyes. "Are you worried about the wedding? About us? Afraid you're making a mistake?"

"Oh, Steve, no. Not that."

"Then what?"

Laura took a deep breath, and managed to speak in a voice just above a whisper. "The phone. He calls three or four times an hour every night for several hours. I never know how often it will be. I can't let the phone wake Susan and Josh."

Steve gripped her arms a little more tightly than he intended. Through clenched teeth he asked, "How long has this been going on?"

She knew he was angry, but was too tired to understand why. Blinking, she answered, "I'm not sure—three, maybe four, weeks. I have to answer. It might be someone who really needs me. He knows that."

Steve clenched his teeth tighter and held her against him. She felt him taking deep breaths and knew he was going to yell at her. He was very quiet for about a count of ten, then softly he asked, "Why are you just now telling me about this?"

"I don't know. I guess I didn't think it was important. And it wasn't every night. He would skip a night or two and I thought it was over. Then he started again. Besides what can you do to stop a person from calling? I can't leave the phone off the hook."

"Laura, darling, I will chalk that comment up to pre-wedding nerves, because I know you are smarter than that. Don't you see what he's doing to you? He's killing you slowly with sleep deprivation and exhaustion. Well, I'll take care of that immediately."

"Steve, I…," she looked up into his eyes again. He wasn't angry, but neither was he teasing. "How…how could I be so stupid? I'm sorry. I don't know if I'm coming or going—too tired to think."

"Of course you are! That's what he wants. Now you march yourself upstairs and get back in bed. And you better be asleep when I come up, or I might have to crawl in with you to put you to sleep."

"I have to give the Thanksgiving message tonight. I can't go back to bed."

"Laura, my love, I know you better than that. You have had that message done for at least a week."

"Well, yes, but…"

"No buts. You're wasting precious time. Go." He turned her around and pointed her toward the steps. "I will be up to check on you in about five minutes."

Laura didn't argue further. He was right. She wouldn't be able to even go to the service, much less give the message, if she didn't get some rest. Her body was shutting down. It had to rest. She slipped out of her clothes and into her nightgown, which lay on the bed where she'd left it, unable to hang it up. When she crawled under the covers, Rascal and Mischief bounced onto the bed and snuggled on either side of her. There was no way she could get up if they decided to keep her there.

"Did he send you up here?"

They ignored her question and purred in stereo.

When Steve checked on her a few minutes later, she was sound asleep. Rascal and Mischief stretched to their full length on either side, protecting their human the best they could.

As he pulled the phone cord from the wall plug, he breathed a prayer of thanksgiving for those two devoted fur balls, and a prayer for protection for the woman he loved.

Back downstairs, Steve called the Glenville Station. "Joe, we've got more trouble over here." He explained the situation and what he was going to do. "Call my cell phone if you need me until I get this business straightened out."

"Are you sure you want to wait another month, Steve." Joe was genuinely concerned. "Maybe you better either just move in, or set the date up—like tomorrow. That man isn't going to give her a moment's peace. He's like a cat playing with a mouse."

"I hear you Joe. And believe me I'm tempted. And gossip or no gossip if he makes one more attempt, I'm moving in if I have to live in the basement. Right now, I'm going to call and get her an unlisted number. She will yell to high heaven, but it will stop the phone harassment. I'll work out something with

Dorothy so her folks can call. She just won't get a lot of travelers looking for handouts. The other churches can handle that."

"If you need me, you know where I am."

"Thanks, Joe."

Steve disconnected from Joe and called the phone company's office. He had Laura's number changed to an unlisted number then called Dorothy. He gave her the new number and told her why it was necessary.

"I knew she's been dragging lately, but she wouldn't say why, just that she wasn't sleeping well. I guess I just assumed it was nerves over the coming wedding. Sorry Detective, I should have been more observant. I'll try to do better."

"Dorothy, you are one in a million. You're a good friend as well as a good secretary. Thanks for all your help. Why don't you call some key folks and have them help you get the word out to the church folks without printing the new number anywhere."

"We'll take care of it."

Steve went upstairs to check on Laura. She was still sleeping—hadn't moved a muscle. The phone rang as he stepped from the bottom step. He grabbed it quickly. Who could have the number already? He'd only given it to Dorothy.

"Hello." He didn't identify himself.

"Detective, this is Dorothy. A man, who said he is Norman Stewart called. He said he was trying to get the pastor but the operator told him the number was disconnected. I took his number and said I would contact her to call him. It sounded like Susan's husband, but I only met him last spring at the picnic. I'm not taking chances with anyone. It could be that Jacobson man trying to get the new number."

"You're right, Dorothy. Good thinking. Give me the number and I'll call him. If it is Norman, he'll talk to me. If it's Jacobson, he'll know he has to deal with me."

Dorothy gave him the number. That's strange, he thought. That's a Glenville number—pay phone near the bus terminal. Norman is in still in Germany.

"Hello." The man sounded like Norman.

"You were calling Reverend Kenzel?" Steve still didn't identify himself.

"Steve, is that you? This is Norman. What's going on there? Is everything all right? Susan wrote me about Laura's accident a couple of weeks ago. I

192

decided I couldn't stay in Germany any longer while people I loved were in danger. I finished up early and left. I'm in Glenville and I sort of hoped someone could come and get me."

"Norman, welcome home. Yes, we've had some more trouble." He explained what had happened and why he couldn't leave right away. "But, I'll get you home some way," he said.

"I can wait here until Susan gets off work. Maybe she would…"

"Why don't you go across to Marie's and have a sandwich and coffee or something. Tell her to put it on my tab. Someone from the department will bring you over here. All right?"

"I don't want to be any trouble, but I am anxious to get home—well at least to Laura's home. I guess I don't have a home right now. We had to sell our home while we were in Germany. You wouldn't want a hoarder for a couple of days until I can find something, would you? Susan and I are talking, but I don't think she's ready for us to sleep in the same house, much less the same bed."

Steve laughed, "Sure Norman. Todd put me up more than once when he lived there. I guess I can do that for the man who is going to walk my bride down the aisle to meet me."

"I still can't believe she really wants me do that?"

"She's counting on you. Get your coffee. I'll call a friend over there who'll bring you to Cottonville. You don't mind riding in a cruiser do you?"

"A cruiser—as in Police Cruiser?"

"That's it."

"Well, I've never ridden in one before. If I can sit in the front not the back, maybe I won't look too much like a criminal." Norman laughed.

Steve laughed with him, then hung up and called Joe. He gave him the new number and asked him to get someone to bring Norman over to Cottonville.

Forty-Seven

Laura opened her eyes to see Steve's blue eyes twinkling at her. "You been sitting there long?" She sat up then threw her arms around his neck.

"Long enough," he said, returning her hug and letting their lips meet. "Do you feel better?"

"Much. Is it lunch time yet? I'm feeling a little empty."

He laughed.

"What?"

"Sweetheart, you slept through lunch. Dinner is on the table."

"Dinner? But…" She noticed the late afternoon shadows across the floor and turned to check the clock. "Five-thirty? Steve, I have to…"

"Relax. There's plenty of time. He held out her robe. "No point in getting dressed until after dinner."

"But…Susan and Josh. What will they think? What did you tell them?"

"The truth."

"You should have gotten me up before they came home."

"Why? They're family. They need to know what's happening. If you don't care enough about me, or them, to let us in on your private wars…" He didn't want to be angry with her again, so he stopped—too late.

Laura glared, took a deep breath, and exhaled slowly. "Of course you're right. I should have said something sooner. I do care about you and Susan and Josh. I want you to fight my wars; make them go away; take me away to paradise. But, I have to fight some in my own way."

"I'm sorry I yelled. Let's go downstairs. We have company."

"Company? Steve, who…? I should get dressed."

"You're fine—only family."

Josh's excited voice reached her before she even got to the bottom step. She gave Steve a curious glance. Who was Josh talking to? Then she heard Norman's voice.

194

"Norman?" Steve nodded and she hurried to the kitchen. Norman all five foot ten inches of him stood by the sink with an arm around Josh. His hairline was receding before he left for Germany, now what he had left, was streaked with gray. He had grown a beard to look older over there, but now was clean-shaven again. His dark eyes lifted from his son to see Laura in the doorway. She saw pain and relief mingled. He released Josh and had her in his arms in two long strides.

"Norman, it's so good to see you, but you weren't coming until next week sometime."

"Well, I kept hearing all these horror stories about what was happening to my favorite mother-in-law and I had to come home to get in on some of the fun."

"You're welcome to all of it if you want it— no, second thought I wouldn't wish my misfortune on anyone."

Susan watched her mother, throughout supper, but didn't say anything. Laura decided she needed to explain—and apologize for trying to *protect* them.

"Susan, Josh," she began, paused, took a deep breath, and exhaled. "I owe you an apology. It was wrong of me to try to carry this latest load alone, when you were both so willing to help. I don't have any excuse. I…"

"That's all right, Grandma. It's that man's fault. Some day we'll get him and he'll be sorry."

"Josh, I know you're angry. I am too, but don't hold on to it. Don't let anger for a no good jerk like Bill Collins destroy you. He will have to answer for his actions."

"I know Grandma, but I don't like him, especially when he hurts you. I love you too much."

"Come here Josh." Laura opened her arms for him.

"Always let that love be your greatest emotion. Don't let your anger overshadow it—ever. You understand?"

"I think so, but it's so hard."

"Maybe you need to learn a little game I used to play when I was your age, Josh." Norman reached for his son.

"What kind of game, Dad?"

'When I felt myself hating someone, I tried to think of something about them I liked. If I didn't like anything, I pretended that person was really someone special a wicked witch turned into a mean ogre. Then I loved the special person and ignored the ogre."

"That sounds like an idea, Josh," said Laura. "Even Bill Collins was once a tiny baby created by God. He was once a minister who must have helped some folks along the way. He made lots and lots of wrong choices. Now he can't see they're wrong."

"Is that why you don't call him by his real name?"

Laura looked startled then smiled. "I guess I hadn't given it any thought, Josh, but that's probably true. Bill Collins I know, Colin Jacobson is only a name to me."

"I hope I can be as smart as you some day. And I hope God loves me as much as he loves you."

"Oh, He does, Josh. He does."

Susan excused herself and left the table, but Laura saw her tears. Norman followed her out of the room.

"Can I go see if Jerome is going to church tonight?" Laura smiled, glad that Josh was still enough of a child that he couldn't dwell long on the horrible happenings, but jumped immediately to what he could do with his friend. Since Susan and Norman weren't there, Laura gave him permission to go, then began to clear the table.

"I'll clear things while you dress," said Steve. He reached for her as she started toward the door.

"Laura…" Words stuck in his throat.

She turned, looking into his eyes, waiting for him to finish.

"What can I say, except ditto to what Josh said?"

"Steve, you are…"

He put a finger to her lips. "Go get dressed."

Forty-Eight

Thanksgiving passed with no further incidents from Jacobson—at least none that were detectable. A decorated tree stood in a corner of the Alpha Room; lights and candles glowed throughout the church mixing with greenery. Angels kept vigil from their perches on the wall. Silver flying angel mobiles watched from the ceiling.

Laura's favorite was the crèche on the altar. She often sought quiet moments alone—well almost alone—meditating near the crèche. Rascal and Mischief sat on a front pew on either side of her like statues appearing to meditate with her.

"Pastor, are you all right?"

Startled, Laura jerked around. Rascal and Mischief didn't move or even blink. "What? Oh, Dorothy."

"I didn't mean to startle you," said Dorothy, "but you seemed so troubled." Dorothy had learned to ask that question often, since the "sleep episode." Her pastor would try to *go it alone* when there was trouble.

"I guess I was lost in a time warp somewhere between here and that long ago Bethlehem night. Did you say something?"

"I asked if you're all right. With the wedding coming up day after tomorrow and everything I thought maybe…"

"Maybe I was getting ready to go off the deep end again?" She smiled at the chubby woman who had become far more than a secretary to her.

"Well, the thought crossed my mind. I really don't have time to pick up the pieces and put them back together. So, I thought I would try to catch you before you fly apart." She laughed.

"You're very perceptive, Dorothy. I guess I am getting more than a little nervous. I'm glad Bishop Giles will be preaching Sunday morning. I don't think I could stand long enough to do it."

"Weak, rubbery knees?"

"Something like that. Now I really know how young brides feel. I didn't have a wedding ceremony the first time—only a judge at the courthouse."

"I'm sure you have a different view of marriage and its responsibilities than you did then."

"Yes, and sometimes I feel guilty that I should be so blessed."

"Why? Don't you think you deserve happiness as much as anyone else does?"

"No, I guess, I really don't." Laura answered honestly.

"Pastor, if anyone deserves happiness, you do. You've earned it the hard way. How many times have you told us, God doesn't put a price tag on his gifts to us? The only price has already been paid at Calvary. Accept His gift and enjoy it."

"Dorothy, maybe we should trade places. You be the preacher and I the secretary. I'm surprised that anyone even remembers any of the words I've spoken."

"We remember what touches us and what is important. And don't even think about switching jobs. I've seen your typing."

"Dorothy!" Laura laughed with her. They were quiet for a minute. "I love Christmas," said Laura. "I like to come in here and just be near the crèche—you know put myself in there, hold the Christ Child to my heart like His mother did, brush the tears from the eyes of that young girl giving birth with her mother so far away, assuring Joseph all will be well. I guess I'm a hopeless romantic."

"You might be a romantic, Pastor," said Dorothy swiping at her tears, "but hopeless? Never. Don't ever change. That's what makes you so special. That, too, is a gift that God has given you. You can enjoy not only the present, but also the past and the future. Your detective man better know how lucky he is or I'll…"

The male voice startled them. "You'll what, Dorothy?" Rascal Mischief blinked, looked at Steve then turned back to Laura and Dorothy.

"I don't know what I'll do, but believe me you'll wish you'd paid better attention!"

Steve laughed as he approached the women.

"We didn't hear you come in. You've been eavesdropping on us," accused Laura.

"Not eavesdropping, just marveling at the wisdom and beauty of my future wife."

"Now there's a man who knows how to appreciate God's gifts, Pastor. You better latch onto him fast. If you don't, I just might take a crack at it myself." Dorothy gave her a hug and started back to her office.

"Dorothy, did you want something, or were you just checking up on me?"

"Just checking," she said and left humming *Joy to the World.*

Steve sat beside Laura and took her hand. "She is truly a friend. I see now why you appreciate her. And she's right, you know."

"About what?"

"Everything she said—you deserving happiness, me appreciating the gift God has given me through you. You *are* a hopeless romantic, but don't ever change. Keep seeing those visions, holding the Christ Child, comforting the mother and the poor, bewildered Joseph. You make the Word of God more real to others when you can do that."

"Steve, are you as scared as I am?"

"More."

She threw her arms around his neck and kissed him.

"What was that for?"

"For being you. For being here. For just—just, loving me through your fear." He kissed her back

"Ditto," he said. "Are you about ready to go for lunch? I'm in no hurry. Just stopped by because I needed to stare at my beautiful bride-to-be."

"Steve!" Her face reflected joy as well as embarrassment. Rascal and Mischief plopped down on their bellies and covered their faces with their paws.

"Let's go," said Steve when he stopped laughing. "The bishop will be here in a couple of hours."

"I'm leaving, Dorothy," Laura called as she grabbed her coat and purse. "Call me if you need anything."

"Sure thing. See you Sunday."

A powdery dusting of snow lay on the steps, sidewalk, and ground. Rascal and Mischief bounced down the steps scattering the snow with each step then chasing the flakes as they fell around them.

"Car's over here—or we can walk and I'll come back later for it."

"Let's walk, if you really don't mind. I love snow for Christmas, but what if we get snowed in and can't get away? What if the bishop can't get to his daughter's. What if…"

"Laurance Ellen Kenzel, you stop the what ifs right this minute."

"But…"

"No, buts either."

She stopped walking, opened her mouth to complain about him ordering her around then started laughing. "I almost did it again."

"What did you almost do?"

"Push a childish argument over something we can do nothing about anyway."

"True. We won't worry about it. If we are snowed in, we'll have a warm place to stay and we'll still have each other. And somehow, I think the bishop can take care of himself. If he can't, he has Helen."

They were almost home when a sudden chill sent a shiver across her. Rascal and Mischief hissed and ran toward the trees.

Steve hadn't seen the cats leave, but felt the shiver. He laid the back of his hand against her forehead. "Laura, are you all right? You aren't coming down with something are you? You don't seem to have a fever."

"No, I'm all right. I just felt…I felt him nearby. Is this cat and mouse game ever going to stop?" Rascal and Mischief returned shaking their fur back in place.

Steve couldn't give her the answer she wanted, so he put his arm around her shoulders and drew her closer to him, held her for a minute, then started walking again.

"What time is Bishop Giles arriving?"

"I'm not sure," answered Laura. "Sometime in the next couple of hours— before dinner. Sophia wants to help cook, so I'll let her. Todd, Carolyn and Jerome will be there."

"With Norman and Susan, sounds like we'll have a houseful." Steve laughed and tugged her hand. "Maybe we better get there before the crowd arrives.

Laura glanced at her watch. "We better hurry if we're going to have lunch before everyone starts coming and Sophia and I have to start dinner. I think school will be out early for the Christmas holiday."

Even so, Laura and Steve took their time leisurely strolling home.

Forty-Nine

Sophia and Laura were in the kitchen preparing vegetables for a salad when Susan and the boys came in. Grabbing a snack Josh and Jerome ran upstairs to Josh's room—"to get out of the way," said Josh.

"And keep from being put to work," added Jerome.

Rascal and Mischief passed them on the steps and sat at the top grinning at them.

Sophia had two pans of lasagna all ready to go into the oven. Carolyn would be home a little later and prepare the loaf of Italian bread with garlic butter for toasting in the oven with the lasagna.

Steve and Norman decided to follow the example of the boys and stay out of the way. They sat in the living room talking about Norman's experiences in Germany; Steve's work, both in Glenville and with the FBI; and the boys, how they were coping with all the violence they had seen and experienced. They heard the car stop then pull into the driveway. Both men rose to answer the doorbell that was sure to ring.

Rascal flew down the steps and stood staring at the door. When the bell rang, he stood on his back legs and wrapped his front paws around the doorknob to open the door for their company.

"How does he do that?" Norman knew the cat could open doors but had never seen him in action.

"Strong front paws with an extra digit, I suppose," said Steve, "plus his higher than usual intelligence."

A feeling of déjà vu swept over him as Steve saw the Afro-American couple standing on the porch. The man was tall, clean-shaven except for a small mustache. His wire-framed glasses gave him a scholarly look.

This time, however, Bishop Matthew Giles brought a small suitcase for their weekend visit. He wore a long, gray woolen overcoat, and felt hat. Helen, neat and trim as before, wore a bright red coat with a double row of buttons down the front. She had a white angora hat pulled down over her ears, but her shoulder length hair curved beneath it. A big smile lit up her face as Steve opened the door wider for them.

"Come in," said Steve, reaching for the suitcase. "I hope you had a pleasant trip."

"All except that mountain," said Helen. "Did I hear someone say the last time we were here that you are getting a new road—one that misses the mountain?"

"Eventually," said Steve. "The highway department is working on it. It'll come through the valley from Glenville, around the mountain and hook onto Main Street west of town. Eventually it will expand to connect to the interstate, giving us a closer route both east and west."

Laura came in to greet them and introduce Norman and Susan then re-introduce the others. "Dinner won't be ready for about an hour," she said. "We just put the lasagna in the oven."

"That sounds wonderful," said Helen. "I wouldn't mind just visiting and letting the vibration of riding for hours have a chance to settle."

"Would you care for some coffee while we wait?"

"Thank you, but only if it's no extra bother," said Bishop Giles.

"It's already brewed," said Steve. "I'll get it."

"Well, Laura," Bishop Giles chided as he settled on the couch with his coffee in hand, "What happened to the running report I asked for in August?"

Laura felt embarrassed and mumbled something about being busy.

Bishop Giles smiled. "Well, I'm not entirely in the dark. Your husband-to-be has kept me informed and up to date."

Laura was surprised, then angry. "Bishop, I don't know what Steve has told you, but…"

"I've told him every thing, Laura. I knew you wouldn't and he needed to know. I've been writing to him regularly."

"And you didn't tell me?" Weeks and months of taut nerves made it suddenly impossible to keep her anger in check.

"Laura…" Steve started.

"Don't Laura me. What about all those pep talks about honesty and…"

"Uh-oh, looks like you opened a can of worms, Matthew, dear," said Helen. "Maybe we better take a walk so they can work this out."

"No," said Steve clenching his teeth the way he did when he was too angry to talk. "We were just going out ourselves. You relax with your coffee. We'll be back in a few minutes."

Laura clamped her jaw shut and turned away from Steve, intending to stalk out of the room. Catching the embarrassment in the bishop's eyes and compassion in Helen's, she thought better of it. She and Steve had to get this settled and there was no point in making a production out of it in front of reluctant witnesses—her Bishop yet!

Grabbing her coat from the closet, Laura ran out the door, closing it before Steve could follow her. He zipped his jacket and ran after her.

Rascal and Mischief, upstairs with Josh and Jerome heard the door open. They leaped over the boys and down the steps three at a time, following Steve out the door. Whipping their tails around them, they barely missed getting them caught in the door as he closed it. Rascal trotted along side Laura and Mischief stayed with Steve. Laura noticed their bushy fur, but assumed it was because of Steve's angry tone.

Laura turned toward the park as fast as she could walk. Steve caught up with her, grabbed her arm, and swung her around to face him.

"Laura, don't..."

"Just leave me alone," she said between clenched teeth. Fighting the anger, she jerked away from him and kept walking. They walked side by side in silence until they neared the park.

Once again, Steve stopped, gripped Laura's shoulders and turned her to face him. Refusing to look at him, Laura stared down at the ground

"Laura, please look at me." The anger was gone; his voice almost trembled with compassion. He waited.

Slowly, Laura lifted her head until their eyes met. She loved those blue eyes that so often twinkled—but not tonight. He wasn't teasing; he was serious. Her own brown eyes began to sting with tears she refused to shed.

Rascal and Mischief had fallen behind chattering to one another. Suddenly, they began to run like thoroughbreds in the final lap of the race. They threw themselves against Steve's back—all 8 paws and forty pounds of cat—sending him off balance. His arms went around Laura and they both fell to the ground. A shot echoed across the ballpark. A bullet whistled past them.

It all happened so quickly that as they told it later, neither Steve, nor Laura, could say for sure which happened first. Vaguely they remembered a thud as the bullet embedded itself into a tree.

By the time Steve got his phone out of his pocket, Todd was already there. "I saw Rascal and Mischief run after you," he said as he gave Steve a hand up. "I knew something was up—something more than your spat."

"Grandma?"

"Pastor?"

Josh and Jerome, ignoring their mothers, had seen the cats' bushy fur, also, and followed. They ran to her and fell on her, choking her with their hugs.

"I'm all right boys," she said, not sounding at all like she was. "Rascal and Mischief knocked us down."

"He…shot at you." Josh looked toward the woods where searchers with flashlights moved around and called to one another.

"And he got away again," said Jerome.

"Mom?" Susan, pale and shaking from more than just the cold, looked down at Laura still on the ground. Norman reached a hand to Laura.

"I'm all right," Laura said. "Take the boys back before they catch cold without their coats."

"I can see why you didn't have time to write." Bishop Giles stood with an arm around Helen.

"I'm sorry, Bishop. I…"

"Don't try to explain here. We'll talk when you get back to the house. Come on Helen, before *you* catch cold." Following the rest back to the house, the Giles left Laura and Steve to finish their argument.

Laura pulled her coat tighter around her, but still trembled—not entirely from the cold. Steve wrapped his arms around her.

"Laura…" he started

"Steve…" she started at the same time.

Together they said, "I'm sorry," then smiled at each other. They needed no other words. When Todd arrived a few seconds later from the woods, they were in a tight embrace, lips together.

"Are you two frozen together? Shall I get something to thaw you apart?"

"I think the ice is broken." Steve laughed as he released Laura.

"He got away again, didn't he?" Laura didn't need to ask. Todd didn't need to answer.

"He's getting bolder," said Todd.

"He's determined to prevent this wedding," said Steve.

"Maybe we better just have the bishop do it at home and not expose the folks at the church to possible terror." Laura looked at Steve then Todd and back to Steve who was studying her.

"Is that what you really want? To let him know he has won at least a major battle?" Steve wasn't angry; he wanted her to think about what she was saying.

"No, I just don't want anyone else to be hurt—or killed." Laura was still trembling.

"Laura, I don't think it will make any difference to Jacobson," said Todd. "He is mentally deranged and you can't be rational with him."

"I think Todd's right," said Steve. "We'll take every precaution possible. With every available officer from Glenville, Cottonville, and the entire county sheriff's department, we'll cover every inch of the area. Thank goodness, there's only one road into town. We'll have that blocked."

"You want me to call Mark to swing by here and give you a ride back?" Todd saw Laura shiver.

"No, I need to walk," she answered. "He won't try again right away. Walking clears my mind."

"All right, see you back at the house." Todd turned and jogged back.

"I owe the bishop an apology," said Laura, taking Steve's hand. "I should have kept him informed, but somehow everything was too horrible to put it in writing. I guess I was being an ostrich. If I didn't admit any of it on paper, it really didn't happen."

"Laura, I shouldn't have written to him without your knowledge. I knew you would feel that way, but he needed to know what was happening." Steve squeezed her hand as they walked.

"I understand. I really do. I was angry, I guess, because I knew you were right and I was wrong and…"

"And I showed you up in front of your bishop," he finished for her.

She stopped and lifted her face to him. Unshed tears sparkled on her eyelashes. "I guess that sounds about right. I'm sorry I…"

She didn't finish the sentence. Snow had begun to fall in giant fluffy flakes, landing on her nose and eyelashes. "It's so beautiful," she whispered. "Thank You."

Steve knew she wasn't talking to him, but that was all right. He agreed with her, except he thought his view was more beautiful.

Laura let Steve explain what had happened while she went to change into warm, dry slacks and sweater.

"Laura, dear," said Helen, as Laura came down the steps, "I'm so sorry for all that you are going through, but I do envy you your faith and courage."

"Faith I have, Helen, but courage is a little shaky right now. But, enough of Colin Jacobson. I'm not going to let him spoil our wedding. Now, until dinner is ready, we aren't going to talk about anything more than wedding plans and what's happening around the conference."

"That's an excellent idea," responded Bishop Giles. "I know it's a little late, but you should have some counseling before the wedding. Maybe after dinner we can go some place where just the three of us can talk."

"We can go to my office," said Laura, not really wanting to go out again.

"Or my apartment," said Steve.

"Or you can just stay here," said Norman. "Susan and I and Todd and Carolyn are going to take the boys for a ride around town to see the Christmas lights." Norman's smile was the brightest Laura had ever seen. The short separation had been good for both of them. She was glad to see them together again.

"Care to join us Helen?"

"That sounds like a lovely idea. I haven't gone out just to see Christmas lights in years."

"You've never seen Christmas lights at all until you see Cottonville," laughed Carolyn. "We do all the holidays up to the max. Almost every home in town has some kind of display."

"Then it's settled," said Norman.

"Now, let's eat," said Sophia coming in from the kitchen. "Dinner is on the table."

* * *

Bishop Giles, Laura, and Steve settled down to talk about the things she had talked with Todd and Carolyn about several months earlier. Somehow, it felt different when she was on the receiving end of the questions.

Because of their ages and different backgrounds, it was necessary to review Steve's first marriage that had ended in divorce in less than a year. "It was a marriage that should never have happened," said Steve. "Vivian seemed lonely and her folks were in West Virginia. I wondered why she wasn't with them, but learned later that she had run away. Anyway, to make a long story short, she said she was pregnant—not by me—and begged me to marry her to give her baby a name. She said we could get an annulment later and like the stupid kid that I was, I believed her. I had my life planned and what would it hurt to stop long enough to help a poor girl in distress."

Steve stared into space and unconsciously reached for Laura's hand.

"Didn't work out that way," he continued. "She wasn't pregnant; had no intention of getting an annulment. She just wanted to make E. J.—whoever that was—jealous. I tried to make the best of it, but I wouldn't sit back and let her run around with every man in town. She fought the divorce, but in a small town, everyone knows everyone else's business. Folks knew me and didn't know her—except by reputation. She lost. It was a nasty divorce and I determined once I had that decree of divorce in my hands that I would never let that happen again. I never looked at another woman until…" Steve grinned and squeezed Laura's hand. "There was nothing helpless about this one."

"Was your marriage so good that it will cause problems?" Bishop Giles looked to Laura. "Sometimes a widow finds herself comparing…" He stopped. Laura was shaking her head.

"Sorry, Bishop," she said, "but, my marriage to Harold was a matter of convenience—his not mine. He only wanted a showpiece—someone to stand beside him at community and church events; someone to help him when it would make him look good. Because of my jokester uncle, Harold believed I was pregnant when we married. I wasn't then, but I was after he took me to a motel to consummate our marriage—the only time he did. He would never believe Susan was his daughter."

Laura didn't look at Steve, but appreciated the pressure of his hand on hers.

"I guess I stayed with him because I'd made a commitment and because he took good care of Susan and me. I'd seen too many young girls trying to raise a child on their own. Most of the time, it didn't bother me. I learned to help with some counseling, hospital and nursing home calls—things that Harold didn't want to do. I learned a lot about the church and fulfilled my desire to work in it until…"

"Until?"

"I felt the call to ministry. I knew Harold wouldn't approve, but decided that I would go to seminary with or without his blessing. He was killed before we had a chance to talk. Sometimes I regret that I didn't stand up to him. Maybe we could have…"

"Laura, you can't undo, or redo, the past. We go on from here. Obviously you and Steve have talked about many things, and have learned how to handle differences." Bishop Giles smiled at her.

"We are learning. It's not easy starting over at this stage of life, but then everyday is a new beginning anyway. We'll make it." She squeezed Steve's hand and grinned at him.

"We both have come a long way, Bishop," said Steve, "and we recognize we have a long way to go—hopefully many years to grow together."

"I understand now more about the evil power at work here, and we'll certainly be keeping you both in our prayers."

Bishop Giles offered a prayer for them, knowing that there was a great chance Colin Jacobson alias Bill Collins would show up at the wedding Sunday to wreak havoc.

Fifty

Saturday morning began with gray skies but soon the sun was bright, the snow melted, and the roads clear. A good omen, thought Laura as she prepared breakfast for her guests. It will be a beautiful day. We'll have a perfect rehearsal. She smiled as she beat the batter for pancakes. She could always dream.

By the time all the parties involved gathered at the church, however, things weren't quite so perfect. It seemed to Laura that everyone's nerves were stretched tighter than the wire holding the tree in the corner of Alpha Room. Everyone was on tiptoes to keep the line taut. Maybe it's not *everyone*, she thought. Maybe it's just me and they're afraid I will fall apart. She glanced at Steve who was watching her with a look of concern.

"Steve…is…is everything all right?"

"As far as I know," he answered.

"Then why is everyone so tense? Even Bishop Giles is frowning."

Steve sucked in a deep breath, took her hand, and looked into those brown eyes he loved so much. "I think we might have too many preachers and not enough brides."

"What do you mean?" Anger flared. Then suddenly Laura paled as she realized she had been trying to do it all—even telling Bishop Giles how to perform the ceremony.

"I just want our wedding to be perfect," she whispered.

"The only thing that will make it perfect is having you say, 'I do.'"

Bishop Giles joined them and Laura wanted to hide—to run away—but she knew she had to say something. "Bishop…I'm sorry…I guess I…"

A sudden commotion drew their attention to the Alpha Room. Laura felt the blood drain from her face. Had Jacobson somehow…?

Then everyone laughed and looked up at the balcony surrounding the room. Suddenly the laughter turned to groans and ohs. Laura held her breath, and knew that others were too. Rascal and Mischief sashayed along the railing, tails held high. They stopped, did a little dance, turned a summersault and continued to dance their way to the corner where the short two-foot, strong, tight wire held the Christmas tree steady.

"They aren't going to go to the tree," Laura said barely above a whisper. Steve tightened his grip on her shoulders. "It looks like they are," he said.

Laura wanted to call to them to stop, but her heart throbbed in her throat. She could only cling to Steve and watch.

While everyone held their breath, Mischief tiptoed across the wire and disappeared into the tree. When she was safe in the tree, Rascal followed. Throughout the room not a sound was heard until two fur balls rolled out from under the tree, each with a piece of tinsel on an ear. They bounced to their feet, did an exaggerated bow then covered their mouths with paws while emitting a sound like, "Yuk, yuk, yuk!"

The room exploded into laughter and applause. The tense atmosphere was gone. The rehearsal continued much more smoothly.

"There will be no problems tomorrow," stated Bishop Giles confidently when they were finished.

"I hope you're right," Laura commented. Somehow, she knew there *would* be trouble.

"Reverend Kenzel," said Bishop Giles, "I am *The Bishop*. If I say there will be no problems, then there will be no problems!"

Amid the laughter, Laura pushed the fear and foreboding to the back of her mind. I won't worry. The only entrance to the town and every church entrance will be covered. The cats will cover the inside. Police officers from both Cottonville and Glenville will be on hand, some inside the church, some outside. Even Jacobson can't possibly get his black Cadillac past the roadblock.

A nagging sixth sense told her Jacobson *would* find a way. He *will* make an appearance. He *will* do something. If I could only figure out what.

* * *

Long after everyone had gone to bed, Laura sat in her darkened room by her window staring into the night. Stars twinkled. Fresh snow was falling. Her thoughts automatically flew to the Psalms. *O Lord, our Lord, how excellent is Your name in all the earth...enemies surround me...how long O lord...how long...? I waited patiently for the Lord... He heard my cry... Be still and know that I am God.*

Laura sat motionless, conscious only of the presence of God. She knew He was there, but she longed for the soft chuckle that would tell her everything was all right. She longed for assurance that those she loved would be safe. She longed for the peace of Christmas to fill her soul. She felt only sadness.

Visions from the Gospels moved about in her semi-conscious musings—the journey of Mary and Joseph to Bethlehem; their flight to Egypt; a vivid vision of Jesus praying in the garden. She saw the sweat like great drops of blood fall from his brow. She saw the anguished, distorted face as he cried out, "Let this cup pass from me." She saw that same face relax into a peaceful, acceptance as he said, "but, not my will, but yours be done."

Laura knew what she had to do. She fell to her knees beside her chair and prayed as she had heard Jesus pray. When she rose, she knew that she too would be sorely tried, beaten, and maybe even die, but she now had the peace she longed for. Whatever she had to endure, God would be with her and her loved ones. She could ask for no more than that.

Fifty-One

Sleep came quickly and easily until Rascal and Mischief let her know it was breakfast time—at least for them. Pulling her plush, green terry robe around her and sliding her feet into waiting matching slippers, Laura said to her furry friends, "Well, guys, this is the day. Let's get started."

By the time Laura descended the stairs, Rascal and Mischief were beside their dishes waiting for their breakfast. Cats fed, coffee made, Laura took her shower and settled with her coffee and Bible. It was still only a little past six when she rose from her chair and went for her second cup of coffee. She stopped by the phone, hesitated, then picked it up and dialed.

"Hello," a sleepy Steve answered.

"Happy birthday, darling," she said.

"Laura? Is everything all right?"

"I was up early and wanted to call you. You don't mind?"

"Of course not. It's the first time anyone ever called me at six o'clock in the morning to wish me a happy birthday. Come to think of it, I don't remember anyone *ever* calling me at any time of the day to wish me a happy birthday. I even forgot I'd told you it was today."

"Want to come over for breakfast?"

"Should I? Everyone keeps saying the groom shouldn't see the bride before the wedding. It's supposed to be bad luck, or something."

"Steve, with Jacobson hounding us, what could possible be worse? At any rate, I think he will show up whether we see each other, or not. And it *is* Sunday, so how are we going to avoid seeing each other if we go to church?"

"Laura," he laughed, "do you want me to come over for breakfast?"

"Yes, I guess I do. I need to talk."

"Not backing out are you?" He tried to sound like he was teasing, but she could hear the fear in his voice.

"Sorry, pal, you aren't going to get rid of me that easily."

"Be there by the time you have sausage and eggs on the table."

Rascal and Mischief ran to meet Steve before the door opened. Laura set breakfast on the table. "We have maybe a half hour before the others are up," she said.

"Something is bothering you. Want to tell me?"

She told him about her vision then asked, "Did Colin Jacobson know Vivian?"

"Where did that come from?" He laughed uneasily.

"I don't know—something you said the other night when we talked with Bishop Giles. Something about her making E. J. jealous."

"Yeah, but…"

"Could she have said C. J. not E. J.? It was a long time ago."

"I don't know. You're right, it was so long ago, I hardly remember…but now that you mention it, she did know the Jacobsons. I remember her saying something about them being losers—except one, who had a crush on her. You don't think…"

"It would make sense. If he had thought he had a chance with her and she dumped him, or completely rejected him for you…and then I…"

"Did the same thing? Laura you might be right. But, surely he hasn't carried a grudge like that around for thirty years!"

"Maybe not so intensely, but when circumstances began adding up and he learned we were getting serious, it brought it all back with a vengeance."

"Laura. How can we stop a warped mind like that?"

"I don't know. I don't think *we* can. We just have to trust and…"

"I don't like where that can lead."

"Neither do I, but it is all I can do at this point—that and prepare as best we can, which I know you and Todd have done. The cats will be there, but I worry about them. I'm sure he will try something to disable, or kill them. Maybe I should leave them home."

Steve grinned at her and said, "Oh yeah? You and what army?"

She laughed. "Then again, maybe I won't. They will be able to take care of themselves unless he shoots, and surely he won't do that in the church."

"I hope you're right, my love. I hope you're right."

The phone rang causing her to jump.

"Jumpy this morning, aren't we?" Steve laughed at her.

"Well, it *is* only a quarter to seven."

"Maybe I better get it in case…"

"No, I'll put it on the speakerphone."

She caught it on the third ring and pushed the speakerphone button.

"Good morning, Reverend Kenzel speaking."

"Tomorrow you will have to change that to Reverend Morgan speaking" laughed the familiar voice."

"Cora, how are you today?"

"I'm fine, Love. I won't be able to make it to the wedding. My heart is acting up again, but I had to call. Laura, God loves you so very much, you and that fine gentleman you are marrying. But, He told me to call because you need to be surrounded by prayers today. Gracious God," Cora began as always just jumping in, "this poor girl has been through so much. Surround her with your grace and your love. Give her your protection. Give her and Steve the assurance of your abiding love. Protect them and keep them safe. Amen."

"Thank you, Cora."

"Pastor, please be careful. Trust the Lord. He will see you through whatever happens."

The dial tone told her Cora was finished. She sighed deeply and looked up into Steve's eyes.

"She's never been wrong. He'll be there."

Steve said nothing. He just wrapped his arms around her and held tightly until a voice from the steps separated them.

"Are you two at it already this morning? Steve don't you know…?"

"I know, Susan. It's bad luck, but, like my beautiful bride-to-be reminded me, we are likely to have bad luck whether I see her or not."

"I hope you're wrong this time, but if past experiences mean anything…" Susan couldn't begin to put her thoughts into words. The rest soon gathered around the table, talking, laughing and even eating a bite now and then.

Fifty-Two

Bishop Giles would preach, and Fred Martin was the Liturgist, so Laura sat in the congregation with Steve. The cats settled on their second favorite perch—the organ, since Laura wasn't in the pulpit.

"I think they're falling in love with my organist," said Laura.

"I don't think George will let them take over." Steve laughed.

Steve hadn't said who all would be there from the Glenville Police Department, but Laura recognized several men from both Glenville and Cottonville. Some milled around outside. Most folks hardly knew police were present except as worshipers.

After church, Josh went home with Jerome and Norman went with Steve to his apartment. Susan and the cats accompanied Laura.

"Would you like a sandwich or soup or…" Susan started rummaging through the cupboards looking for something simple and easy to fix.

"I'm not sure I can eat anything, Susan. Maybe some tea and toast. I hope I'm not coming down with the flu or something."

Susan laughed but put her hand against her mother's brow. "No fever," she said. "I would say it's just a good case of bride's nerves with a little fear of what Jacobson will do thrown into the mix."

"You're probably right," said Laura. "I am concerned. He will try something. I know he will. I just hope I'll have the strength to stand up to whatever it is."

"Mother…," Susan threw up her hands in despair. What could she say to ease the worry when they all knew what Jacobson was like? "Surely he won't get past all the roadblocks and security in and around the church."

"I hope not Susan, but deep down, I know he will. Susan, whatever happens, keep a firm hold on Josh. Don't let him try to save me."

"Mother, you don't think…"

"I don't know what to think. Just keep your son safe."

"I will guard him with my life, if I must. I've learned that much from you in the last few months."

"Enough of this scary talk," said Laura. "Let's see if that white suit I bought two months ago still fits."

"I still think you should have gone for the traditional wedding dress with a long train and veil."

"Why? So Rascal and Mischief could play with the train or sit on it while I walk down the aisle dragging them along for the ride?"

Susan laughed and followed Laura upstairs to dress. The white wool suit was a perfect fit. Susan gave her a tiny bouquet of baby's breath for her hair. She swiped at the tears in her eyes as she watched in the dresser mirror behind Laura. "I can't believe you're my mother," she whispered. "You're so young and beautiful—more like my sister."

"Thank you for the compliment, but I feel every bit old enough to be your mother and maybe even your grandmother. Sometimes I wonder what Steve ever saw in me and why he…"

"He loves you," said Susan, "just as much as you love him. It's too bad you didn't meet when you were both younger, but you'll have a wonderful life together. You have a lot of years ahead of you."

"I hope so," whispered Laura. "I hope so." She shivered as if the evil presence of Jacobson had somehow seeped into the room. "Let's get back to the church," she said, hugging herself and rubbing her arms.

"You felt it too?" Susan said, shivering.

"Must be nerves," said Laura and they both tried to laugh it off. "Besides," said Laura, "I'm sure *some*one over there needs me to tell them what to do and how to do it."

* * *

Two o'clock Laura was back to oversee things—but found they really didn't need her. Martha had the kitchen under control. Karen, with George's help, was ready with the music. She certainly wasn't going to tell Bishop Giles how to do his job—again! Settling in her office with Rascal and Mischief, she tried to relax while they slept on the couch. Everything was peaceful and quiet. It was a beautiful day. Roads were clear. Snow was predicted for later, but folks would be able to come to the wedding and return home before the snow hit. What could possibly go wrong?

"Rascal, Mischief, what do you think? Is he going to show up? You will be careful if he does, won't you? I don't want you to get hurt in the process."

They opened their emerald green eyes and blinked at her, closed them and settled down for their nap. Laura chuckled in spite of her misgivings. Surely, she was worrying for nothing. It would be all right. The smells from the kitchen were wonderful. The sounds from the sanctuary were just as wonderful— music mingling with laughter and conversation. Laura leaned back in her chair and dozed.

Fifty-Three

Until the new road through the valley was opened sometime next summer, the only road into Cottonville went over Gopher Mountain Road. Glenville and Cottonville police set up roadblocks on each end of the mountain—a double check on cars leaving Glenville and entering Cottonville.

"What's the trouble?" More than one motorist asked as the police in Glenville asked to see a driver's license and registration. When they arrived in Cottonville and had to go through the same process, some got angry. "We're going to be late for the wedding."

"Sorry, folks, just a traffic check."

"Well, you could have chosen a better day than the Sunday before Christmas."

Most were patient as they went through the motions of doing what they were asked to do. Neither police department had sighted a black Cadillac driven by a large man in his early sixties, hazel eyes, thinning hair. Scars on his face and hands from cat scratches and a scar on his right hand or wrist, where Laura had shot him, would have further identified Jacobson.

Several cars waited on the Cottonville side while the young officers did a thorough check of each one. At last, the red Taurus with West Virginia plates moved to the checkpoint. The driver was possibly seventy-five or eighty, dark eyes, white hair, medium height and about one hundred sixty pounds. A blind man sat in the passenger seat; a large black Doberman Seeing Eye dog lay across the back seat.

"You folks new around here?" The police officer asked.

"We're here for the wedding," said the driver. "My cousin asked me to drive him up for our Cousin Laura's wedding. We haven't seen her for some time. Thought this was a good opportunity."

"Can I see your driver's license, please?"

"Sure." The man leaned forward to get his wallet from his hip pocket. Handing the license to the officer he asked, "You got a problem up this way, officer?"

"No, just doing some research." The young officer smiled as he read the name, "Thomas Calvin Sizemore, Glen Jean, West Virginia. I had an aunt that used to live in Whipple."

"I know the place—maybe even knew your aunt."

"Maybe so." The officer entered the name and registration number in his notebook and waved them on. "You folks have a good day," he said.

"Very good," said the blind man as they pulled away from the roadblock. "Now drive down the street to the right and I'll show you where you can park the car, then I'll pay you. How much did I say?"

"You offered me five grand," said the driver, "but you didn't say anything about roadblocks. You said you had information about my daughter's death. When are you going to give me that? This is more dangerous than I thought it would be. I just want to get my money and information and get out of here. I think ten grand is more like it."

"You will be well paid. Now pull in behind those trees by the park then I will give you what I promised."

The driver did as he was told. "Do I have to wait for you here? I'd rather get on back home."

"Yeah, you do that," said the blind man, who was Colin Jacobson in disguise. He pulled a gun with a silencer on it from his coat. "You wanted information well here it is old man. Your daughter was a slut. She ignored me, laughed at my attempts to woo her. Then she snagged that all-star hero, who didn't care a hoot about her. He kicked her out and she came running to me, as if I would be interested in used merchandise.

"You want to know what happened to her?" Jacobson asked the horrified, speechless man. He laughed at the fear in the old man's eyes as he pointed the gun at him.

"I gave her the same thing I have for you. Thanks for getting me through the roadblock." Jacobson smiled his crooked, wicked grin as he pulled the trigger, shooting Thomas Sizemore through the heart.

"Come on, Brutus," he said to the Doberman. "Let's go to a wedding."

He laughed his eerie laugh and hurried down the street, slowing his steps and letting the dog lead, tapping the street with his cane when he saw anyone near him. He arrived at the church. It was almost three o'clock—time for the wedding to begin. A few stragglers moved up the steps. He could hear the music playing as he started up the steps. The dog led him into the building, where he removed his coat and stood in the shadow of a doorway watching and waiting for the bride to appear before he made his move.

"Easy, Brutus," he firmly pulled on the dogs chain. "It won't be long, now."

Fifty-Four

One eye on the clock, the other on the cats, Laura paced anxiously. Rascal and Mischief, in their *catnap* positions on the organ, were her barometers of trouble. They seemed relaxed, but also wary. Suddenly alert, they sat up, ears twitching. Still wide eyed, they cased back, paws tucked under them, staring at the back of the sanctuary, ears turning like a radar screen. The organ started the pre-wedding music and the sanctuary began to fill, overflowing into the Alpha Room.

The Presbyterian Church tower clock sounded: Bong! Bong! Bong! Laura glanced at Norman and tried to smile, but something *felt* off—wrong. Carolyn and Susan, unaware of any tension other than their own fear of tripping, marched into the sanctuary. Jerome and Josh carried the rings. Bishop Giles, Steve and Todd waited at the altar.

Karen adjusted the stops on the organ for the *Wedding March*. Throughout the congregation, plain clothed officers from both Glenville and Cottonville scanned the room constantly. Joe sat with Clarissa near the back of the overflow, also scanning for trouble.

Norman squeezed Laura's arm and smiled at her. "Okay?" he whispered. Laura nodded, but felt as if her heart were going to explode.

Before Karen hit the first chord, Rascal and Mischief in synchronized action flew off the organ and sped down the aisle, hair bristling, tails straight up and three times their normal size. Steve and Todd saw them and without a word, both fell in behind the cats. Someone in the back row of the overflow screamed. Hisses and growls mixed with a dog barking as pandemonium erupted. Those in the sanctuary could see nothing and those in the overflow were helpless to stop the attack.

The blind man with his dog had moved as if to take a seat. Without warning, he pocketed the dark glasses, swung his cane around like a majorette twirling a baton, and caught the crook of it on Norman's ankle, pulling him to the floor.

He then kicked Norman in the side and hit him on the side of his head with the cane. The Doberman snarled, bared his teeth, and lunged for Norman's throat while he lay helpless on the floor. Rascal and Mischief flew at the dog.

Steve and Todd arrived on the heels of the cats, but the blind man—Colin Jacobson—had Laura around the waist with his left hand, his gun—minus the silencer—pressed against her right side.

The Doberman snarled at the cats, which spit and hissed back. They divided their prey and circled the big animal from two sides. The confused dog, snapped at Rascal; Mischief landed on his back. He shook her free and Rascal was at his head. Between the two of them, Rascal and Mischief scratched his eyes, nose, and even clawed his tongue. The poor dog yelped in pain and ran. Someone opened the door and he raced out. The cats stopped at the door as if an invisible barrier prevented them from going further. They turned back, but they, also, were too late. Jacobson, his arm tightly around Laura, a gun pressed to her ribs, was forcing Laura toward the sanctuary.

Joe moved to help Norman up.

"Don't anyone move a muscle or you will be picking up the pieces of your precious pastor," barked Jacobson. "Now tell that organist to play the *Wedding March.* And let's continue the wedding—with a change in the cast of players." His high-pitched manic laugh echoed around the sanctuary.

Karen's fingers froze over the keyboard then began to tremble. "I can't," she cried.

Jacobson fired a shot toward the organ, intentionally missing, but scaring Karen nonetheless. She screamed, as did several members of the congregation.

"I said play the *Wedding March*," he bellowed. "And if anyone so much as lifts a finger the next shot won't miss." He jabbed the gun back into Laura's side.

George jumped to the organ bench, slid Karen off the end and started playing something that sounded like a march—not the *Wedding March.* Colin Jacobson stared at him, shrugged, and started moving with Laura down the aisle toward Bishop Giles.

Norman, back on his feet, helped Todd and Joe hold Steve back.

"You can't rush him, pal," said Joe. "He'll kill her in a heartbeat."

"I can't just stand here and let him hurt her."

"He'll hurt her a lot worse if you try to grab him. We'll have to wait it out."

"The cats are slithering toward the front as we speak," whispered Todd. "I saw them slip under the pews on either side of him. When there is any opportunity, they'll be there."

Colin Jacobson marched to the altar with Laura, his face set with his evil grin. Carolyn, Susan and the boys stood like frozen statues. Jacobson stopped in front of Bishop Giles; George abandoned the keyboard and slid off the seat to wrap his arms around Karen.

"Well, Bishop, it was good of you to come and perform this little ceremony for my true love and me."

Steve with Todd, Norman, and Joe keeping him under control, followed and stood near the front pew. Laura knew they were there, but couldn't turn to look at them, and would not if she could. She needed all her power of concentration to do what she had to do.

"Collins, or Jacobson, or whatever your name is, you can't be serious." Bishop Giles was playing for as much time as he could, hoping for a miracle. What could anyone do?

"Oh, I am very serious, Bishop. Now cut the gab. Skip over all that stuff and nonsense and get to the wedding vows. Laura, dearest, I'm going to release you so you can turn and face me. I want to see your face. I want to see you look at me the way you look at *him*. Don't try anything funny, or you won't live to even see your detective again." Once more, he laughed as if he had told some huge joke. He released his hold on her, but jerked her around to face him.

"Look at me dearest."

Laura refused to look into his face. She stared at the wall behind him. His left hand shot out and slapped her across her face with a crack that echoed around the room. Gasps followed muffled sobs from the congregation. "I said look at me!"

Laura steeled herself to keep from raising her hand to her face that stung as if a swarm of bees had landed and left their stingers. She would not give Bill Collins the satisfaction of knowing he hurt her. She still refused to look into his eyes, so he slapped her on the other side of her face—with his gun hand. The butt of the gun left a knot rising on her cheekbone.

Clenching her teeth, she held back the tears that threatened. She refused to acknowledge the pain that filled her head.

Steve lurched forward.

"One more step, Morgan, and you can bury her instead of marry her," Jacobson bellowed not taking his eyes off Laura then laughed wickedly at his attempted joke.

Fists clenched as tight as his jaws, Steve allowed his friends to hold him back. There were more gasps around the congregation, but most sat like frozen statues—afraid to even breathe.

"Now, Laura, dearest, you must get over this stubborn streak. You know I could kill you just as easy as I slap you around." With that, he hit her again sending a trickle of blood from the corner of her mouth.

"Why don't you go ahead and kill me, Bill. You will anyway, so why go through this mockery?" Laura's voice was controlled. She would not raise her voice and shout or scream at him.

"Brave, aren't we?"

"No. I'm not brave. But, neither am I afraid to die."

"Oh, spare me the lecture on going to heaven and all that nonsense." Jacobson sneered.

"There is that," she said, "but there's a more practical reason. I know that before my body hits the floor, you will be a dead man—or wish you were."

"They don't have the guts to shoot a man inside a church." He laughed, nodding toward Steve and his friends.

Laura used every once of strength to stay focused on the man with the gun pointed at her.

"I wouldn't count on that if I were you," she said quietly.

"Well, well, well. If *you* aren't afraid to die, then maybe you would be more afraid for the kid." He nodded toward Josh. "Get over here kid. Now! Or I will shoot her right here in front of everyone."

Josh started to move. Susan put her arms around him to hold him back.

"Stay where you are, Josh." Laura ordered without turning to look at him. He knew when she used that tone of voice he dared not disobey—no matter what the consequences. He bit his lip. Tears ran down his face, but he didn't budge.

"You can't shoot both of us, Bill. Take your pick, him or me. Either way, you're a dead man as soon as you pull that trigger. It's me you really want— or is it? She must have hurt you pretty badly thirty years ago."

Colin Jacobson looked startled then laughed again. "So, you figured that out, too. I always said you were too smart for your own good. Yeah, Vivian knew

224

I wanted her, but she ran off to *him*. Then when he kicked her out, she thought she could run back to me, but I fixed her. I won't be second to anybody."

"You killed her, too." Laura didn't ask a question; she stated what she believed to be a fact.

"Laura, dearest, how do you do it. You seem to know more about me than anyone I've ever known. But, enough time wasted. Do your thing Bishop. I want to have some fun with my bride before I kill her."

"Bill, how could you turn your back on the church?" Bishop Giles tried to reason with him.

"Don't try your psychology stuff with me, Bishop. I never was really a part of the church. It was a good cover for me. That's all. Now, let's get this over with. These folks want to go home and I want to get out of here. This place gives me the creeps."

A slight movement under the pew behind Jacobson caught Laura's eye—Rascal and Mischief. She tried to brace herself for whatever they did, but could never have been prepared. Jacobson momentarily dropped his guard as he talked to the bishop. That was all the time Rascal and Mischief needed.

Fifty-Five

Mischief flew to Jacobson's gun hand, sinking her teeth into the flesh of his thumb, and her claws into the back of his hand. At the same instant, Rascal leaped from the front pew, hit Laura in the chest, used her for a springboard, twisted his body and flew onto Jacobson's face. There he dug in his claws as far as he could and let himself slide.

Jacobson dropped the gun and grabbed at his face to pull Rascal free. Mischief let go of the hand, dropped to the floor, and flew at him from behind digging her claws into his back while sinking her teeth in his neck.

Steve pulled away from his friends and slipped to his knees beside Laura where she had fallen from the impact of Rascal's weight. Todd and Joe pulled guns out and tried to get cuffs on Jacobson, but Rascal and Mischief weren't about to let go this time.

"Laura, darling," Steve caressed her bruised face and bleeding lip. She gasped for breath.

"Rascal really packs a wallop," she said still gasping for air, "but I think I'm all right. Help me up."

Steve stood and lifted her to her feet.

"Laura, can you call them off so we can get him out of here?" Todd said. "No big a hurry, except they we're in the church and we still have a wedding to finish.

"Yeah," said Joe. "No hurry, mind you."

Colin Jacobson was yelling and screaming all the profanity he knew.

"Rascal. Mischief. Come here sweeties. Good kitties."

They spat at their enemy, gave him one last swipe of their claws, dropped to the floor, and raced to Laura. Taking a flying leap, they landed on her shoulders, licked her bruises and then flew to the front pew where they proceeded to clean themselves, grumbling and chattering all the time. Before anyone could stop him, Steve took the opportunity of that brief second between the time the cats left and Joe got the cuffs on him, to sock Jacobson in the jaw, knocking him to the floor. He would have done more, but Todd and Joe held him back.

They got Jacobson on his feet. As they cuffed him, he turned to Laura, his face and hands dripping with blood. "Too bad, dearest. It wouldn't have lasted anyway." His laugh this time was a cross between a sob and a cackle. "But, I still accomplished my purpose. You and Morgan will never have peace. Your hatred for me will destroy your marriage." He laughed again and Joe started to take him out.

"Wait," Laura called to them. "Bill, you're wrong, you know."

"I'm not Bill Collins. I'm Colin Jacobson."

"To me you will always be Bill Collins. That's how I will remember you. That's why I can forgive you and put this behind me. You were my superior for a time and I respected you even if I didn't like you. Colin Jacobson, I don't know. He's someone who is a little mad. I forgive you Bill Collins because of who you once were. I also forgive Colin Jacobson because he is mentally deranged."

"I don't want or need your forgiveness. I won't accept it. You will still have to live with the fact that I won't accept your forgiveness." He sneered. "And I know you well enough, Laura Kenzel, to know you will hold on to your anger forever. You still haven't forgiven that kid who killed your first husband."

"You're wrong, mister," Tom Martin stood in the congregation. "She did forgive me, even though I only *thought* I killed her husband. And what's more she's helping me prepare for ministry."

"You've not only lost the battle, but also the war, Bill. Let God help you."

"Don't preach to me, Laura Kenzel. I don't want any part of your God."

"I'm sorry Bill. I am truly sorry for you."

"I don't want, or need, your pity. Maybe you think you have forgiven me, but he hasn't and never will. I will always be there between you."

"No, Jacobson," said Steve. "Laura's right. You're mad. I can't hate a mad man. I can only pity you. You have truly lost."

"Get me out of here before I get sick," Jacobson said to the police officers who held him.

"Read him his rights and watch him. He's tricky," said Joe.

Several police officers led him out. Other officers joined them, surrounding Jacobson.

The congregation sighed as if they had been holding their collective breath. But what came next? Would they continue and finish the wedding? Would they cancel and reset the date? Laura was pale and looked as if she might pass out.

"Steve, I need to sit down. I think I'm going to…" Darkness began to close in. She heard Doctor Jonathan say, "Get her back to her office. Give her a few minutes. I think she'll be all right, but she's had quiet a shock."

Fred Martin stepped to the pulpit microphone. "Folks, there will be a short intermission while we revert back to the original cast of characters. Please be patient. Stand up and move around a little if you want. The organ will begin playing when we're ready to resume. Our pastor has coped with worse battles from that man. She'll bounce back. Just give her a few minutes. Thank you."

Fifty-Six

Laura opened her eyes; she was on the couch in her office. Family and friends hovered around her. Doctor Jonathan sat beside her with his blood pressure cuff on her arm.

"Steve?"

"I'm here darling." He spoke from above her head.

"Doctor Jonathan? What's happening to me? I've never fainted in my life." She tried to sit up, but fell back holding her head.

"You're all right, Laura," said Doctor Jonathan. "I'm not surprised you fainted. I'm more amazed you didn't do it sooner. You took quite a beating—physically and emotionally. You're going to *need* a two week rest."

"The wedding! We have to..." Once again, she tried to sit up. This time she managed to bring herself into a sitting position before the nausea and dizziness returned. She closed her eyes and started to fall back. Steve had slid into the corner of the couch and put his arms around her. She lay back against him.

"Laura, maybe we better just have Bishop Giles do a quick service here and..."

"No, we can't do that. Too many people will be disappointed."

She swung her legs off the couch and tried once more to sit up. Josh plopped himself beside her.

"Josh, I think Grandma and Steve need to be alone for a few minutes."

"He's all right, Susan. I need some reality pegs right now."

"Grandma! I'm not a pig!" Josh giggled.

"I didn't say pig, I said...never mind." She tousled his hair and laughed.

"Now, I've got to go comb my hair before I walk down the aisle again. We *are* going to do it again aren't we?"

"Sure we are. Just give me a few minutes to get myself together. Okay?"

"All right. Mr. Martin said we're having an intermission."

"I know you're all concerned, but I would like to see my patient alone if I could," interrupted Doctor Jonathan.

"Sure, Doc," said Todd. "Come on guys. She's going to be all right. Let's give her room to breathe."

Laura heard what sounded like gunshots from somewhere outside. She glanced at Steve and wondered, did he get away—again?

Understanding her look, he said, "I'll go see. Be back in a couple of minutes."

Alone with Laura, Doctor Jonathan checked her bruises and cut lip, took her blood pressure and pulse again. "Blood pressure a little high and pulse a little fast. Considering that little scene, I'm not surprised. Sure had me scared to death. He could have killed you."

"I know, and I was ready for that. I wasn't ready to let him kill my grandson or anyone else in there. I knew if he shot me, the police would be on him before I hit the floor. He knew that too. That's why he wasn't willing to shoot. I was his only means out of there."

"Laura, if you insist on continuing with this wedding, take one of these tranquilizers. Here are several. You can take another later. They'll help you get through the rest of the evening. You still have a reception to endure."

"Thanks Doctor Jonathan, but, I can't take those. I want to be fully conscious and know what I am doing. If it's the same thing you gave me once before, one pill will put me to sleep."

Steve returned in time to hear her refuse the medication. "Darling, if you go to sleep, I'll carry you home and put you to bed," he grinned. "I can do that now."

"Not yet, you can't. Not unless we get this wedding over with."

"You won't go to sleep that quickly."

"I don't *want* any medicine."

"I'll take them, Doctor, and see that she gets them later if she needs them."

Once they were alone, Steve sat beside her with his arms around her. "Laura, you're shaking like a leaf."

"Oh, Steve." She threw her arms around him and all the tension began to drain through her tears. She could not have held them back if Colin Jacobson himself had been standing there with his gun on her.

Steve didn't try to minimize the terror by clichés. He simply held her next to him until the tears abated and she reached for a tissue. He got up and went into her rest room, returning with a glass of water. He held out a pill for her.

"Take this and I won't have any argument about it. You really are human, my love. Enough is enough. You can't do any more tonight without some help."

"Steve, I don't want…"

"No arguments. I don't like ultimatums, but you will take it now, or we will postpone the wedding until later tonight or tomorrow, when you've had time to recover.

"Steve, that's not fair."

"So, who said life is fair?"

Laura felt the old stubbornness rising. It was overshadowed by a soft, gentle chuckle. The stubborn set of her jaw softened into a smile that just about brought tears to Steve's own eyes.

"I'm sorry, Steve. You're right. I'm not thinking clearly. I need you to think for me—at least until we get through this day."

She took the pill and the water.

"Shall I tell Karen to begin again, or do you need a little more time?"

"Give me about five minutes. I need to talk to my Boss."

"I'll get everyone in place again and tell Karen to start playing in five minutes. Norman will come and get you."

"Steve, the shots? Did he…?"

"Yes and no. He did manage to break lose. They don't know how. He also got one of their guns. He ran, shooting at them as he ran. They had no choice but to shoot back. He's dead, Laura. I'm sorry."

"So am I," she said brushing away the tears. "Oh Steve it must be awful to die such a violent death and not have a single person to mourn that death."

"It looks like he has one," Steve said softly as he brushed away her tears and kissed her gently avoiding her cut lip.

"Five minutes," he said and started out the door.

Laura remained on the couch. "God, I don't think I could get up if I try to kneel. I can't believe it's really over. Did I do all right? Will You truly bless our marriage? I do love him so much, but I don't want to ruin his life with my problems."

Laura felt the familiar chuckle and deep within her soul heard the words, "Well done my good and faithful servant."

"Thank you," she whispered.

Norman knocked on her door and stuck his head in. "Karen is starting to play. Jody is going to sing again then we'll be ready for the processional again. You can stay here until it's time for us to go down if you want. I'll come and get you."

"I'll be all right, Norman. How about you? How's your head? He cracked you pretty good with that cane."

"I've got a thick head." Norman laughed. "It'll be sore for a couple of days, but it's nothing compared to what you went through. I don't know how you did it."

"You do what you have to do and trust God to give you the strength to hold on."

They walked to the back of the overflow area where they could hear Jody beginning her song, "I asked the Lord to comfort me…"

Jody finished her song and Karen reached for a tissue before beginning the processional. Once again, Carolyn, Susan, Josh and Jerome moved forward to meet Steve, Todd, and Bishop Giles. This time Karen played the *Wedding March* and the congregation stood for Laura's entrance. Taking Norman's arms she let him guide her down the aisle, glad that she had opted for a suit, not a long, flowing wedding gown. She was glad too, that Norman was there. She was still shaking and didn't think she could have made it on her own.

When the Bishop asked, "Who presents this woman for the blessing of this marriage, the entire congregation joined Norman with, "We do."

The rest of the ceremony went as scheduled. They exchanged the rings and the vows and knelt for the prayer of blessing after which Jody sang *The Lord's Prayer.*

Steve was prepared with a clean handkerchief. He gently wiped her tears, being careful of her bruises. The song was over and he helped her to stand.

Bishop Giles said, "Friends, I want to present to you your new pastor, Reverend Laura Morgan, wife of Detective Steven Morgan. Steve you may kiss your bride, very carefully." He smiled at them.

Steve looked into that pool of cocoa brown eyes, drinking in the love he saw there. Then he very gently took her in his arms and kissed her, being careful, as the bishop had instructed.

Suddenly, a sound like a dozen cats fighting came from the organ. They separated; Steve looked alarmed; Laura began laughing until tears streamed down her face. When Steve realized what it was he, too, went into peals of laughter, as was the entire congregation.

Rascal and Mischief, perched on the organ *sang* a duet for them. When they finished they each placed a paw over their noses and made their sound of, "yuk, yuk, yuk, yuk, yuk."

"They're laughing up their paws," said Fred Martin who had taken the opportunity to go to the microphone again. "This has been a most unusual wedding for a most unusual couple. You have all been kind and considerate with Reverend Morgan. I'm going to ask one more indulgence. I know they are prepared for a receiving line in back, but at the risk of overstepping my bounds, I am going to change all that and ask the wedding party to process directly to the fellowship hall down stairs where Reverend Morgan can sit and greet you folks. I think she's had enough exhaustion and tension for one day."

"Bless him twice," whispered Laura.

"Amen to that," whispered Steve back to her.

Karen, having stopped her own laughter—almost—began the recessional. Rascal and Mischief leaped from the organ and fell into step behind the bride and groom. They marched side-by-side, tails in the air, curled at the tips.

Fifty-Seven

Martha and her crew slipped down the back stairs to the fellowship hall and met Laura and Steve as they entered by another door. "You want me to get Frank to bring one of the soft chairs from your office down for you?"

"Thank you, Martha," said Laura, "but I'm afraid I'd fall asleep if I got too comfortable. Doctor Jonathan gave me a mild tranquilizer."

Martha laughed. "You sure needed something. I don't know how you…" she stopped and shook her head. "Well, the good Lord got you through the tough part and me and my crew will get you through the rest. You just sit right over here."

Martha took Laura and Steve to two chairs with enough room for people to file by and greet them on the way to the buffet table. Laura, grateful for Martha's take-charge attitude, sank onto a padded folding chair.

Did everyone in both Glenville and Cottonville come to congratulate us, she wondered. Will the line ever end? I would give anything—well almost anything—for a cup of coffee.

His friends from Glenville surrounded Steve and Susan and Norman were talking to Todd and Carolyn. Even the boys were in the corner with some other kids. Only Rascal and Mischief sat attentively on either side of her. Rascal's green eyes stared into her brown ones then he trotted off to join Josh and Jerome. He smacked Josh on the hand to get his attention. Josh glanced her way then disappeared among the guests. Laura sighed and turned her attention to Clarissa, who was congratulating her and giving her sympathetic murmurings for her ordeal.

"Excuse me," said Josh squeezing between two men who moved aside for him. "Rascal said you wanted some coffee," he said, handing the steaming cup to Laura and giggled at her surprise. Steve glanced down at them and Jerome handed him a cup. He heard what Josh said and grinned.

"Thank you," said Laura as Rascal took up his guarding stance beside her again.

Finally, everyone was in the fellowship hall eating sandwiches, salads, and assortment of foods. Laura and Steve sat with their wedding party while Laura nibbled at the food—too tired and weary to feel hungry.

Martha approached them. "Everyone isn't finished eating, yet, but would you like to cut the cake. Then you can leave when you need to. We can skip it if you don't feel up to it," she said. "We can take care of it."

"I think I can manage that," smiled Laura, "as long as I have a strong arm to lean on."

"Shall I call Norman to help you," Steve teased.

They laughed and went to cut the cake, so the photographer could catch the action. Steve took her back to the table before anyone could corner her for conversation. Karen and George sat beside her.

"We want you to be the first to know," Karen said, as she held up her hand for Laura to see the ring on her finger.

"Karen, that's wonderful. Have you set a date yet?"

"Sometime next spring," said George.

"After Easter. I wouldn't want to go through this kind of commotion at Easter time."

"We'll talk when I get back," said Laura.

"There are a couple of things that George and I both agree on," said Karen trying to look very serious.

"What is that?" Laura knew these young folks were both extremely serious about their music.

"We don't want any dead bodies turning up, and we definitely don't want a tone deaf Maine Coon duet."

They broke into giggles and laughter as they moved over to the table where Karen's parents sat to share the news with them.

"Darling, you look like death warmed over. I think we better leave."

"Steve, I can't just walk out."

"Shall I carry you out?"

"Steve!"

Fred Martin approached them pulling something from his pocket.

"Fred thanks for taking charge up there. I owe you one—or more." Laura tried to smile and look like she was really enjoying things, but the tranquilizer Doctor Jonathan gave her was making it difficult to stay alert.

"Glad to help out. You look like you need to get out of here—or ought to at any rate, so

I thought you might want these." He held out a set of keys.

"Keys?" She looked perplexed.

"To the new parsonage. We still need to do a number of things yet, but it's livable, at least for a couple of days. The master bedroom and bath and the kitchen are all set up—food in the fridge for breakfast. We won't do any more to it until after Christmas, while you're gone."

"You mean we can stay there tonight?" Laura was confused. "But…what about the bishop?"

"I think the bishop can take care of himself, Reverend Morgan." Bishop Giles had walked up behind her. "Helen and I won't be leaving until sometime tomorrow. Susan said we're still welcome at her house. Personally, Detective, I think you ought to take your wife home and put her to bed."

"I've been telling her the same thing. She thinks she ought to stay until the last person leaves."

"Well, I say she goes home immediately," said Doctor Jonathan who also slipped among them. "Unless you want to end up in a hospital bed again."

"I don't *need*…" Laura started to protest. She knew better. She *was* exhausted and knew it. She shook her head and sighed. "Of course, you're right—all of you. I am at the point of exhaustion. I'm feeling light headed. Let me tell Susan then I'll be ready to go."

"That was too easy," said Steve. "What do you have up your sleeve?"

"Nothing. I'm too weary. I think I'm going to break down and have another crying jag if I don't get out of here. I told you I needed you to think for me."

"Let's go."

Rascal and Mischief walked with them to the door of the new parsonage, then turned and ran back to Josh and Jerome. Steve unlocked the door and carried her over the threshold and up the stairs to the bedroom, where he closed the door and put his exhausted bride to bed.

Jacobson was dead. She could settle into simply being Reverend Laura Morgan, wife of Detective Steve Morgan. Couldn't she?

Somewhere in the fading conscious of her mind, she wondered if Jacobson had any other relatives who would seek revenge.

Epilogue

The young police officer at the roadblock had been suspicious of the red Taurus from West Virginia. He radioed information in and discovered the car was stolen. The driver was Thomas Sizemore, Vivian's father. He had moved from Glenville shortly before his daughter married that nice young Morgan boy. He never expected the marriage to last. He knew his daughter had tricked the kid in some way. They were divorced a few months later and he never heard from his daughter again.

Todd's men began a search for the car and found it in a grove of trees by the park. The driver was dead, the blind man and his dog gone. By the time they figured it out, and got to the church, Jacobson had already made his move.

Later, when they were leaving the church with Jacobson in handcuffs, one side of the cuff popped open. No one knew for sure if he had a pick of some kind up his sleeve or if the cuff was defective and just sprang open. Either way, it took Colin Jacobson only a split second to grab the gun from one of the younger, inexperienced police officers near him. He shot the young man then ran. The Doberman emerged from the hedge by the church and ran beside him.

The other officers called for him to stop. When he fired back at them, they had no choice but to open fire on him. He was still close enough there was no way even an inexperienced, mediocre marksman could have missed. It was almost as if he had planned it that way. The dog bared his teeth and lunged for one of the officers, who shot him in mid-air.

The young officer was taken to the hospital with serious wounds, but he would live.

Bishop and Mrs. Giles left the following morning to spend Christmas with their family in South Carolina. They would never forget that wedding or the Reverend Laura Kenzel—now Reverend Laura Morgan.

"I think we'll hear a lot more from that woman of God," the bishop told Helen as they drove away from Cottonville.

"I certainly hope so," she laughed, "but no more murders!"

Norman and Susan bought the house Laura had been living in and settled down in Cottonville. They both taught at the Cottonville High School. They loved the town, its people, and their work almost as much as they loved each other.

Laura recovered from her encounter with Colin Jacobson. She and Steve led the Christmas Eve service together. They celebrated Christmas Day with Susan, Norman and Josh. Todd, Carolyn, Jerome, Sophia, SaraBelle and Cora all joined them for Christmas Dinner.

Laura and Steve left the day after Christmas for two weeks of well-deserved time together. No one knew their destination, not even Susan—at least she wasn't telling if she did.

Also available from PublishAmerica

BEHIND THE SHADOWS
by Susan C. Finelli

Born into squalor, Raymond Nasco's quest for
wealth and power shrouds two generations with
deceit, murder, rape and illicit love. Setting his
sights above and beyond the family's two-room
apartment in a New York City lower eastside
tenement, Raymond befriends Guy Straga, the
son of a wealthy business tycoon, and they
develop a lifelong friendship and bond. Caught
in Raymond's powerful grip, his wife, Adele,
commits the ultimate sin; and his son, Spencer,
betrays himself and the woman he loves and
finally becomes his father's son. Years later Kay
Straga stumbles upon the secret that has been
lurking in the shadows of the Straga and Nasco
families for two generations, a secret that tempts
her with forbidden love, a secret that once
uncovered will keep her in its clutches from
which there is no escape.

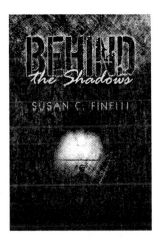

Paperback, 292 pages
6" x 9"
ISBN 1-4241-8974-8

About the author:

Susan C. Finelli has lived in New York all of her life and
has been a Manhattanite for over thirty years. She, her
husband John, and Riley Rian, their beloved cavalier King
Charles spaniel, currently reside in Manhattan, and together
they enjoy exploring the sights, sounds and vibrancy of the
Big Apple.

Available to all bookstores nationwide.
www.publishamerica.com